The Hallelujah Side

The Hallelujah Side

RHODA HUFFEY

A MARINER BOOK

HOUGHTON MIFFLIN COMPANY

Boston • *New York*

First Mariner Books edition 2000

"Sunday School Room Three" was previously published in
the *Santa Monica Review*, Fall 1999.

Reprinted by arrangement with Delphinium Books, Inc.

For information about permission to reproduce selections
from this book, write to Permissions, Houghton Mifflin Company,
215 Park Avenue South, New York, New York 10003.

Visit our Web site: www.houghtonmifflinbooks.com.

Library of Congress Cataloging-in-Publication Data
Huffey, Rhoda, date.
The Hallelujah side / Rhoda Huffey. — 1st Mariner Books ed.
p. cm.
"A Mariner book."
ISBN 0-618-07471-6 (pbk.)
1. Girls — Fiction. 2. Singers — Fiction. 3. Pentecostals — Fiction.
4. Rock music fans — Fiction. 5. Iowa — Fiction. I. Title.
PS3558.U3443 H35 2000
813'.54 — dc21 00-040785

Printed in the United States of America

QUM 10 9 8 7 6 5 4 3 2 1

Grateful acknowledgment is made for use of the lines
from "Send Me Some Lovin'" by John Marascalco and Leo Price.
Copyright © 1957 Sony/ATV Songs LLC (Renewed). All rights
administered by Sony/ATV Music Publishing, 8 Music Square West,
Nashville, TN 37203. All rights reserved. Used by permission.

For Norm Leander

"Feet don't fail me now."

— *Willie Best*

All the Saints

IT HAD BEEN a Second Coming sky all day, which meant they might be in heaven by this evening. Roxanne stood by the mirror trying to make spit curls. Stupidly, her red hair hung there, causing her to glare out at her sister, Colleen the beautiful. Roxanne dropped the spit curl (which went straight), turned to the piano, and hit high C. Then she walked her fingers on the white keys, five notes up the scale and four notes down. Each rang. Over on the couch Roxanne's mother, Zelda Fish, sneezed again, especially hard this time. Sister Fish had the flu, but if they went up she would be cured instantly. Roxanne picked up her doll, Miss Jennifer Smith, and walked back and forth across the living room, back and forth, ready to go. It would happen in the twinkling of an eye, the dead rising first, then the saints going up to meet Him in the air, no time to get your belongings.

"Shhh," said Roxanne to the doll ear.

Out the window a few big drops of rain fell, but the setting sun shone hard, a giant spotlight. Around it the whole sky had darkened. The spotlight made the Second Coming clouds glitter. Holding to the Fish family priscilla curtains, Roxanne squinted, but so far she couldn't see the archangel Gabriel or his trumpet, which was gold. Roxanne allowed Jennifer Smith to look. One leaf of corn was growing almost through the window where the screen was missing. Roxanne's father, Pastor Winston Fish of the First Assembly of God Church of Ames, Iowa, had removed it to paint while he was thinking about world affairs. Outside nothing stirred. The corn hanging from the stalk should be ripe enough to eat in a few days, if the Lord tarried. Picturing the corn on a plate, she hoped He did — a sin, putting idols before God.

"Sorry," she whispered to the ceiling. Surreptitiously she added butter and salt.

"Was that a trumpet sound?" said Colleen.

Roxanne jumped.

"Chick Woolworth's car horn," said Pastor Fish. The Woolworths lived next door, just across the driveway.

Sister Fish turned on the lamp, which they kept off to save electricity. Her pink rollers jumped into prominence, as did Colleen's loose curls. There was the wood piano, with bright sheet music. Roxanne watched the whole room. There her father sat in his blue chair.

"A trumpet sound is higher," he said.

Sister Fish coughed, resigned to the difficulty of being in her mortal body. On the coffee table in plain sight lay *Das Kapital*, a shocking book that Sister Fish rushed to hide each time the doorbell rang, for fear it would give someone the wrong impression. Pastor Fish, to be stubborn, always put it back. He was readng it in order to refute it point by point with Scripture, for his own edification. Human beings had to get their blood boiling each day, he believed, to stay in top working order. A seemingly impossible fight, flying, and fishing were his three great loves.

The couch squeaked. Sister Fish, surrounded by Kleenex, was turning the pages of the new *Pentecostal Evangel*, the magazine of the Assemblies of God. It had color pictures every month and told the truth, giving out information you could trust.

"I'm bored," said Colleen.

"Speed-the-Light has bought an airplane. Amen. Why don't you write to Grandmother?"

"I *hate* Grandmother." Colleen's beautiful nose wrinkled.

"Careful, young lady," said Winston. "I wonder what sort of airplane."

"It doesn't say."

Speed-the-Light was Christians giving money to take the news of Jesus to the unsaved, fast. "Go ye into all the world, and preach the gospel to every creature," read Scripture. This airplane was for Africa so the heathen might hear before it was too late. The missionaries had Speed-the-Light jeeps and Speed-the-Light bicycles and Speed-the-Light speedboats. There was not much time! For Christ was coming back. Picking up Miss Jennifer Smith, Roxanne thought of the whole world. This morning Jennifer Smith had been bicycle riding up and down the streets of Rome. In a flash the rug under the piano bench became Paris, and Roxanne walked Jennifer up the Eiffel Tower steps.

"We need to pray for Speed-the-Light," said Zelda. She raised both hands. "God *longs* for the souls of men. Hallelujah! We are going to meet Him in the air!"

They took good Christian families in total, as long as the children were still innocent. Kids did not have to get saved until they reached the Age of Accountability. So far Roxanne could play all day. The Fish family would go up together, holding hands, ascending through the sky. These were the Last Days. Some Christians sold their furniture and moved out on the lawn to show their faith, a behavior Pastor Fish ridiculed. They had to move back in when it snowed. Pastor Fish laughed and called them fanatics. The Fish family, by contrast, sanely went about their business, mending torn clothes, washing their faces, but they were ready every instant of the day. They didn't steal or take the name of the Lord in vain, including the abbreviations "gee," "gosh," and "golly." God knew all the Christians personally, but He especially counted on the Winston Fish family.

"Oh, I wish we could afford a new church carpet." Zelda turned another page of the *Pentecostal Evangel*. "Someone's going to trip on that bad spot."

"I'm *bored*," said Colleen through her nose.

"C.M. Ward has a sermon here on perfection." Zelda waved the magazine. "Look. With a picture. Now, this sermon is complete from the Revivaltime radio show. My, C.M. can preach! 'Christians, Be Ye Perfect!' it is called."

"I am b-o-r-e-d," said Colleen.

"'Be ye therefore perfect, even as your Father which is in heaven is perfect,'" quoted Winston Fish. A finger marked his place in *Das Kapital*. "This is God's command. God tells us it is *possible*."

"Well, C.M. doesn't keep house. His wife does." Zelda blew her nose. "There's too much to do. Roxanne? Pick up your socks."

It was hot, and beads of sweat sat on Roxanne's face. Winston went back to his reading, his suit coat off.

"This Marx fellow has some strong ideas."

"Oh, I wish you'd hide that, Winston. What if people think we're Communists?"

"Let them."

Roxanne glared across at Colleen, who with her eyes closed did resemble a movie star. Between them the Missionary Box spilled out good clothing gathered from all around America and sent to Pastor Fish. Preachers got first choice, missionaries second, natives third. Sideways, the word "Missionaries" looked Japanese. Roxanne pulled out a scarf, soft material covered with zebras and giraffes. The box was huge. On the floor she was making up an outfit, a navy blue dress and one white high heel so far. She added the scarf.

Roxanne continued to rummage through the sturdy cardboard, looking for the other flash of white shoe. She wiped sweat from her face again. She had sixteen pairs of high heels lined up in her closet, all too big. There it was! She grabbed it and carefully put both high heels upright next to the dress. Their beauty shocked her.

"Mom," she said, happy, "can I sleep in the bathtub tonight? With two pillows?" The bathtub stayed cool when even the living room floor was too hot to breathe.

"I don't see why not."

"Weirdo," said Colleen.

Roxanne's foot shot out to kick Colleen, but she hit her shin on the coffee table, hard.

"Weirdo spastic in the bathtub. Help!"

"Girls!"

Hopefully Colleen would go to hell if the Lord came this very moment. Roxanne smiled secretly. People said Colleen had the looks and personality of Shirley Temple, but those would not help you in hell.

"Look at that corn!" cried Zelda. "It's decided to come in!"

"Ripe in two more days," said Winston.

Teetering, Roxanne stood up in the white high heels, huge on her bare feet. She walked around the living room without falling, an acrobat, her arms out.

"I'm bored, bored, *bored*!" declared Colleen, bouncing on the red chair. Her red lips sparkled, and so did her eyes. Colleen talked to sinners without a second thought. "Can't we go ice fishing?"

"That's what we do with Grandmother up in Minnesota," said their father. "We used to fish all night when we were boys. But it's for winter, not a July heat wave. Wait a few months." He looked up at the other Fishes from *Das Kapital*, his face illuminated by the lamp, his finger at the top of the left-hand page, willing as always to discuss fishing.

As a rule Christians had to stay away from worldly things, but Pastor Fish was sufficiently strong in the Lord, and regularly read *Newsweek* and *Life* magazine. There he often found fodder for his sermons, the abhorrent things Americans were doing. Not very many people living were going to go up. Episcopalians thought they were, but Episcopalians were just as lost as the killer on the street. The apostles would be there, and the Foursquares, and Martin Luther, because he spoke directly to God.

"Let us practice your harmonica and cello duet," said Winston. "You can play it Sunday night. Girls, get your instruments."

"I am too bored," said Colleen.

"You won't be bored if Daddy spanks you." Zelda sneezed.

The girls ran into the church, where the musical instruments were kept. The Fish living quarters were behind the back part of the tabernacle, starting at the end of the platform where their father preached. You could walk through the whole house in a circle, except for the two bedrooms Pastor Fish had built for the girls, which were ex-platform space. During church the platform was holy, but a door from Colleen's room opened directly onto it, and now the girls raced out onstage, Colleen turning two somersaults and jumping down to land on the Communion Table, where she sat for ten seconds. That was sacrilegious. Roxanne hopped onto the first pew and stepped up on the narrow back, starting along its length, arms out, eyes forward, a tightrope walker in the circus. From the circus tent the crowd gazed up, spellbound. When she reached the end she turned around and started back the other way. Her toes felt every swirl in the grain of the wood.

"Let's get going!" came Winston's voice.

They retrieved the instruments from the church orchestra corner and trudged back across the platform to Colleen's bedroom and into the living room, where their father sat waiting. Colleen waved the cello bow and wiggled her hips behind his back.

"'Just a Closer Walk with Thee.' Let's begin." Pastor Fish plunked out the melody on the piano.

Laboriously the girls played. It sounded terrible, but no one said so.

"Help!" Colleen laid down the cello and waved her arms and kicked her legs, her head jerking wildly. "I can't stop dancing! Satan has me!" Her eyes rolled up in her head. "Help!"

Roxanne grabbed the white high heels and jumped up on the piano bench. Possessed! Desperately she got the heels on and wiggled her knees, arms extended. She shook her red hair back and forth in a demonic frenzy.

"You ain't nothin' but a hound dog!" she screamed.

"That will be enough," said Pastor Fish. "*Stop.*"

The girls tried, but they were in hysterics. Behind the *Pentecostal Evangel*, Zelda fought to read.

"Satan and his tribe are not a laughing matter." Winston Fish's face was deadly serious, but the girls laughed on.

"It is very dangerous to ask him in. I'm going to spank the daylights out of you until you both have some sense. Colleen, you first. You girls are going to see the light here. I don't care if we stay up all night."

He stood. *Das Kapital* landed with a thud. Two large hands hung, the skin rough. When he spanked, it made your inner spirit droop. Roxanne looked toward her mother, who was trying to sit up against the couch arm.

"March!"

Colleen walked toward the piano bench, her eyes wet, hiccuping. She could not quell her laughter.

"Lord, give us a burden for Africa," intoned Sister Fish, the *Evangel* open on her chest. "Send the gospel."

"Ha-ha-ha," giggled Roxanne, hardly able to breathe, her hands over her mouth.

Just as Colleen reached her father's knees by the piano bench, someone knocked on the front door, which was really on the side of the house facing the Lutheran neighbors' hedge.

They all stopped.

"My, it's late," said Zelda Fish.

At this hour it could be an angel. It could be anything. They stared at the door, Satan and his antics relegated to another universe. The girls could breathe now, except for the occasional hiccup. Winston opened the door, and the three female Fish family members leaned, straining to see wings. Instead it was a couple, the boy's arm around the girl. Sinners. You could tell by her earrings.

"Good evening," said Pastor Fish.

"Can we come in?"

"My wife has the flu."

"We want to get married. How much do you charge?" The young man looked nervous. He smoothed back his hair, which was already oiled flat.

"Ten dollars. Well now, I don't know."

From the couch, sitting partway, Zelda made frantic signs that meant the Fishes did not have money for groceries. The church paid almost zero.

"Close the door," mouthed Zelda. "Close the door. Close the door."

Pastor Fish excused himself. When the door was shut he turned toward her.

"We need the money, Winston. Ten dollars."

"The Lord will provide."

"Maybe the Lord provided *them*."

"Well, we can at least talk to them."

He opened the door again. Outside, Iowa smelled fabulous. There were no stars because of the Second Coming clouds and the full moon. The corn would not be ready for two days, her father had said. Roxanne's mouth watered. She apologized to the ceiling again. In heaven you ate manna. Sugary, it fell out of the sky all day long. There was no night up there. If the trumpet sounded Roxanne planned to grab Velveeta out of the refrigerator.

The young couple looked hopeful.

"Generally," said Pastor Fish, "I do not like to marry people who are not saved."

"We go to church," said the young man.

"That's not enough!" cried Zelda Fish, tightening her robe belt. Her cheeks looked pinker. Her arm waved. "You are on the edge of a great gulf!"

She motioned and they stepped inside. How exciting it would be if they got saved, and only seconds before the Rapture! But they were not sincere. Neither one was even crying.

"We've got our papers," said the young man, reaching into his shirt pocket.

"Would you like to kneel down now and ask Jesus into your heart?" Zelda sniffled. "Don't get too close. I don't want to get you sick."

"Well," said the boy. The girl clung to him.

"Zelda," said her husband. He observed the lovebirds. "I'll tell you what. I'll marry you, but will you come to our Wednesday night service and hear the Word?"

"We'll be gone by Wednesday," said the young man. The girl's eyes had become huge. "We have to make California by Friday."

"Will you look up an Assembly of God church? And aim to be there by Wednesday night?"

The couple exchanged glances. *Das Kapital* was still lying on the floor, but they were too in love to see it. The man laughed.

"Wednesday, Reverend. Yes. All right."

All at once the Fish living room seemed to be bathed in light. Sister Fish directed from the couch, and the girls ran around cleaning up. *Das Kapital* vanished. Suddenly humiliated, Roxanne scooped up the new outfit and pushed the Missionary Box backwards out of the living room with her hip so the writing did not show, "Missionaries" written in pen. The Fishes wore used clothes! With a pop she shoved the box through her parents' bedroom door while Colleen polished the end tables until the tops shone. The two young people beamed. Roxanne ran back in. How beautiful it all was! The girls sat on the piano bench side by side, striped bows in their hair. Ten dollars was a large sum. Pastor Fish put on his suit coat and stood holding his big Bible.

The lovers faced him, trembling.

"My goodness. Flowers!" cried Zelda. "Girls, the sweet pea! Run. Run!"

When they got back, Pastor Fish preached a short sermon. The young woman, Doris, held the trailing sweet pea vines in her arms like a baby. The fragrance washed everything, and lamplight glowed. Their father's voice was a good voice, deeply satisfying to the ears. Colleen swung her legs. Everything was perfect, Pastor Fish's voice, the crickets. Roxanne began crying. They endowed one another with their earthly goods. As they did not have rings, they pantomimed that part.

"With this ring, I thee wed," said Pastor Fish, entering the home stretch.

Roxanne wiped away a tear.

"Baby," whispered Colleen.

"Bob, you may kiss the bride."

They touched lips, the room absolutely silent. They pulled back. They turned around, an entirely different entity than when they walked in.

"May I introduce Mr. and Mrs. Harro."

Everything was a madhouse now. They signed papers and passed one crisp ten-dollar bill. The sisters stood, pulling out their skirts. Since it made her dizzy to get up, Sister Fish stayed on the couch, but she was as animated as ever.

"I can't *believe* I'm in my pink rollers," she laughed.

"Well. We don't want to keep you up," said the new Mr. Harro dazedly. The new Mrs. Harro nodded. They were in shock.

"Nonsense!" Zelda Fish waved. "We have to have a reception. Girls, get out the dishes and the ice cream and cake."

"The Harros may be tired." Winston shook his head and looked at Zelda. "It's ten-fifteen."

The Harros paused, their arms linked.

"Winston! Not that tablecloth, Colleen! You only get married once! Everybody sit! I'll stay here on the couch." She laughed again. "You don't need germs."

Silverware clinked. They passed the cake around, one white and one chocolate, with ice cream and chocolate syrup. They always had plenty of dessert for missionaries. Bob and Doris Harro stole delicious looks. Under the table Roxanne felt her knees. They had an interesting shape. Animatedly, everyone ate cake. You were only here below for a short time. The bride had her elbow in the sweet pea. It was perfect.

"Don't miss the Rapture," warned Zelda, lifting one finger. She sighed. Her face glowed. "My. I believe I will take one small slice."

Blue Nose Walking

ZELDA FISH looked like a girl when she got excited, and she could enthrall a crowd merely by raising one hand. Roxanne sat on the carpet watching her mother as she moved around the dining room table, humming and tossing manila folders into stacks. Zelda was the Welcome Wagon hostess for Ames. Her face was not exactly beautiful, but it became absolutely irresistible when the power of God consumed her. At such times she left a trail of people calling out to be saved, and not at church exclusively. It might be in Raker's Hardware Store or down at the bandshell where the Ames Brass Band gave free concerts.

"Seven families to welcome this week!" She waved a folder. "I am not supposed to witness. And I try. But sometimes I can't help myself!"

"Teach us the Charleston!" said Colleen brazenly.

"Oh my, no!"

Last week, after visiting a chum from Bible school, Zelda had forgotten her Christianity and done the Charleston in the living room, all wild arms and legs. Their father wandered in via the bedroom from his nap and woke up too suddenly, changing from a man who looked sleepy to one who was beholding the gates of hell in his living room. Although he was helplessly in love, he threw up his hands in despair.

"I will not have such goings-on in this house!"

Roxanne and Colleen jumped. Winston stood there with his hair sticking up. His eyes burned. He was fully dressed except for his shoes. One sock was empty in the toe, partway off.

"Oh!" Their mother froze, still bent over with her hands crossed, glued apparently to either knee. Finally she straightened, and a look of righteous indignation flooded her face. "A boy taught me that back in my Southern California Bible College days. I tried not to let it take hold." You could see her struggling to locate her personality as a preacher's wife.

"I have never been so surprised in my life." Pastor Fish shook his head. His cuffs were still unbuttoned.

"His name was Harmon." Zelda too shook her head, in Christian disbelief. The young man, a ministerial student, while in Bible school! Carefully she straightened her knees, and shook her head again. "Somehow it must have *lodged* in there." She blinked and rolled her shoulders, slowly wiggling her long fingers.

"I hope the girls were not influenced."

Their father stormed out, and their mother went into the kitchen to clean things. Roxanne and Colleen could hardly breathe.

"Wow," said Colleen. "She looked like Little Richard."

"Little Richard?"

Colleen rolled her eyes. She was older, and very sophisticated. She was born that way. "That guy on television we saw out at the Ransoms'."

The Ransoms had a TV, but at least they were spiritual. As Christians you didn't watch it. Instead you played on the staircase, bumping down for hours on your rear end. Pastor Fish preached against TV as the one-eyed monster, but Brother Ransom needed it for crop news. Corn was going up and down like a yo-yo. You got it all on the *Farmer's Report.* Then you turned it off, but sometimes Little Richard was too fast for you. Even the adults had watched, mesmerized, while his hair shook and he played the piano.

"I *wish* she'd do the Charleston," said Colleen again.

Their mother had left the Welcome Wagon folders in stacks on the table, and they could see her at the sink now, washing chicken, both legs itching to kick out and begin swinging. Zelda's face was round and clean, but her body you could easily imagine as a sinner's. Sometimes you could almost imagine what God had saved her from. Between her thumb and finger she held chicken skin.

"Do you believe in angels?" Roxanne asked, suddenly excited.

Colleen rolled her eyes. Angels bored her, to tears. Colleen was trying to find out about her true family, questioning her false parents endlessly.

"You aren't adopted," they always said.

"I *am*."

"Do you?" repeated Roxanne. "Believe in them?"

Colleen looked through her. She was sporting three new plastic rings from cereal, holding up all ten fingers. Her real family didn't live in Ames but in a larger city, and they went out to dinner regularly, once a week, and bought gum every day for the children to chew, Juicy Fruit in a yellow wrapper.

Roxanne went into the kitchen. Zelda Fish, one leg raised slightly behind her, was holding up two drumsticks.

"Do you believe in angels?" said Roxanne. "Mom!"

"Angels?" Zelda put the loose foot down, her attention on some step from the Charleston. "One for Dad and one for you girls," she said, placing the drumsticks in the refrigerator. She scooped up the chicken garbage, brightening slowly. Angels were her favorite subject. Outside the window the weeping willow branches shimmered in bright sun. Sometimes the girls played there, pretending to be Tarzan and Jane. It was late October, but they were experiencing Indian summer, a rare and lovely one.

"Angels," Zelda said dreamily, looking younger by the minute.

"Regular ones," said Roxanne. "Not Archangel Gabriel."

Her mother wrapped the chicken innards neatly in newspaper. She picked the package up, stared at it, and set it down.

"Like the kind that come to the door dressed as housewives," Roxanne went on. "You know? And deliver chicken to just the amount of people who are hungry?"

"Oh my. *Angels*."

Zelda pushed the folded newspaper away, although Roxanne knew from being yelled at that ants would come. Her mother was a perfect housekeeper, but when the Spirit entered she forgot housework.

"Lillian Trasher, the missionary to Egypt, has had car angels for years. For years! One sits on each bumper, and I think what she said is that they're each responsible for one-quarter of the car. Of course they're men. When something goes wrong she just sits there and prays, and then the angel on that section gets to work and pretty soon the car's running. She knows each of their personalities. When she came to California they went with her on the freeways."

"Really?" said Roxanne. The idea fascinated her.

"Hallelujah! Amen!" Her mother clapped her hands, laughing. "Are you going to bake a cake today? It's Saturday."

"I might!" Roxanne could feel the angels' presence. "Chocolate cake with I don't know what kind of frosting. Dad likes the cake to be chocolate. White frosting. Or pink. White!"

"They're all around us all the time!" her mother said, chicken forgotten. "They go with you when you go to school. That's the only reason I don't worry about you. They're with you when you're climbing up on the cupboards. Praise God! They're with your father when he drives the way he does."

At that instant Pastor Fish raced through, hair combed, cheeks shaved. His cuffs were buttoned at the wrist under his suit coat.

"I've got to get to Boone for Winona Johnson's funeral, and I can't find my glasses. I can't be late."

"Well, let's look for them."

They found the glasses on the dining room table, where Colleen sat drawing pictures of her real family. Their name was Whittaker.

"Your finger's bleeding, Winston. Take a Band-Aid."

"I'm going to make chocolate cake," said Roxanne. "What kind of frosting? White or pink?"

"Well now." In his suit Pastor Fish was the handsomest man in Ames, perhaps the world. A head taller than his wife, he looked aristocratic, like someone from a rich family, his nose large and definite, his eyes alert, although his hands suggested farming.

Zelda tapped her wrist. "Winston. Time."

"Let me think." He put on his hat. "Pink. By the way, Roxanne needs a baseball bat." He was teaching her how to swing down in the Sunday School hallway, using one leg of the flannelgraph holder as a bat. A flannel Peter, walking on flannel water, lay discarded on the floor.

"We'll talk about it later. Don't be late! Take a Band-Aid! And watch for slow traffic."

"Wait!" He patted his coat. "My wallet is missing!" He turned his pockets inside out frantically.

They all rushed around the house, looking everywhere. Even Colleen checked under the dining room table on her hands and knees, but the wallet could not be found.

"Oh, Winston! How much was in it?"

"Twenty-five dollars. I cashed a check for it down at the bank. The funeral's going to start! It was right here in my pocket."

"Twenty-five! Go!" cried Zelda. "We'll pray. Run!"

He slammed out and gunned the car down the gravel driveway, gone with one wild screech.

"Dear God," said Zelda. "We need Winston's wallet. Oh dear. This chicken will draw ants in a minute." She picked up the package.

"In the Charleston," said Colleen, posing, "do your arms cross this way?"

"Stop that!"

"But your hips move when you play the tambourine, Mom!" Colleen stood wiggling her pelvis.

A dreamy look crossed Zelda's round face again. "Aimee Semple McPherson's teacher taught me how to play the tambourine. Sister McPherson herself used to stand there in the doorway mimicking me. We will see her up in heaven with the

Foursquares. Oh, Sister McPherson could touch sinners' hearts. Amen!"

Sister Fish put the chicken package back down and lifted both arms, pretending to play her tambourine although it wasn't there. When her wrists flashed you could almost see it. The instrument and she were the same thing.

"I would hit it with my thumb like this, *zip!* And twirl around. *Twirl* around!"

Now she was moving with a clarity all over the kitchen, hitting the magic tambourine against her hip. Her hands flew everywhere as she scooted back and forth.

"'That tambourine is *anointed!*' Sister McPherson used to call out when she watched me taking lessons. She stood in the doorway against the sun. *Bam!* Oh, her voice was lovely." Zelda hit her tambourine against her palm. "*Zambo!* I was quite the tambourinist in my youth. *Tring! Ring! Chinnng!*"

She let the tambourine fall and stood with her hands on the sink, staring at the backyard. The house felt good. Roxanne had climbed on the kitchen counter and was trying to touch the ceiling with her fingers, but her mother knew the angels were holding her. Her mother didn't notice she had her street shoes on.

"Sister McPherson founded the whole Foursquare Church. What are you doing up there? Get *down.*"

Roxanne disobeyed, stretching higher, not holding on. Sunlight fell in white stripes across her black patent leather Mary Janes. Of course they were slightly too big from the Missionary Box, but they looked cute. She could almost touch the ceiling if she balanced perfectly.

"Oh!" Her mother hit the tambourine that wasn't there against her left hand, softly. Something banged in the other room.

"Colleen?"

"I want my family! Where do they live?"

"You are not adopted! Oh dear." Zelda paced. "Oh! Grandmother and I used to walk to Angelus Temple from where we lived."

The tambourine hand described an arc in the air, and Roxanne could see them walking along those California streets. There were avocados everywhere.

"You know, that's where Grandmother was saved, under Sister McPherson's ministry."

"Were there palm trees?"

"Oh yes." Her mother swayed, hitting a chair lightly with the palm of her hand, listening. "Sister McPherson had the Holy Ghost. She used to go out in the streets toward downtown, where it was crowded, a few blocks from the temple. I was just a little girl then. I remember one day when Grandmother and I followed her. Suddenly Sister McPherson stood stock-still. Suddenly she pointed up."

Roxanne and Zelda Fish both looked toward the ceiling, at the blue Los Angeles sky.

"She took off running toward Angelus Temple with her finger pointing overhead, looking up, and more and more people started to run behind her. They were looking up too. Oh, they were curious! Pretty soon there was a huge crowd running and looking up and trying to watch their feet, although Sister McPherson didn't watch hers. I suppose there were angels. She ran across the street and right into the temple, up the aisle onto the platform, and then she turned around and waited for the temple to fill. And there they were. Standing there lost and dying! Staring up."

"And?" Roxanne already knew. She balanced on one foot.

"And then she preached. And when she gave the altar call they ran down sobbing. Then later my best friend Florence and I went out in evangelistic work. Man, I used to love to start up street meetings! Sister McPherson was gone by then. Florence and I would come home from holding our revival meetings in the Midwest, fresh off the train, right at Union Station in downtown Los Angeles. We were still excited! We locked our luggage up and walked straight to City Hall, we had so much zing. Florence played her accordion and I got my tambourine, *tring!* and hit it on my hip, *bam!* and hit it up here on my hand, *wham!* Sparks would fly. And the people started gathering with that Holy Ghost look in their eyes. Oh! I could feel them right here in the palm of my hand." She held the palm out. "Now, Florence was good on the accordion. And when we had them gathered I began to preach. And they found Jesus! Right there at First and Main! On the sidewalks around City Hall!" Zelda laughed. "We preached salvation and we preached sin. We ate ice cream! Then I met your father."

"And you heard wedding bells!" Roxanne teetered.

"Can we get a TV?" yelled Colleen.

"Young lady? I would be very careful if I were you. God smote the Egyptians." And Zelda dashed out the door to throw the chicken package in the garbage.

Roxanne landed on the floor with both arms out. She found two baking pans, smeared them with lard, and used a chair to thumbtack a chenille bedspread over the doorway to the dining room so Colleen could not come in. Now the kitchen was her own. In utter freedom she could climb along the cupboards, precariously holding on and touching the ceiling, surrounded by angels. She turned the oven on to three hundred and seventy-five degrees. Zelda pulled the back door open, letting in a late breeze. The chenille bedspread blew.

"Some people slandered Sister McPherson, but they didn't know what they were saying. There was nobody like her." The ghostly tambourine was in her hand again, so real you could hear it. *Ching!*

A loud ringing jarred them both, but it was only Sister Beverly Cedars wanting prayer on the telephone for her hives. Because she was not married you said her first name. They all gathered around the phone, praying in their separate voices, including Colleen, who mumbled her words on purpose. The spell of California had been broken. Roxanne opened the yellow cake mix and tasted it.

Her mother pulled the chenille bedspread back, ready to go

off by herself and wrestle with God in earnest about Winston's wallet. "Well, Winona Johnson is in heaven. I hope the Boone church gets a pastor soon so your father can rest. Winona Johnson has gone on ahead. I didn't know her, but she knew Jesus. I guess we'll all meet up there."

Standing on tiptoe, Roxanne could feel her own muscles. She was full of something yellow. It was fun just breathing.

"Man!" Zelda cried. "If Jesus hadn't found me I would be a hoodlum in a prison somewhere. I just know it! The devil is strong, but God is stronger."

Roxanne broke two eggs.

"Now, where in the *world* is your father's wallet? Twenty-five dollars!" She sighed. "Well, I'd better get down on my knees before the Throne."

"And Colleen isn't my real name," said Colleen.

• • • • •

If she did grow up, Roxanne would marry Elvis Presley, and so would Superba Andrews, her best friend. The two girls planned to live together always. Of course, growing up was not that likely, with the Lord coming back.

"I'd like to live outside when we grow up. On the grass with the furniture," Roxanne explained. "With a lamp under a tree."

"And butterflies."

"And our husband Elvis Presley."

Roxanne and Superba lay between the bushes and the Beardshear School brick wall, staring blankly at the sky, free from all responsibility. On Saturdays the school was deserted, except for the ants and ladybugs and butterflies. On your back the clouds became wild animals from Africa, a few elephants and many rhinoceroses. Across Carroll Street was the Assembly of God Church, white cross sticking up, and behind it the parsonage where the Fishes lived. So far the Christians were still on earth. If the Lord came, Roxanne would be sucked across the street to go up with them. Superba was not really a Christian, but she was not a sinner either. Roxanne could smell her slightly olive skin. Superba had short brown hair and was special, someone in a category all her own. Boys all over Ames followed her helplessly, up and down the Beardshear School stairs and the fire escape leading to the roof, shocked devotion in their eyes. Roxanne was not nervous with Superba. They relaxed. The clouds shifted. A giraffe appeared.

"Water Lily Maidens?" Superba spoke first.

The two girls jumped up and ran out onto the huge school lawn. Water Lily Maidens was their favorite game. They played it every day.

There was a storm on the surface of the lake because men were coming.

"Help!" shrieked Superba.

They dove. The world was full of green grass, which was how Iowa smelled. Here you could breathe. They dove down to the very bottom of the lake through the grass, which encouraged them. Safe at last, they smoothed their golden clothes.

"How do these earrings look?" demanded Superba, holding up imaginary rubies.

"Quite fabulous."

Roxanne turned toward her own ornate dressing table, where she began dusting her nose with a large powder puff from Younkers Department Store in Des Moines. It had a pink ribbon on top. Unlike Christians, they wore earrings, for they were Water Lily Maidens. Of course everything was waterproof. At the bottom of the lake was a crystal palace, but without a roof, so you could swim up. Even though they were underwater, they could breathe. They were not mermaids, exactly. They had legs. But the men were calling their names, and they were afraid it might be that killing thing, love.

"Oh, hold on!" cried Superba, grasping a Greek pillar.

"My fingers are slipping! Help!"

"Do not listen! Oh, help! Stuff this cotton in your ears!"

Roxanne and Superba held fast on the lake's bottom, their long hair pinned with barrettes, lace around the low necks of their gowns. Their breasts gleamed. In their underwater palace, despite their yelling, they could still hear the men.

"Superba! Roxanne!"

"We must not listen to them! Hold on tighter!" they screamed. The oak tree cut their grasping fingers.

"Come to me! My darling!" the fierce hunters cried. Handsome, with beards, they had chanced on this lake and seen the maidens bathing. They had fallen in love instantly, blindly, with a passion such as they had never known.

"Eeeeek!"

Their maiden fingers slipped, and as they neared the surface they writhed and clutched in desperation, for they were creatures of the lake and could not bear dry land. They were Water Lily Maidens. The passionate hunters with liquid eyes reached toward them in anguish. Flesh touched. A horrid pain seared them. Their preternatural shrieks split the air.

Superba stood up. "I better go eat."

The two girls walked across the lawn toward Carroll Street, with its white line. The woman standing on the grass was someone they had not seen approach. Pretty, she looked slightly old-fashioned.

"I found this," she said, holding out a wallet.

Superba, who was the closest, took it.

"Oh!" said Roxanne. She grabbed the wallet. Inside were two ten-dollar bills and five ones. When she looked up, the woman was gone.

"Where is she?"

"I don't know." Superba's mouth wouldn't close. "I think she had a blue nose."

The two girls ran up Carroll, almost flying. They waited for a car to pass and raced across the street, then down the side path along Roxanne's friend the hedge, which said hello to her in hedge language. Reaching out, Roxanne brushed it with her fingers. They leaped up the steps and in the screen door, slamming it.

"We got Dad's wallet!"

"Well, praise God!" said Pastor Fish, who had returned while the girls were underwater powdering their noses. He held up the painted window screen, finally ready to hang it. Zelda, who was in the dining room peeling carrots, added one more to the pile. On the piano bench Colleen continued to brush her hair.

"Where did you find it?" asked Pastor Fish.

"A woman handed it to me."

"She had a blue nose," added Superba.

One by one the Fishes stopped what they were doing.

"Was it an angel?" said Sister Fish.

"I think so. Afterward she just disappeared. I never saw her before."

"Superba? You saw her too?"

Superba nodded vigorously.

"A blue nose," said Winston. "It is true they are not human." He took his wallet and examined it, counting out the bills. "Angels often have one feature that is wrong." He put the wallet in his pocket. "The money is all here."

"What was she wearing?" Colleen was peering out the front door.

"A navy blue dress thing. I can't remember her feet, but the dress had buttons, and her hair was in a bun. It's out of style now."

"It's funny, but heaven does seem behind about two years, according to most accounts."

"Now, Zelda. Heaven is not about high fashion."

"Was her hair brown?"

"Bright yellow," said Superba.

"We are protected *at all moments* by the love of God," said Zelda, tears coming suddenly into her eyes. "Hallelujah."

Roxanne turned a somersault.

"By the way," said Winston. "Which reminds me. At the funeral today an old navy chum came up to me. Not a chum, really. I have to say I hardly knew him. Engstrom. Claims he wants to kill me."

"Kill you?" echoed Zelda.

"He's still mad from when we were both wrestlers on the base in Pensacola. He said I stepped on his right hand and broke his grip. His life went downhill, he claims. Well, he may be right. There was one year I drank and had many a blackout. Jesus saved me on September eighth."

"But you do remember him?" asked Zelda.

Colleen hit middle C on the piano.

"Well, yes. Somewhat, anyway. Engstrom. He was a quiet man, and he took off his glasses to wrestle. He was heavier then. I would say he was above average. Somewhat. Barely. The muscles of his jaw were working like a maniac's when I saw him today, just chewing away."

Zelda bit a carrot. "He came right up?"

"No. He waited until they lowered the coffin down in. He was polite as far as that goes, but I doubt he's living for the Lord. His fingernails were filthy. I remember now he was out of Colorado. As a wrestler he called himself the Badger. Claims I ruined his career."

"Well, me," said Zelda. "Let us ask God to protect you."

The Fish family knelt, as it was serious, everyone leaning elbows against various furniture, Superba kneeling at the couch, back straight, holding her hands flat together like a Catholic. Real Christians raised both hands to God or rested their faces against their palms or wove their fingers into fists, for these gestures were sincere, but they let Superba be. Colleen lifted the seat of the piano bench and looked inside. To get extra faith, Roxanne squeezed her eyes impossibly tight.

Zelda prayed. "Dear God, protect Winston from this Badger man."

They stood up.

"God is a very present help in time of need." Zelda's face was lit from inside. Now you could see she was immortal.

"By the way, we thank you, God, for this wallet," said Winston, holding the slight object out before him.

It was brown, cracked, simple, but it had the air of heaven around it.

Each standing in a moment of eternity, they floated in the living room, aware of Blue Nose, grateful to be going up, grateful for Iowa, grateful for the piano with its white keys.

● ● ● ● ●

The next night, Sunday, Pastor Fish preached against getting hysterical over angels, but the congregation had heard about the sighting and was looking for Blue Nose in every corner of the sanctuary. Sister Witter actually held up her gold compact, flashing the mirror toward the back, on the pretext of powdering her nose. People stretched and scratched their ears and looked for songbooks on any chance of turning around. On the left, seated behind pew two and facing the giant map of Africa on the church wall, the entire retarded Nedley family bounced and pushed, making no pretense of listening to the sermon. On the center aisle their smallest boy wiggled the loose threads of the worn church carpet with his toe until his father's dirty hand descended on his head. It was not really dirt. Brother Nedley worked on cars. All their mouths hung open, and Roxanne opened hers too.

Pastor Fish looked at his flock. "I want to ask you something. What if Jesus should come back tonight? Oh, you may go up, but what will Jesus say? Will He say, 'Well done, my good and faithful servant'? Souls are dying and going to hell up and down the streets of Ames, Iowa, yet you twist around and look for blue-nosed angels. Shame on you!"

"I am adopted," Colleen wrote with a pen on her own hand. Zelda, nodding encouragement at her husband, could not see. "HELP."

"Glory!" cried Brother Witter, who was almost deaf.

On the platform Colleen's bedroom door was slightly ajar, and now it blew open. All the congregation jumped. Pastor Fish walked over and closed it. When he came back he stared at them again. He was wearing his red tie and his navy pinstripe store-bought suit.

"God isn't all fancy tricks. If Jesus comes back tonight He's going to ask you what you've done to spread the gospel, Christians. This is the First Assembly of God Church, not Barnum and Bailey Circus. Don't anybody turn your head."

Everyone held still, for the moment at least.

"Oh, it is true that we have miracles, and there are certain Christian groups who will not talk to us because of that. They think we are dangerous. Because we have the Holy Ghost!" Pastor Fish banged his fist on the pulpit.

"We all know what happened years ago at the conference of the National Association of Evangelicals. Can you imagine how it felt? There the Pentecostals were — Holy Rollers, they were called — new members eager to participate. These Holy Rollers were farmers mostly, people who earned meager livings. There were no doctors. But these Holy Rollers spoke in tongues. They prophesied. They practiced divine healing and they cast out demons! This was a whole new thing." Pastor Fish's cheeks were pink.

"The three Pentecostal delegates took their seats, fine men chosen carefully by the newborn congregations that had sprung up. Excited, they sat up straight while the National Association of Evangelicals conducted its business. Finally it was their turn. At the podium President Bingham turned their way and pointed. There they sat in their three wooden folding chairs. They scooted forward, eager to stand and be introduced. I suppose one chair creaked.

"'These three are of the devil! We are asking the delegates from the Assembly of God Church to leave! Out!' The three delegates blinked. 'You people are the Last Vomit of Satan!' Bingham bellowed at them. So out they went, their tails between their legs, and all the Evangelicals pointing at them. For this was a respected body. They were a respected body, but they did not have the power of God in their midst! Oh, they may make heaven, but they do not have the Holy Ghost. They do not have miracles! Angels do not visit them!

"The Holy Ghost scares people, people! The Holy Ghost is a wind that blows where it will. The Holy Ghost can speak to us directly, and that scares the Nazarenes. It scares the Baptists. It doesn't scare the Foursquares. The Holy Ghost speaks to them too." Pastor Fish was getting hoarse, from the volume of his voice. "Sometimes our neighbors even call the police when we make noise. Holy Ghost power scares the world!" He leaned forward, attempting vainly to make eye contact. "Yet what is this power for?"

The congregation faced front, staring at him blankly. Their torsos strained sideways, ready to greet Blue Nose if she flew in. They had not heard a word he said. Next door Chick Woolworth slammed his window shut.

"'But ye shall receive power, after that the Holy Ghost is come upon you: and ye shall be witnesses.' Acts 1:8."

Sister Witter worked her fan, using her whole arm because her wrist was crippled from arthritis. The Witters had a farm south of town, but now they were retired. They had sold off all the cows and most of the pasture.

"The time is short, people." Pastor Fish swallowed, his throat dry. He did not keep water at the pulpit. This practice he found theatrical. "How many in Ames are saved? How many are going to hell?" In one furious gesture he threw his Bible off the pulpit. It landed on the Communion Table.

"Jesus may come before this service ends. We do not have *time* to look for angels in the audience. Yes, they exist. Oh, they visit us. But who did you tell about eternal life today?" he shouted.

Now the congregation was listening. They had never seen their pastor mad before.

"*Power.* Power to witness!"

"Amen!"

"Power to save souls!"

"Yes!"

"Oh yes! It is true we are going to meet Jesus in the air. But souls are lost! The grocer! The librarian downtown! We are Pentecostal, people! We have power to talk about the Second Coming to the postman. Angels!" Pastor Fish shook his head. "Christians, we have work to do."

Thelma Nichols turned around to recapture her broken belt (she was getting fat), and there the angel was. Sister Nichols simply stared, her belt hanging down from one loop.

Pastor Fish stopped thumping with his fist and gazed toward the back.

The woman from the lawn at Beardshear School stood behind the last pew, her golden hair pulled into a bun. Her nose did seem slightly blue, and her dress was definitely dated, the hem too long. Roxanne and all the saints looked at her.

"Which way is downtown?" said the angel.

"It is to my right," said Pastor Fish. "That would be your left. Three blocks, then turn right by the power company."

Not a Christian moved.

"Thank you," said the angel. She turned and departed.

"Whoop!" said Brother Witter.

When the fire fell that night, there was hardly a saint left standing. Roxanne waited in pew one, her body limp, feeling the Holy Ghost move around the room. Her eyes got bleary. The Christians lay sprawled every which way with their feet turned out, possessed, utterly helpless. Roxanne swung her legs, thinking of Blue Nose. Angels hardly ever showed off by flying. They often had a sense of humor, and did not carry purses.

Pastor Fish stepped among his congregation, tending the sheep, calling for a revival in Ames. For souls were going to hell. Satan waited outside the door, camped on the Ames, Iowa, battlefield. Tonight the Christians were filled. The Holy Ghost had visited them. Slain under the power, Sister Beverly Cedars went down. Limbs lay twitching in all directions as the saints spoke in tongues, talking to God in a heavenly language. Their voices were beautiful, sometimes guttural, sometimes high as a bird's.

Roxanne swung her legs and listened. Sister Fish found a blue sweater and covered the skin at Beverly Cedars' waist where her blouse had ridden up. The pastor and his wife stepped over bodies, careful not to squash anyone, Zelda gently clapping her hands. God was here. Roxanne fought to stay awake. Tomorrow they were going downtown to buy the girls fabric for new dresses, if the Lord did not come tonight. All listened for the trumpet, which was gold. How eternal the air felt! The Woolworths' kitchen lights were on next door, their shades down. Happy, Roxanne sat still. God was real. It didn't matter what the science teacher said. Death was not real. At the piano Sister Weston quit playing and knelt down at the altar, falling on her back almost at once. Her face softened. Hallelujahs filled the sanctuary.

Finally the Holy Ghost departed. One by one the Christians got up, their cheeks flushed, their eyes clear. Even the retarded Nedley family didn't look retarded, their faces gathered into something different. People collected their things and went outside. Sister Beverly Cedars still lay on the carpet, the blue sweater over her midriff. Her arms still reached toward heaven, and the peace that passeth understanding made her face young. Small cat sounds came out of her small mouth. At last her arms came down and consciousness returned. Sister Beverly Cedars sat up.

Roxanne went outside.

Christians peppered the lawn, speaking of croquet if the Lord tarried, looking for their various automobiles. Brother Ransom kicked his tires for good measure. The stars were bright, sharp, the sky black. You could smell plowed dirt out on the edge of town. Iowa soil was the envy of the world. The saints stood on the grass and the sidewalk, saying good night. Seams went up the women's legs, crooked now. They were all still on earth, waiting for the trumpet sound. Ames was quiet tonight. Car headlights crisscrossed Carroll Street, illuminating its white line. Sister Beverly Cedars came out carrying her Bible and purse, blouse tucked in but hair wild, the Holy Ghost about her still. Her Bible was zipped.

"Look," said Pastor Fish.

Thelma and Lyle Nichols and the Fishes stood on the side path, the last to leave. Light poured out the open double church doors, illuminating Ames, Iowa.

"Sputnik."

They craned their necks.

"Where?" said Thelma Nichols. "I don't see it."

"There." Pastor Fish pointed overhead. "Flashing on and off."

And there it was, invention of the Union of Soviet Socialist Republics, directly over the church. Of course, the Russians would be crushed in time.

"That Khrushchev is a pill," observed Sister Fish.

"It seems to be working." Pastor Fish stood rooted, looking up.

"The Russians are trying to destroy us. Communists! And that man's finger sitting next to that red button all day long." Thelma Nichols sneezed for emphasis.

"My," said Zelda. "I would think a sinner would be sorely *afraid* with the atom bomb flying toward him. To miss out on eternity!"

A rustling made Roxanne look left, toward the hedge, and there was Blue Nose in the Lutheran neighbors' yard. The others were looking up, including Thelma, who was peeking through her hands. She did not want the Russians to photograph her. The angel looked directly into Roxanne's eyes.

"Lo, I am with you alway, even unto the end of the world." She pinched Roxanne's nose.

"Ouch!"

"What's wrong?" said Sister Fish.

The angel vanished from the hedge.

"They think there is no God," said Winston.

Thelma Nichols took one final look at Sputnik. "Blink, blink, blink to you," she said.

Welcome Wagon Day

ZELDA'S JOB as Welcome Wagon Hostess was to greet new families who had just moved to Ames. Today was Wednesday, and they had to hurry in order not to miss the midweek service at church.

"We want Three twenty-three Duff," said Zelda. "This is Nine hundred." She hummed, checking the curb for house numbers. Already three out of four women had been home, and she had just picked Roxanne up at Beardshear School.

It was fun to drive around Ames in the pink Pontiac. After 323 Duff they would rush to eat tomato soup and Saltines before church. Roxanne's mouth watered as she added butter. Colleen was secretly visiting her friend Maria, a sinner, and although Roxanne disapproved, she would not tell. Colleen was going to hell.

"Roxanne! You are going to freeze us. Roll that window up!" Zelda hummed and drove slowly, happy to be out and about.

People new to Ames did not realize you weren't sinners, and sometimes you could just sit lounging on their couch and looking around. As Zelda passed the house of Jason, the boy with black hair from school, Roxanne blushed and fiddled with the radio, careful not to linger on rock and roll, which was the devil's drumbeat from Africa. You had to move the dial fast, for the pulse could actually lodge in your head, the way the Charleston had with Zelda. Roxanne located *The Great Gildersleeve*, her father's favorite radio play, just as Zelda pulled over.

"Here we are. The Bells, Three twenty-three Duff."

Roxanne pushed the Pontiac door against the November snow. She put her mittens on and picked up the Welcome Wagon bag firmly. At dinner she would observe Colleen to see if she had committed the Unpardonable Sin by watching television. Roxanne stepped into the snow on the curb and felt it crunch. Her job was to dig into the Welcome Wagon bag and find just the right gift at just the right moment. She looked up, stamping her feet. This house had yellow shutters, which were beautiful.

"Do you have the bag?"

Roxanne lifted it.

"Now, the Bells are from Arizona, but their folder doesn't say what the husband does. Stand up, Roxanne, don't hunch."

There was no car in the driveway, which had been shoveled quite recently. It had not snowed since morning, and the sky was the clearest blue imaginable. Iowa in the winter had completely different smells except for one, the smell of Iowa itself, the dirt, which you could get through everything if you concentrated and sniffed lightly.

Roxanne sniffed. "Can I make a snow angel?" she said.

"No. Not in other people's yards."

Zelda rang the doorbell, and Roxanne shifted from foot to foot, regarding Mrs. Bell's yard with longing. It was perfect, with its untouched thick snow, and made her toes itch. She stepped in place while Zelda rang the doorbell again.

"Go ahead," said a voice behind them.

Mrs. Bell came around the corner without gloves or boots, cradling two logs against her coat. She was round, petite, gorgeous. Her teeth were like pearls, her eyes intelligent, and she wore both lipstick and earrings, the trademark of sinners. Now she laughed at her predicament, unable to shake hands.

"Welcome to Ames, Mrs. Bell. My name is Zelda Fish, and this is my daughter Roxanne."

"What wonderful red hair she has!"

"Yes, that comes from my mother's side out in California." Zelda lifted up Roxanne's cap and squashed it back down. "May we give you some gifts from the merchants of Ames?"

"Yes, but first a snow angel." Mrs. Bell smiled widely. "That is exactly what this yard needs." She held the logs. "Go on!"

Blushing, Roxanne looked at her mother, who nodded.

Carefully she walked out into the yard. Falling backwards, she landed stiff, flat, arms at her sides, without losing her nerve and bending at the last minute. She lay still. Snow came out on all sides of her. It was going to be beautiful. Elbows locked, she moved her arms up and down, up and down, scooping out wings. Carefully she got up.

"Perfect!"

Both women laughed.

"The furnace is way high!" Still laughing, Mrs. Bell pushed the door open with her hip and stepped in. The Fishes followed, struck by the heat. "Coming from Phoenix, I can't adjust it properly."

One of the logs slid sideways, but when Zelda went to catch it the other log slid the other way. Their arms flailed, and the logs tumbled to the floor. Mrs. Bell burst out giggling, and Zelda joined in. Roxanne watched the two women as if they were a strange species. Grownups were hard to fathom.

"At least it wasn't your best china," said Zelda, and the women started in again.

"And you're from California?" Mrs. Bell washed her hands, which were red from the cold. Pink fingernail polish flashed. "I suppose you miss the warm air."

"More the mountains. This flat land seems empty, but I wouldn't change places with anybody. We live about a mile away."

"Excellent. Let me get you some coffee."

The women laughed again, as if they were children. This house had real woodwork, and Roxanne's eyes followed it around the floor and up the doorways. Phoenix! No wonder Mrs. Bell was missing gloves and boots. While she was heating the coffee up, Roxanne took off her rubbers. Zelda put them next to hers on the doormat and hung their coats on hooks. Roxanne wandered into the living room, where two couches stood askew. Curtains on rods lay around the floor at odd angles. Cardboard boxes stood unopened in three stacks along one wall, like Missionary Boxes, only smaller. They were marked "Books."

"Too hot?" called Mrs. Bell.

The living room was sweltering, and the Fishes unbuttoned their blouses at the collar. The heat made it difficult to breathe. Zelda walked over to the stacked boxes and began arranging the papers in her folder.

Mrs. Bell entered, carrying a tray. She wore capris, another sin. "It *is* too hot."

She looked around for a place to set the refreshments down, but the only thing resembling a table was the stack of cartons that had just been taken over by Welcome Wagon papers. Both women laughed again, and Roxanne did too. There was no place to set things! Mrs. Bell put the tray on the floor.

"Let's move this furniture," said Zelda.

They dragged the big couch with the flowers to one wall, Roxanne on her mother's side, and then eyeballed the whole room for beauty.

"No," said Mrs. Bell. She pointed. "It has to be that wall."

They dragged the couch again. This time, they agreed, it looked as if it had been made to fit there, against the wallpaper with thin pale-green stripes. All three nodded. They started on the second couch, solid beige, and changed their minds halfway across the floor, sliding it to the right of the fireplace. Mrs. Bell smelled good. It was true she was a sinner, something you could tell from the ashtrays as well.

"If we don't turn that furnace down we'll faint." Zelda looked around, hands on her hips. "Where is it?"

They adjusted the furnace and went back to work, dragging

furniture, stepping back to look. Slowly the room took shape, except for the stacks of boxes and the curtains scattered around the floor. The room was cooling, although it was too late not to sweat.

"I met someone I like," said Mrs. Bell. "*Quelle* relief."

The coffee table was in place now, and they moved the tray. The coffee was cold, but the three of them ate cookies, Oreos with frosting in the middle, munching and admiring their efforts.

"Yes, yes, yes," said Mrs. Bell, leaning back.

"Now I would like to welcome you to Ames."

"You already have." Mrs. Bell stretched out her capri legs, but Zelda, who abhorred such clothing, seemed not to notice. She motioned for Roxanne to grab the bag.

"Now, what does your husband do?" Zelda wiped her forehead with a handkerchief.

"Doctor." Mrs. Bell licked her fingers. "He's taking over Dr. Harvey's practice because Dr. Harvey wants to retire."

"My!" Zelda Fish too licked her fingers. "Are they acquainted?"

"Since my husband was at medical school. So Ames is a far cry from Phoenix, but I think we'll like it here."

"Ames is a good town. It has a good air. Plus it has concerts in the bandshell all summer, and the college on the other end, in the part we call Dog Town." Finger on her list, Zelda sat up straighter, and Roxanne followed suit. "Chickin Lickin Family Restaurant out on the highway has two free meals."

"Yum," said Mrs. Bell. "We can use those this evening."

"Yes. And Emmet's Cleaners has a coupon for a man's suit and two women's dresses, free of charge. Emmet's is a good cleaners. There's another one west of town, but they don't give anything."

Roxanne had the Emmet's coupon ready, and she held it out, a pink one. It was fun to concentrate. Mrs. Bell's pink fingernails glistened as she took it, and Roxanne tried to see if the fingernail moons showed, to tell Colleen. You could definitely see them. Roxanne extended each coupon without a mistake: Raker's Hardware, a free rake; J.C. Penney, which gave socks in all sizes for both males and females. There were free brake inspections and a free permanent. Mrs. Bell set the coupons out on the coffee table in a fan shape, which came from playing cards, a sin also, and blew Roxanne a kiss.

Zelda held out the mayor's official letter of welcome. "This tells where all the parks are. We have several, but the largest one is Brookside Park, out by the college. It has a nice tennis court."

"Dr. Bell plays tennis. He'll be happy to hear that."

"It has a swinging bridge," added Roxanne, and blushed, surprised to hear her own voice. She was usually shy with sinners, but Mrs. Bell had said her hair was wonderful.

"Do you have children?" said Zelda.

"No, but we're trying to. Is this your only one?"

"We have two." Zelda put her papers in the folder. "Roxanne and her sister, Colleen." Slowly she stood up, stretching, and for a moment Roxanne thought she might do the Charleston, but she was only working stiff limbs.

From the foyer near the front door, the two grownups cast a backward glance at the living room arrangements. A clock chimed four times. As they were putting on their coats, Zelda smoothed her daughter's red hair. Roxanne wished Mrs. Bell would call it wonderful again.

"Are you sure you have to leave?"

"We'll let you move in. You were awfully good to locate those refreshments." Impulsively Zelda picked up a floor lamp and moved it closer to the couch. It looked right immediately.

"Let me just unpack this china and I'll cook us all dinner." Mrs. Bell leaned back against the foyer wall, legs spraddled. "We have a cat en route that Roxanne can play with. What does your husband do?"

"He's a minister here in town."

"How nice." Mrs. Bell discreetly drew her knees together. "Presbyterian? We're not very religious."

"Assembly of God," said Zelda. She paused. "I am not supposed to do this, but I would like to invite you out to church."

"I've heard of that." Mrs. Bell pursed her red lips and turned away to fiddle with the shade of the floor lamp, which did not need fiddling with. When she turned back, her beautiful face was distant. You would not guess they had just moved furniture.

"The snake people?" she said casually. She stepped toward the front door, one arm out to open it. "You put them on a pole? And pray?"

"Oh my, no. Snakes." Zelda's voice was calm. "We believe in the power of God to save sinners' souls."

"Now I remember. You pray instead of going to the doctor. The Assembly of God." Mrs. Bell was staring at them, her eyes cold. Her capris were green. "You try to heal diseases by praying. My husband is a doctor."

Zelda had been putting on her boots. Now she stopped. "Your husband is a doctor? My! I'm surprised he does not investigate divine healing."

"Divine healing!" Mrs. Bell laughed, a squeaky sound.

Zelda looked her directly in the eye. "Mrs. Bell, I am going to invite you out to hear my husband's brother when he preaches next time. Roland Fish has the gift of healing. Your husband ought to investigate it. Isn't he a scientist?"

"I need to unpack," Mrs. Bell said, smiling like the dead, her face stretched tight. She adjusted each earring.

God didn't like earrings, but Mrs. Bell thought there was no God.

"Dr. Bell will be home soon. Goodbye." She picked out a cigarette from a gold tray on the umbrella table.

Zelda's eyes burned into hers, narrowing. "Organs start to function. People who had blurry vision see."

Mrs. Bell held up a hand to stop her, but Zelda kept on.

"Yes! Limbs straighten! Stomachaches disappear."

"Quacks," said Mrs. Bell to Zelda's coat lapel. "Goodbye."

Zelda took Roxanne's hand, mitten to mitten. Her voice was powerful, and it echoed.

"I am here to tell you God is real."

They stepped out into the snow, and the door stayed open behind them. Roxanne glanced left. In the waning light the snow angel looked stupid, not beautiful. The sky was pink. How Roxanne wished the Lord would come tonight! Then the Bells would be left. But it did not look like it.

"Please don't bother us," said Mrs. Bell from the doorway.

Roxanne and her mother walked down the neatly shoveled path, a tall and a short Martian, and got into the pink Fish Pontiac. The doctor's wife was still watching, and indeed she did look lost, her mouth frozen in a little smile.

"She's shaking her head," said Roxanne, peering into the rearview mirror as they pulled away. You couldn't see the snow angel.

"She does not believe in God," said Zelda. "Oh! I once felt as she does. I was lost and blind out in the world."

Zelda drove slowly through the snow, and Roxanne watched as long as she could, staring into the mirror at the doctor's wife, who hadn't moved. Jason was in his front yard talking to an older boy. Roxanne slid down in her seat. They turned the corner, and the car engine whirred.

"She was nice at first." Roxanne touched her red hair. "What does 'cat en route' mean?"

"In a cage. Most of Ames will not go up. Strait is the gate, and few there be that find it."

They turned again, and there the church was, the double doors, the white cross sticking up, the flat roof, the Lutherans to the left, the Woolworths to the right. The church walls needed new shingles. Zelda rolled up to the curb without pulling into the driveway.

"Get Colleen," she said. "I feel like ice cream."

Colleen was back in no time, for the Fishes never bought ice cream except on sale. Roxanne sat in front. Zelda drove directly to the end of town, where the Dairy Queen was, blue against the darkening sky. In the distance you could see snow on silos and two cows.

"If Jesus hadn't found me!"

With one hand Zelda hit the steering wheel. When Roxanne looked back, Colleen shrugged. Zelda swung into the Dairy Queen.

"Any flavor we want?" said Colleen.

"If God hadn't found me you girls would not be here. I would be in a jail cell! Oh! I have done terrible things." Zelda's eyes looked dangerous. "But God found me and I got saved. And all my family. We're going up!" She turned the car off, and they sat there. "Mrs. Bell cannot see."

Colleen leaned forward. "How many scoops?"

The girls both got chocolate, double scoops, and Zelda got vanilla, and they drove out to the country eating them.

"Terrible things?" said Colleen.

"Awful things! Sins! Roll the windows down!"

The girls did, and cold air rushed in. It felt exhilarating.

"Oh, I used to love to minister to men down in their cells in the prisons. As tough as they were. Oh! I could have been one."

Both girls looked at her admiringly.

"Which sins?" said Colleen.

Zelda turned toward the small town of Gilbert, thirteen miles west. "For all have sinned and come short of the glory of God. God can forgive anything. Glory."

"Robbing banks?"

"Oh! Much worse."

"Killing people?" Colleen took a bite of ice cream.

"I hope you never find out!"

With that Zelda turned into a ditch, neatly, as though she had planned it. Deep and broad, the ditch cradled them, and snow from up above fell on the windshield. All the Fish women held their breath. The headlights shone out beautifully. For the second time that day Zelda Fish began to giggle, but stopped to lick her ice cream cone so it wouldn't drip. The girls giggled for her. The ice cream tasted fabulous. They were in the ditch, but they were saved. Nothing could hurt them. Zelda's foot touched the accelerator, but the tires merely spun.

"Praise the Lord," she said.

They all climbed out and walked toward the nearest farmhouse, where a man was already looking out the window at them.

"I need to call my husband," said Zelda.

"Come in," said the farmer, who wore coveralls. "I see you went off the edge."

• • • • •

"We had a good day," said Winston.

Tucked inside her tent, Roxanne watched her parents' feet come and go. The blanket house was draped over the furniture and went all the way to the piano. Jennifer Smith stood against the bench leg waiting for her boyfriend Paul to pick her up. It was almost eleven o'clock.

Assistant Pastor Weston had driven their father out to where the car was stuck, then gone back to church to preach. The Fishes had waited for the tow truck together, talking about Ames. Zelda and Winston spoke softly, holding hands. With their parents' permission the girls climbed up the snowbank on the farmer's side and slid down. Angels watched, of course. It was past dark when the tow truck arrived at the ditch, and just before the altar call when the Fishes arrived at Wednesday night prayer meeting. Now, warm and dry, they were having Campbell's tomato soup and Saltines. In church Saltines were the body and blood of Christ, but not here. Roxanne ate one with globs of butter on it as her mother's hand reached down and extended a bowl of soup.

"Zelda!" said Winston. She could just see her father's feet. "I don't know why you let her put these blankets over every chair in the house. We can't even get through the living room."

"It's a tent house," said Roxanne, dipping her spoon in the soup.

"Well, take it down tonight."

"I told her she could leave it up three days." Zelda handed Roxanne another cracker. This butter was even thicker.

"Three days! Why, we can't get in our bedroom this way. We'll have to go around."

"Winston."

Roxanne went back to eating. Mrs. Bell seemed right, but she was wrong, even if the kids at school said your mother looked like a ghost without lipstick. Christians had been persecuted since the time of the lions. Christians were going up, and the saints from Ames would meet the saints from Boone in the air. Roxanne's father got saved as a young man, sitting in a Buick up in Minnesota with his brother Roland, a Christian of three weeks. God had blinded Roland with a light so bright it hurt. Convinced, Roland reached across the Buick and shook his brother by the shoulders, telling him to pray. To his own surprise, Winston did. Suddenly God's presence filled the car, and Winston, a new man, looked out the windows and knew that he was eternal. The boys' mother, who liked poetry, was furious. Struck by the gospel, both men changed their lives. Winston dropped his plans to be a navy pilot and went to Bible school, and Roland went out west.

"Make those animal sounds," said Colleen now, her bare feet appearing outside the door blanket.

Roxanne put down her soup bowl and got on all fours in the tent house. "Oink, oink."

"Oh, stop that!" Zelda cried. "You sound like a real pig."

"Moo-oooo!"

"Demons!" screamed Colleen.

"Very funny. I am serious. Winston! Remember when we met?"

They retraced their early romance, Zelda and her friend Florence, young traveling evangelists from California, getting off the train at Oelwein, Iowa, to be greeted by young Pastor Fish, newly out of Bible School, ordination papers three months old. He had driven two hundred miles south from Minnesota to take this church. At the Oelwein station Zelda knew at once that she was going to marry him.

"We all went down the plank sidewalk toward the car," said Zelda dreamily.

"And you heard wedding bells!" both girls yelled.

"My whole life started there, at sunset. Oh, the devil tried to get me, and he still tries. I stole cars when I was a teenager! I drove them to Pomona or San Berdoo and hitchhiked back, and no one ever caught me. I still itch to get my hands on a Cadillac. I could be in jail today! Then you girls would not be here. Thank goodness God has washed my sins white as snow!" Zelda's voice seemed to echo around the house.

Pastor Fish stared at his wife, whose hazel eyes still sparkled from the ditch adventure. She picked up a cracker.

"But your father swept me off my feet, and we both knew it. Then we all went out for ice cream. Florence cried all night, but I didn't care."

"Vanilla, if I remember," said Winston.

"No. There were little bits of chocolate caught between my teeth."

In Roxanne's tent, yellow light came through the yellow squares of the blankets, making life look promising. Her mother took the empty bowl, and Roxanne's eyes closed by themselves. She had not brushed her teeth. This pillow was delicious. The whole Fish family was going up, except possibly Colleen. At this point Roxanne had not yet reached the Age of Accountability, twelve if you were stupid, ten if you were exceptional. Colleen, at twelve, so far showed no signs of anything. On the day you reached the Age of Accountability, you realized you were a sinner and you had to ask Jesus into your heart, quickly. Then He saved you as an adult. Roxanne sighed. Still nine, all she had to do was play and sweep the back porch once a day. Light hit her eyes and she blinked. Her father's hand held the blanket door back.

"Roxanne? Time to go to bed."

"Let's leave her here." Zelda's face appeared, and both her parents stared down.

"She has those one-eighth Icelandic eyes," said her father, who was going to let her stay put, "like my great-uncle Edgar's. His looked like they could see right through you, just like hers. I'll get out the pictures of him sometime."

The blanket flap fell back, and Roxanne tried to remember what her eyes looked like. She attempted sitting up, but nothing moved. The mirror by the piano seemed miles away.

"Sleep tight! The Lord bless you."

Footsteps receded. Roxanne hugged Miss Jennifer Smith tight in case the Lord came, for they might wake up here or there. At this moment Jennifer Smith was actually in Paris on her job as a parachute jumper. Just as Jennifer pulled the ripcord, Roxanne fell fast asleep.

Sunday School Room Three

AS USUAL, the service was boring. In pew three Roxanne leaned back, spying on the Woolworths next door, wiggling left for a better view. Colleen, being older, was babysitting in the nursery. It was getting dark outside. Chick Woolworth stood in his kitchen window, deliberately drinking a can of Pabst Blue Ribbon beer, his hairy belly exposed. Catching Roxanne's eye, he raised one finger, and she immediately looked away. The Christians ignored him, of course, but it took lots of energy. Now Chick Woolworth disappeared. Alcohol precipitated the Woolworths' insane behavior. Once it touched your lips you could not control anything you did. Roxanne waited curiously, but the window remained maddeningly quiet.

Some sinners were nice, of course. A few of the kids at school were friendly, but still, you would not be seeing them after death. The way was strait and narrow. Lutherans, Presbyterians, Episcopalians, they flouted God, sitting in movie theaters, wanton. Roxanne sighed. Unfortunately there were not that many kids her age going to heaven. In her father's Announcements from the Pulpit, Africa was in turmoil, which was a sure sign of His quick Sooncoming. In the Last Days there would be wars and rumors of wars. With the dark falling, Roxanne opened her drawing pad, something all children were allowed to have in church so they would not make noise. In heaven the Fish family was going to live in a huge house with three bedrooms and wall-to-wall carpeting, a mansion like the houses on the outskirts of Des Moines.

How she hoped the Ransom girls lived nearby. Of course, heaven wasn't that big.

Suddenly Roxanne sat up in the pew. Sister Beverly Cedars had seen the devil in the laundromat, staring at her from behind a dryer.

"He kept right on lookin' at me!" Sister Beverly Cedars cried. Her voice was wild and her eyes were wide. A chill traveled down the congregation's spine.

"Get thee *behind* me Satan!" Sister Beverly Cedars' voice rang out. "Glory!"

Now the congregation jumped. Only Lyle Nichols, as always, looked straight ahead. Employed at the electric company, he was an important man in Ames. He never moved, and it was hard to tell if he was listening or thinking about electricity. Sister Beverly Cedars stared, holding to the pew in front of her. Her knuckles were white. Several people looked around for Satan, but he wasn't in church. Except for Lyle Nichols all the congregation leaned forward.

"He gave a flinch, but he still stood his ground. The dryer kept right on goin'. Right on goin'. He smiled, and his teeth were white like in that Colgate picture. *Bright.* But when he tried to move and come at me? God Almighty paralyzed him!"

Voices went up.

"Holy Scripture did the trick, hallelujah!"

"Amen! Praise God!"

"Every word of God has the power of a two-edged sword!"

The congregation gave thanks, holding up their Bibles for Satan to see. Bibles had mysterious power. That was why you never set the salt and pepper on them, as Colleen was wont. Roxanne's Bible was white and looked like it belonged to a child. She wished she had a black one like her father's.

"Shondala seeleo! Heeleo! Praise God!" Sister Beverly Cedars sat down.

Roxanne breathed deeply. Weekdays were perilous for Christians, with the devil hiding even behind clothes dryers. Luckily they had midweek service every Wednesday. Even downtown Ames was not safe! Interested, Roxanne kept her ears perked. She had never seen the devil personally, although she knew he was there. She made a mental note to check the stacks of lumber at Raker's Hardware Store.

When the sermon started, Roxanne picked up her drawing pad. It was going to be a long evening, judging from the text, something about evil thinking, which meant Darwin. If the Holy Ghost interrupted, of course, things could pep up. Darwin was Survival of the Fittest, which meant Satan. Darwin, a scientist, went around trying to pry people away from God, and especially schoolchildren. At Beardshear Elementary her teacher Mrs. Brittain was nice, but being nice did not save you. Almost all of Ames was going to hell. Only Christians were safe. Roxanne wiggled all her fingers and toes, twenty at once, like an insect.

Today she drew a Sinner Climbing Trees, starting with the hair, a flip, and the face in profile with the nose sticking out. This sinner had a cute chin. After some consideration Roxanne drew a long neck. So far it looked good. She added dangly earrings. Roxanne thought she might be an artist if she weren't a Christian, but the Lord was coming, probably before Saturday. Nervously she looked out the window. However, Archangel Gabriel was absent. Gratefully she traced in arms upraised to a tree limb, pleased at the prospect of the bust. Roxanne glanced at her mother. Then she drew them: two enormous, stupendous, gargantuan melons bursting out of a cashmere sweater. Next she added on a leg with a bent knee, climbing up. Roxanne's ladies always wore heels, impossibly thin ones, four inches high. The other leg was on the ground. She wore capris, but of course she was a sinner. Roxanne put stripes on them. Cupping her left hand to hide the bosom, Roxanne drew in clouds and a sun, then hovered over the page, surveying her work with piercing admiration.

"Pssst," said her mother. Her thumb came down over the offending protuberances.

Blushing deeply, Roxanne erased. Her own chest was flat.

What a mystery it was to have those objects! Her eraser flew. Her mother nodded, still listening. Roxanne drew the sinner's chest flat. Then she tried drawing fireflies, but it wasn't interesting. She added big bows to the sinner's shoes.

"I'm going to the nursery to check on Colleen," said her mother.

Alone, Roxanne redrew the bust, bigger than before, more magnificent and huge, sticking far into the tree's bark. She erased the tree and moved the trunk back. She drew grass and added dimples in the woman's cheeks, then leaned back. These were the largest two breasts ever drawn by her. A noise made her jump, but it was only the usher returning the offering basket. For fun she drew the woman's face to smile. This was indeed a masterpiece. Quickly Roxanne slid it in her notebook, to hide it. Checking both ways, she opened the notebook again. She stared at them.

"Hoo," she said.

· · · · ·

When Sister Fish came back, Habakkuk in the person of her husband was saying something to the people. The prophet yelled that God had laid waste the wicked, which was what was going to happen to Darwin's followers. All the high priests were old men, and Roxanne couldn't remember whether they would be in heaven or burn eternally. They did not believe in Jesus Christ, because the Messiah had not come yet.

"Can I get a drink of water?"

"Sit up straight," said Sister Fish.

Roxanne tried crossing her legs to get the Northern Lights between them. Staring straight ahead, she pressed. At least the woman with enormous breasts was safe. Her father went on about Habakkuk this and that. She stopped breathing.

"Pay attention."

She gave up and uncrossed her legs. Picking up the hymnal, Roxanne went through it, taking the titles and adding "Under the

Bed." "Jesus, I Come, Under the Bed." "Come Ye Sinners, Under the Bed." "What a Friend We Have in Jesus, Under the Bed." "Rescue the Perishing, Under the Bed"! That was a hysterical one. If she twisted she could just see Eileen and Ramona Ransom, who were her age. She held up five fingers and then seven, for the hysterical songbook page number.

"Face front," whispered Sister Fish.

The truth about Habakkuk droned on. Looking left across the church aisle, Roxanne studied the retarded Nedley family. Two rows back, as usual, they were plopped down with nothing but an empty pew between them and the huge map of Africa, which said "*Afrique.*" With five kids and five teenagers, they comprised the biggest family in church. Squashed into the same pew, their shoulders pressed together, they sat with all their shoes untied. Roxanne looked at each face, fascinated. Their mouths hung open, and drool dripped off their lips. Being retarded, they did not have to do anything. They did not have to carry Bibles or witness to kids at school. They did not have to memorize the books of the Old and New Testaments. Because they were stupid, God was just going to let them in. Roxanne let her mouth drop and rolled her eyes up in her head. It felt good, but drooling was not that easy, she realized.

She sneezed.

She was trying to read the tithing admonitions on the offering envelope in Pig Latin, sounding out each word, Ithway Anksgivingthay, when something smashed her in the left side of her cranium.

"ROXANNE IS A FILTHY SINNER."

Roxanne sat up, the offering envelope between two fingers. The thing that hit her had taken her wind completely. Gingerly she inhaled. The sermon from Habakkuk went on. She swallowed.

"God? I am too young. I am still innocent. My name is Roxanne Fish."

"Don't correct Me, you evil parasite! Ha! Do you think you are holy? You are not holy. Your righteousness is as filthy rags. Depart from Me, for I am God Almighty. Phew. You stink."

Suddenly she felt it, sin crawling on her arms like maggots. She brushed hard, but the sin remained. Roxanne Fish a sinner! Sin went up her arms and back, covering her with gray slime. For it filled the world and men were born in it. Black goop flowed in her veins, not blood. Sin crawled over her elbows and stuck between her fingers. It crawled up her neck, the foul odor hurting God's nostrils, an unthinkable stench. Satan didn't care if her father was pastor of the First Assembly of God Church. Sin was sin. Putrid, Roxanne sat where she sat, not daring to move or put the offering envelope back.

"You can no longer go to heaven just because you are a Fish. You are filthy! Depart from Me, I never knew you. For I am holy."

"Habakkuk *interceded*," said Pastor Fish.

If she died now, she would never see her family again, for they were going up. All the Christians sat listening to the sermon, but a great gulf separated them. She was on the other side! She could smell her mother's White Shoulders perfume. If the atom bomb went off, she would wake up in hell, where five billion years was nothing. Five billion years was but a drop in the bucket of eternity.

"Jesus?" Roxanne said carefully.

"Read Holy Scripture," He instructed.

She leaned across her mother for the large black King James Bible, but her arms weren't long enough. She must be sure not to hurt or puncture any vital organ while trapped in this sinful state. Again she stretched toward the King James Bible, which stayed out of reach. In the air Jesus Christ waited for her, holding out his nail-scarred hands, exactly as in the Sunday School flannel-graphs. He had her age confused, but that didn't matter. White Shoulders filled her nostrils. Stretching farther, careful of her heart, she almost had the Bible. Anything could stop: your lungs, for example.

"Settle down." Her mother looked perturbed.

"Bible," she croaked.

"You better hurry," said God.

"Here." Her mother handed the Bible to her absently, writing "Habakkuk *tried*!" on the church program. "Don't *jiggle*," she added.

Roxanne grasped the Holy Scripture with both hands, sitting up straight. Heavy, with a soft cover, it was hard to hold open on your lap. Jesus' promise of salvation was in John, in red, somewhere toward the back, but she could not find it. Sinful, weeping in despair, Roxanne tore a page. The paper was so thin. Nothing looked familiar. The Bible books had changed places. Mark! Esther! Acts! Song of Solomon! She let out a cry.

"Roxanne?"

The situation dawned in Zelda's hazel eyes not gradually but all at once. The Age of Accountability! Sin! Roxanne an adult! They must act fast. Her mother's arm, eternal, reached out for her. Her mother watched her intently, the sermon forgotten.

"John 3:16! Hurry!" pleaded Roxanne.

"Here," her mother said, and steadied the big Bible on Roxanne's lap. Her cool hands turned the pages, the fingers moving under Jesus' words in red. She didn't care that one page was torn. John 3:16 leaped out at them, underlined in pen. Her mother's fingernail, calm and beautiful, pointed to it, and she watched Roxanne's lips while she read.

"'For God so loved the world, that He gave his only begotten Son, that whosoever believeth in him should not perish, but have everlasting life.'"

Roxanne Fish's finger, pink, dead, touched the printed words. Gray slime was everywhere, but she looked up at Jesus and felt hope of life. "Whosoever" meant Roxanne Fish.

"I am not saved," she whispered, her nose touching her mother's ear. Tears welled in her eyes and made it hard to see.

"Would you like to go downstairs?"

Together the two women stood. Together they walked down

the aisle, past the congregation, which tried not to stare at them. Only Lyle Nichols looked up. Habakkuk wailed. The bad part of the carpet was ahead, threads sticking up where it was worn through. If she tripped! Her neck could break. She lifted her feet absurdly high in order to meet Jesus in the basement. Her mother held her hand tightly. Snot was running into her mouth now. They reached the landing of the stairs and turned the corner. Sin covered Roxanne like a dark cloud.

Downstairs her mother hurried forward in her blue high heels, straight out of the Missionary Box. "Room Three has chairs," she said, clicking on the lights.

Sunday School Room Three jumped out at Roxanne from childhood. A room for little kids, it had the easel with the flannelgraphs, now standing up, its leg no longer a baseball bat. Noah welcomed animals onto the flannel ark, two giraffes and two zebras. The two women, both adults, sat down, their chairs facing. The metal was cold on Roxanne's legs, but that did not matter. In a moment she would be incorruptible. She looked at her own arm, the soft hairs, which in a moment would be saved. Following her mother, Roxanne folded her hands in her lap. At the ground-level window Ralph, the Woolworths' dog, ran by. In the moment just before eternal life Roxanne waited.

"Tell me again what you told me upstairs," said Sister Fish, her voice throbbing with emotion. Her eyes were bright.

"I am not saved."

Zelda closed her eyes. Sin was all around, cold as death. Man was born into it, but God could wipe the slate clean. She leaned forward, completely alert. She touched her daughter's hand. It was filthy, but not for long.

"Do you believe Jesus can take away your sins?"

"Yes."

"And give you eternal life?"

"Yes."

Her mother stood. "Roxanne, let us pray the sinner's prayer.

Jesus wants to come into your heart and write your name in the Lamb's Book of Life. You will live forever with the saved in heaven! Kneel down."

It was a relief to reach the portal of salvation, now that she was there. The women knelt. The chair was ice cold. The wonder of eternal life filled her as she laced her fingers together, almost a Christian. She knew the prayer, but her mother said each phrase and Roxanne repeated it. Heaven waited. It was eight o'clock on Sunday night.

"Dear Lord."

"Dear Lord."

"I know I am a sinner."

"I know I am a sinner." Roxanne closed her eyes harder. A frog had appeared, and she had to clear her throat.

"Thank you for dying on the cross."

There was a rushing sound as Ralph ran by.

"I am sorry for my sins." She bent her head. Dangling between worlds, she knew not whence the miracle would come, as a rushing mighty wind, or peace, the peace that passeth understanding, or light. She pushed her knees out more, to be set.

"Please forgive my sins and come into my heart to live, and give me everlasting life."

Two voices echoed in the empty basement.

"Amen."

"Amen."

"Praise God," said Sister Fish. Tears were running from her eyes, which saw Jesus. "Glory to God."

"Save me," said Roxanne, clenching her fists. She waited for Jesus, her heart's door wildly open. "Save me!"

"God doesn't like you," said an irritating voice. "Oh, boo hoo."

"Who are you?"

"Fred. I'm a demon's assistant. Hello, Roxanne."

Roxanne looked around. She knew immediately who they were, though how they got through the crack in visibility she had no idea. It must have been her prayer, she realized. Her blood ran cold. All in a row they looked at her, their eyes unblinking, which was how you knew they were dead.

"What are you doing here?"

"Hallelujah, Jesus!" said Zelda, her eyes shut.

The left one had the shape of a small black bat, slimy feet curling on the children's chair back. On the right was a disembodied pair of eyeballs. How malevolently they regarded her! In the middle was the one that took her breath away with fright. It was a stuffed toy horse, soft and fluffy, blue with pink ears and a green ribbon around its neck, balanced on the children's Sunday School table on all four pink feet. The pure evil intent in its eyes made Roxanne's throat close.

"We are Abba, Babba, and Mo," said Eyeballs.

Roxanne jumped to hear his disembodied voice. Her mother was still praying and weeping for joy.

"Of course, those are not our real names."

"Just our names for children," said Abba, the bat. "We love children. So fresh."

"Glory!" Zelda Fish stood up, hands raised. "My little girl! Do you have something to tell me?"

"I got saved," cried Roxanne, her voice flat. The three demons watched her. For God saved all who came, but He had not saved her. There must be some heavenly error. Roxanne could hear the voices of the agonized in hell coming through the linoleum. Her mother looked up and through the ceiling.

"Let's praise God together!"

Both women raised their hands.

"How do you feel?"

"Washed clean." Sin circulated inside her.

"Shondala seeleo!" Real light streamed from her mother's face, which was why Christians did not need makeup. "Right now the angels are writing your name in the Lamb's Book of Life!"

"Save me!" prayed Roxanne, turning away from her mother

in order to hide her lips. God had not heard her! Being saved, her mother could not see the demons. Her tearful eyes looked through the ceiling at the Throne of Grace, but all Roxanne saw was the plaster, green, with two cracks running on the diagonal. She strained her eyes.

"Let's go upstairs and tell the congregation," Zelda said.

Roxanne's eyes widened. She wiped snot off her face with her skirt bottom.

"God won't save you," said Eyeballs, who was Mo. "He doesn't like you for some reason. Possibly your red hair? Fred will accompany you and report back to us."

"Where did that horsie come from?" said Zelda. She picked it up and put it back down. "My oh my. It's a new one. Come."

Together they went up the church stairs, hand in hand, their feet clicking.

"Pastor Fish?" said Zelda from the back of the sanctuary.

She looked over the congregation, which had turned around to stare at her, the whole Nedley family with their mouths open.

"Winston? Roxanne has something to say. She would like to come up on the platform, wouldn't you, Roxanne?"

"Yes." Roxanne walked down the aisle, her heart beating fast. Perhaps God was busy! For God saved all who came.

Fred had plopped down in the first pew and was lying with his head propped on one arm. Extremely thin, his expression derisive, he watched her, amused.

"Liar," he whispered.

At the platform's top step, her father took her by the shoulders and looked into her face. Above his pink tie concern flickered. Then he turned her around.

"What do you want to tell us?"

Roxanne looked out at the congregation, and eternal souls looked back at her. The saints were smiling. She tried to see what they were wearing. If the Rapture happened she must grab the full skirt of a Christian, fast. That way she would be dragged up, up, up with the hosts of the Lord. Sister Nichols shifted in her seat. Leaning forward, Roxanne could see what looked like strong fabric gathered at Sister Nichols' waist. She gauged the distance between them.

"Roxanne?" Her father's hands squeezed her shoulders. "Do you want to speak?"

"I got saved," lied Roxanne in a loud voice.

Babysitter Schmitz

"PLEASE PASS THE GREEN BEANS," said Winston Fish.

Roxanne handed her father the bowl and sneezed. When Zelda Fish had preached her once-a-month sermon today, three souls were saved, very unusual for Sunday morning. Sister Fish had been inspired. But by one o'clock the entire congregation was hungry, their stomachs growling audibly. Roxanne had raced back to the parsonage to take out the pot roast.

It was December, and Jesus had not come yet, so she might get six tomatoes for Christmas. Her favorite food on earth, they came from California each year, mailed in a long box tightly wrapped in cellophane. At times the Fishes were extravagant. Roxanne swallowed. Mashed potatoes she loved, but string beans had a terrible taste, more like string. She moved some around in her mouth. Jesus was coming when you least expected it. For example, He would never come right on Christmas or Easter, when you were thinking of it, because He was going to surprise the sinners, all the people who made fun of the Fish family and called them crazy. Then they would know. Mr. Woolworth next door was going to be running around like a chicken with his head cut off, grinding and gnashing his teeth, but it would be too late.

"More mashed potatoes, Winston?"

"I believe I will. These are good. Are these those little onions?"

Sister Fish smoothed the tablecloth, especially happy today. The once-a-month she preached showed you a whole new side of her.

"Shallots. Sister Witter brought them yesterday out of her garden. By the way, that was she on the phone before. Praise God. She says she can't sit down. She claims the sermon got her going. She's marching up and down the dining room eating burned meatloaf! Takes a bite, up and down. Then she takes another bite. Praise God!"

"Praise the Lord! Sister Fish can preach! I'm going to take my text from Hebrews tonight. 'Faith is the substance of things hoped for, the evidence of things not seen.' These onions are good."

"My, yes. Faith is the victory. Shallots. She said they come out of North Dakota."

Colleen held out her hand. "Pass the ketchup."

"Please."

"Please," said Colleen in a nasty voice.

Ketchup went from hand to hand.

"Pray for souls!" Zelda's voice broke, and her hands flew up to heaven. You could see she saw God. Although their father was the pastor, she was more like Aimee Semple McPherson. When she preached her monthly Sunday, the unsaved were pried out of their seats and the Christians hung on the edge of their pews.

For a moment the Fishes lifted their hands in prayer, their faces toward heaven, speaking in a heavenly language. Eventually they went back to eating.

"Amen. Roxanne, is something wrong with your neck?"

"I love everything flat." Roxanne tipped her chair back. "Like I wish we lived on the ceiling."

They all looked up, and her father nodded. "Plenty of room, anyway."

At this exact instant Roxanne picked the ketchup up and shook it, and the lid flew off.

"Duck!" yelled Zelda.

Red squirted everywhere.

"Oh my!"

They all stared, amazed at the sight of ketchup all over the table, the books, the china cupboard, Winston's Bible. It had missed *Das Kapital*, but every wall in the dining room had some. Ketchup adorned Roxanne's hair and dripped off her ear.

"It looks like modern art," said Pastor Fish.

Colleen, untouched, continued to eat her dinner as if ketchup were not everywhere. She was extremely beautiful, but everything bored her and she wanted to become a Baptist. Colleen looked like someone from a better family than this, richer, without food all over the walls. With her stunning curls and snapping eyes she looked exactly like a movie star, except for her red nose from the cold she'd caught from Roxanne. Their grandmother lived in California, where the movie stars were. However, movie stars were going down, not up. Roxanne wiped ketchup off her own straight hair.

"The red walls! Oh!" Their mother grabbed the table edge and laughed. "Oh! Our good things!"

Roxanne burst out laughing too, and finally even Colleen shattered, sophistication lost. The ketchup looked so madcap in the dining room, against the Reader's Digest Condensed Books and *Strong's Concordance of the Bible* and the works of C.M. Ward of Revivaltime Radio Show. C.M. had shaken Roxanne's hand once at Camp Meeting, and the anointing flooded her, a mighty wave. C.M. walked like a duck. They laughed on, occasionally able to breathe. God was real. Ketchup dripped down over the window with snow outside.

"Oh!" Zelda stood up. "I need to spot my white collar."

Roxanne froze where she sat. "What?"

"My white collar. Daddy and I will be home late. We're having that joint service with the Boone church, and you girls both have colds. I don't want that night air in your lungs."

"Yippee!" Colleen slid off her chair.

"Help your sister get the rags and wipe this up."

"I didn't *do* anything." Colleen sneezed. "*She* spilled it."

"March, both of you. The babysitter will be here any minute. Be nice to her if you know what's good for you."

"Be nice to who?"

"Whom. You don't know her. She lives up the street next to the crab apple tree."

"Is she a sinner?" Roxanne tried to sound casual, merely curious, but her voice cracked.

"Yes." Zelda sighed. "I do hate it that Sister Nichols can't stay with you like she usually does, but she's in Pennsylvania visiting her Dutch relatives. And Colleen, and I *mean* this, you will *not* throw pillows. Get that little bit of ketchup right there, Roxanne. No, up. Colleen, do you hear me?"

Colleen, eyes at half-mast, kept on lazily wiping a clean spot of wall.

Sister Fish fixed her with the evil eye. "Colleen!"

Roxanne rubbed, fighting to suppress a cough. She swallowed hard. With Sister Nichols gone, there would be no Christians to grab on to should the Rapture occur. Sin seethed in her veins.

"I feel better," Roxanne yelled to her mother, who was rushing around in the bedroom. "Can I go?"

"No. I want two healthy girls."

Roxanne concentrated on the ketchup, trying to keep her face normal. A cold was nothing as compared to hell. Pastor Winston Fish jiggled his keys, ready to go.

"How far up is heaven?"

Sister Fish pinned an artificial flower on her lapel and kissed Roxanne. She put on black gloves.

"Five hundred miles. What do you think, Winston?"

"The Bible does not say. The Bible does not *say*. Why do you women *persist* in these things?"

"Are any Christians sick?" said Roxanne. "The Westons?"

"Check me for lint. No, I think everyone is going to Boone. They're all excited. The missionaries from Tanganyika are there!"

"How far is Boone?" said Roxanne.

"Twenty miles? Winston?"

"Now, *there's* a question human man can answer. Finally. Eighteen, I think."

At the sink Roxanne washed the red rags out in water, not caring about tomatoes for Christmas, not caring about her stupid hair. There were only Baptists left in Ames, and you could not count on them. Sin oozed from her pores. Her terror grew. The ketchup looked like blood swirling down the drain.

"Mommy's Little Helper," sneered Colleen.

• • • • •

Lying awake in her parents' bed, Roxanne listened for the trumpet. Archangel Gabriel was going to blow it. She shivered, despite the furnace. If the Lord came tonight she was in trouble. Beneath her legs the double bed sheets stretched away, huge and empty. She did not as per usual have Miss Jennifer Smith and the new baseball bat and softball her father had bought her. Tonight she had to pay attention. She was doomed. She could hear them moaning down in hell. She stuck both fingers in her ears and pulled them out immediately. With your ears blocked you could not hear the trumpet! Her parents should be home already, if they were still on earth. Of course, service lasted later when missionaries appeared in their native African costumes. Roxanne hugged her knees. She could smell her mother's White Shoulders on the pillow, her father's whiskers. She pushed down beneath the covers and sat right up. For it would happen in the twinkling of an eye.

"Save me!" she said.

In the kitchen she could hear the babysitter singing "Wake Up Little Suzy."

Roxanne took a deep breath.

Oral Roberts was an expert on the Second Coming. Once, at church, they saw his film *A Thief in the Night*, which showed exactly what would happen to the sinners who were left. Black and white, it did not lie like color movies. *A Thief in the Night* showed some men's and women's feet going up in the Rapture, all different shoes, and then you saw cars crashing on the highway, the contorted faces of those left behind. Left behind! Roxanne bit her thumb. The people on the ground were screaming and frantically pulling drawers open.

"'Two shall be sleeping in a bed,'" Oral intoned in the film, reading from the Bible. That was his real voice. "'One shall be taken; the other shall be left. Two shall be plowing in a field.'"

Roxanne, eyelids open in the dark, smelled her underarms. How the two holes stank! Her parents' bed was huge, but you could not hang on to it. Her father and mother gone! Breathing too fast, she looked around the dark room.

"Save me!"

"A dead red head," said Fred.

From the kitchen, where the sinner sang, she could hear faint strains of the Everly Brothers, happy in two-part harmony, as if there were no God.

Suddenly a sound pierced the night.

"Jesus?" Roxanne jumped out of bed and ran toward the window. The drapes tried to swallow her, but she could hear the trumpet echoing, feel it right down her spine. If her parents were no longer on earth! She wiped the windowpane with her forearm. When it cleared, Chick Woolworth was opening the refrigerator in his kitchen. For a moment they stared at one another, two lost souls. High up, her parents were not visible in the air. She could not see Archangel Gabriel, but the trumpet still rang inside her ears. She looked up for the dead, who would be rising first, from the cemetery. The room felt cold. No Christians! Without her parents she did not know how to get food or water. Oh, she could stand on a chair at the sink, but the loneliness! *The trumpet shall sound!* A cowlike groan came out of Roxanne Fish's chest. All the people rising through the air, gracefully, some holding Bibles and some holding handkerchiefs and some holding purses, some without their coats. They were rising from the Boone church! Eventually her parents would remember her, but they wouldn't care. There were no tears in heaven. She grabbed the pillow, ran to the kitchen door, and jerked it open.

There the babysitter was.

"Oh! Hello," said Babysitter Schmitz.

She was still singing to the radio, leaning back in her chair, waving one finger, earrings on her ears. Jesus would see those. And no one wearing orange lipstick could possibly help you now. The blond floozy sitting at the kitchen table didn't even realize what was happening. The Antichrist was coming! Roxanne dropped the pillow and stepped into the kitchen.

"Hey, what's wrong?" said the babysitter. "Did you see a ghost?"

Roxanne coughed. "Did you hear a trumpet?"

"Trumpet? Yeah, I did hear something. Nah, why would you hear a trumpet? That was a stuck car horn."

The babysitter's eyelashes blinked, lost and dying, bent up where the eyelash curler had been. You could see mascara. Her chair was tilted back on two legs. She turned the radio down.

Roxanne thought fast. "Can I have a drink?"

"Your mother said not to." The babysitter stood up and ruffled Roxanne's red hair.

Roxanne flinched. Soon those painted fingernails would be on fire.

"She said you'd wet their bed," the babysitter added.

Roxanne blushed, swept by shame. But occasional bedwetting would not matter in hell! She forced herself to stand still and smile.

"I won't swallow. I'll spit it out. I just want to get my mouth wet."

"Well," said the babysitter doubtfully, "you have to promise, okay?"

"Okay," said Roxanne.

Babysitter Schmitz's keys sparkled on the kitchen table. There were several, in a circle on a key ring. There was still music on the radio station, but people would start screaming soon.

"What a nice night," said Roxanne.

"Isn't it?"

Babysitter Schmitz went to the sink for water, and when her back was turned Roxanne picked up the keys. She held them tight in her fist to keep them from jingling.

Babysitter Schmitz turned around. "Here."

"Thank you." Roxanne rinsed her mouth, spat, and returned the glass with her free hand. "Good night."

"Good night," said Babysitter Schmitz. "Now, don't wet the bed. I don't want to get in trouble with your parents."

Roxanne closed the kitchen door, pleased to hear Babysitter Schmitz singing again. She had not missed the keys.

"Sweet dreams!" called the sinner.

Roxanne moved fast. There was no time to dress or put on shoes. She crept into the living room, keys cutting her flesh. The Antichrist would be here soon! This trip was a matter of life and death. She opened the front door quietly and looked across at the doomed Lutherans' house, which was dark. There was snow on the ground, but in heaven they would warm up your feet. She ran down the side path, stopping to consult her friend the hedge. The hedge knew everything.

"Which car belongs to Babysitter Schmitz?" she said.

"Yellow," said the hedge.

At the yellow car she got in. Out on the highway, terrible crashes would soon begin as Christians rose up through the roofs of their automobiles. Roxanne tried not to think about that. By sitting on the extreme edge of the seat, she could just touch the gas pedal. She stuck the long key in as she had seen her father do a million times before. The car growled, then roared. She must not quit now. Luckily the windshield wipers sprang to life without her doing anything. She had to hurry before Babysitter Schmitz came out. The Christians might still be there.

"D for Drive," she said.

The car, impossibly, was moving. Roxanne's eyes widened. She was going to reach her mother's skirt despite everything. Concentrating, she moved with the car into the intersection and pulled the steering wheel with superhuman strength. Magically, the car turned right, toward the highway that led out of town to Boone. Even without headlights it was easy to see in the full moon.

"Wait for me!" she prayed.

"Don't forget the brake!" cried the hedge back on Carroll Street.

But Roxanne Fish, unsaved, was not stopping for anything. She drove by Superba's house, peering up over the dashboard. It had knobs. Even in the cold this car smelled like cigarette smoke, but that wasn't her fault, she reminded God. It began to snow lightly. She heard the Andrews Sisters coming out of somewhere.

Boone, 18, said a sign with an arrow.

She turned left, tugging, barely missing the curb. Her clenched teeth hurt. Snow came down like cotton candy, but sinners would be screaming soon. Her hands gripped the steering wheel. You drove on the right, she remembered. Headlights came toward her. The road stretched on. More headlights approached, then faded.

Boone, 15, said a sign.

She pushed her foot down on the gas pedal.

"Liar, liar, pants on fire," chanted Fred, who could not be seen.

If the Christians had left, there was still one more way, which involved chopping off your head. This was in Revelation, the horrible book. She did not want to think about it. The Antichrist rode up on his dark horse to brand your forehead with the Mark of the Beast, 666. If you refused, he cut off your head with a hatchet and you went to heaven immediately. So there was nothing to be afraid of. It had begun to snow so hard that she could no longer see the road, although she could see fences. She sat rigid. The windshield wipers flopped merrily. She pushed the gas pedal farther down, leaning toward Boone.

"The Antichrist is behind us!" cried Fred.

Bright lights blinded her. They came from everywhere. If the Antichrist was here, the Rapture had taken place! There was only one option left. Her foot of its own accord stepped on the gas, and the car began to turn gracefully, like an ice skater. Roxanne kept her hands on the steering wheel. A snowbank appeared in front of her; gently the car entered. Her mother had gone into the ditch, but now her mother was in heaven. The yellow car stopped. The windshield wipers wiped, and more snow fell. The car tires spun.

"Get out with your hands up!" yelled a voice.

Once the Mark of the Beast was on your forehead, 666, you belonged to Satan for eternity. In the rearview mirror she could see that her forehead was still clear. Red lights flashed across her face. She sneezed, which forced her eyes closed. Blood would get all over the nightgown, and her head would fall down on the fresh snow.

Thump. Something hit the car and rocked it. A hand came to the window.

"I do not accept the Mark of the Beast," Roxanne said, teeth chattering. How sweet life was!

The hand knocked on the window. "What the hell?"

"I do not accept the Mark of the Beast," she whispered.

She squeezed her eyes shut tighter, not looking at the dark horse or the hooded figure or the axe, which must glisten. Aimee Semple McPherson was up there, and the apostle Paul. In a moment she would see her mother and father. She didn't know about Colleen. Of course, her head would roll on the ground. She tried to think about White Shoulders perfume but could not remember how it smelled.

"It's a midget."

She had not pushed the lock down! She lunged, but it was too late. The door opened.

"Help!" The car rug she clutched was giving way. Out she slid.

"Grab her! Turn off that damned key!"

She fought demonically, kicking her bare feet out beneath her nightgown, palms over her forehead, which did not say 666. But the Antichrist had helpers. The helpers' hands restrained her. Her forehead was exposed!

"I do not accept the Mark of the Beast!" she said in a clear voice.

Red flashed on her closed eyelids.

"Wrap her in my coat. Okay, check the registration. Move."

Warmly she wet her pants. It hardly mattered at a time like this. In the French Revolution they were guillotined but did not go to heaven. The French were sinners. With her eyes closed Roxanne thought about pancakes.

"Where do you live?"

She peeked out. Three policemen stared at her, in police uniforms. They didn't look like the Antichrist. She checked the surrounding area. They had no dark horse.

"Nine thirteen Carroll Street."

One of them wrote that down.

"Her feet are bleeding."

"Check that girl missing where the mother was yelling at us. I think they live on Carroll Street. Trout. Or Perch."

The joy of playing baseball with her father filled Roxanne's soul. Her swing was getting better by the week.

"What time is it?" she asked, never having stayed up this late.

"Jesus H. Christ. A girl, joyriding in the middle of the night! We got the car. Ten-four."

Roxanne smelled deep, dark dirt, the smell of Iowa, all the way beneath the fresh snow.

"Take her home," said a voice.

In the police car she moved her head on her spine, happy to be in Ames. Christmas decorations sparkled on one farmhouse, something she had not seen on the ride out. She had driven a long ways. Wrapped in someone's jacket, Roxanne felt warm. How she loved this police car, the bump in the middle of the floor. How she loved their uniforms, the sweet fabric of their navy blue coats, the car upholstery. They said "Schmitz" on their radios, speeding toward Carroll Street. When she sneezed, a blue arm handed her a Kleenex. The six tomatoes might still arrive. They drove by where the Andrews Sisters were singing, which must be a record. Then Beardshear School hove into view. Out the small cracks in her eyes she saw the dear pink Pontiac parked in the long driveway, everything covered with dazzling whiteness. Peace filled her. Next door Ralph barked. Now that it had stopped snowing, the moon sailed out. Her mother, running down the driveway in her one elegant suit, looked like a fashion plate.

The door opened and the police got out. "We've got her."

Roxanne snored girlishly.

"She's asleep." Zelda's soft hand brushed her forehead.

As her father took her in his arms, she saw Chick Woolworth peeking out his kitchen window without a shirt. He lifted a Pabst.

"We aren't going to file charges, but technically your daughter stole a car."

Pastor Fish shook his head, holding Roxanne like a sack of potatoes. "I don't know what to think. She must walk in her sleep."

"I don't believe I've seen a case like this," said the policeman who had pulled her out of the babysitter's car. "You've got to hand it to her." He looked from the street to Roxanne, she saw through squinted eyes. "How in hell did she turn the goddamn thing?"

"Thou shalt not take the name of the Lord thy God in vain."

"Pardon me, Reverend."

Snoring, Roxanne listened.

"God hates swearing. Well, it looks like we'll have to do something about this. For tonight I'll barricade the outside doors."

"Where's my car?" demanded Babysitter Schmitz.

"Here she comes, no worse for wear."

The yellow car turned into Carroll Street, driven by a police officer.

"Halfway to Boone. She said something about the naked priest. Or beast."

"My poor little girl." Her mother kissed Roxanne's cheek and wrapped a soft blanket around her scratched feet as Winston carried her toward the house.

"Schimflact," murmured Roxanne, to throw them off.

"She's dreaming again." Zelda touched her hair.

"I won't be back here," said Babysitter Schmitz.

"Lock her in good!" called the policeman. "No offense."

Zelda's laugh was musical. "No offense taken!" She lifted both arms up into the Iowa night. For some reason there was no snow in heaven. "Praise God. Thank you, Lord, for finding my little girl!" She waved to the three policemen. "Goodbye! Goodbye!"

Woolworth pulled down his shade.

In her own bed, listening to her father move furniture across the front door, Roxanne continued snoring as her mother came in with a wet washcloth. How warm it was on her feet. After her mother left she snored a little more for insurance. She might send Jennifer Smith to Italy on an important spying mission. From the kitchen came her parents' voices, exclaiming over the events of the night. How God had protected her! They moved on to which missionaries were on furlough. Colleen appeared at Roxanne's bedroom door, standing in a shaft of light from the hallway with a gold trumpet. Assistant Pastor Weston's trumpet, from the church orchestra pit.

"I was sleepwalking." Roxanne bounced up.

"Liar. I scared you to death!" Her sister made a face and waved the trumpet. "It was easy. You just spit in it. Car thief!" She ran out of the room with a toss of her curls.

Roxanne closed the door and turned around. Every bone hurt. She fell flat onto the bed on her stomach, deliciously conscious of pancakes in the morning. Downtown the train whistle blew, on its way to California where her grandmother lived. Next to her Jennifer Smith's head stuck out. The baseball bat was by her feet, and the softball pressed into her stomach pleasantly.

"You forgot to pray," said Fred.

She got out of bed. It was cold, but she knelt and folded her hands.

"Please save me!"

She waited, counting up to sixty on her fingers, but God was angry, possibly with her red hair. She remembered how the car felt carrying her to Boone. She could hardly wait to tell Superba and the hedge. She put the covers over her head.

"Wake up Little Suzy," sang Roxanne.

War on Carroll Street

THE WOOLWORTHS NEXT DOOR were not redeemed. They were sinners. So were the Lutherans on the hedge side, but you never saw them. Reverend Kelsey, who lived in back of the Fishes, was also lost, a famous Episcopalian. He was writing a book about tongues-speaking, which he called "glossolalia." He preferred Greek. But who were the experts? The Fishes spoke in tongues every day! And he did not so much as come over to say hello, which told you something about the value of a Harvard education. Sinners filled Ames, drinking at the water fountains in shorts and bending over, likely to pick up a gun and use it if the devil said "Shoot!" And in this respect the Woolworths were only typical. The Woolworths lived not twenty feet away from the driveway-side windows of the Assembly of God Church. Chick Woolworth hated all real Christians with a violent fury, and this too was typical of sinners fighting God's convicting power. Lately Chick had been complaining in a loud voice that members of the Assembly of God Church were insane.

"What is he going to do today?" fretted Zelda, not yet dressed for Sunday morning service, brushing Roxanne's hair and scrambling eggs. "Colleen? Move my Bible out from where the syrup is."

"Mom?" said Roxanne.

"Get your father's shoes. We have to polish them."

"Do you know any red-haired people who are saved?"

"You."

With a final stroke of the brush, Zelda pushed Roxanne to the table to eat her scrambled eggs. Believing hard, Roxanne pulled the yellow butter toward her.

"I'm just worried!" Zelda cried.

Last Sunday morning Chick had fired up his power lawn-mower, the first in Ames, as soon as Pastor Fish began to preach. He mowed up and down for the entire sermon, up and down, drowning out the text and all Pastor Fish's carefully prepared thoughts. He had purchased the mower at Raker's Hardware Store downtown on May first. Mr. Raker was not to blame. Although he was a Methodist, he deplored Woolworth's agnosti-cism and would not have sold it to him if he knew. Unfortunately, Mr. Raker and the Methodists would one day be surprised to wake up next to Woolworth in hell.

So far the lawnmower was not visible. It was red, like Satan. Wednesday Colleen had witnessed the two Woolworths, in bed, with whiskey, planning some shenanigan for Sunday morning, and today was Sunday. Colleen had seen them through a crack in their shade. It was not inconceivable that God in His infinite mercy might someday save the Woolworths; the congregation prayed with hearts that were broken. But God had given man free will, and if the Woolworths chose hell there was nothing anyone could do about it. The Christians flinched for the Woolworths, almost feeling the fire. In the meantime, the early Christians had faced the raging lions with a song, and anything Chick might do was as nothing to the saints of Ames, Iowa.

"Roxanne, you like to run. Go check if you can see anything," said Zelda, scraping strawberry jam off the breakfast plates. She saved everything. The Fishes had no money, but the family looked fabulous. Zelda made the girls one dress each year from remnants on sale, and magically caused her single good suit, brown, to stretch into a vast wardrobe. But the Woolworths were driving her crazy.

"Roxanne? Don't wait."

Roxanne was kneeling on a chair pouring Welch's grape juice

into tiny tumblers for communion. Episcopalians drank real wine and then staggered out into the church aisle, unable to stand. She put the grape juice down.

"Go! Run before your father gets home."

"Zelda!"

Sister Fish jumped.

Winston Fish stood in the doorway looking like a handsome stranger. One hand in his pocket, he exhibited a slight frown, his hat at that rakish tilt their mother loved. Women all over smiled at him, even in Des Moines, but he ignored them. Only Zelda thrilled him heart and soul. He was just back from his sermon on the radio, WHMO, Ames 47.2, exhorting sinners and saints to turn to I Corinthians. His sermon had been on love.

"I have a handsome husband, Winston Fish."

He didn't budge. "Zelda, this spying on the Woolworths has got to stop."

Zelda's eyes flashed. "Winston, I cannot stand this one more second. Roxanne?" She gave a small push. "Go."

Roxanne stood up on her chair and jumped off. The little glasses jiggled in their holders, but nothing spilled. She wanted to be perfect, as Jesus said you could be, and so far she had not spilled a drop.

"Mom? Don't let Colleen *do* anything."

"I think I had a good radio show," said Pastor Fish. "I preached on I Corinthians 13."

"Mom? Mom?" Roxanne's voice rose urgently. Maybe God would save her if He noticed she had not spilled. In the sun the purple Welch's looked like jewels. "Colleen doesn't get to!"

"You can pour mine for the rest of your life!" yelled Colleen, who was in the living room playing "Three Blind Mice" on the piano. "I'm a Baptist! I just found my real parents."

"Colleen!"

Roxanne went out the door rapidly to avoid Colleen's sarcastic remarks. She always felt ugly around her sister. Mrs. Bell had called her red hair wonderful, but that was so long ago, last winter, and Mrs. Bell was a sinner. Colleen even laughed like a movie star. Out the screen door the fresh air felt good. Perhaps today Jesus would step through her open heart's door. On the side porch Roxanne stood on all ten tiptoes, arms overhead.

"Play something spiritual!" called their father.

The girls' eyes met through the window.

"Criminal," mouthed Colleen. "Car thief. You will go directly to jail."

Roxanne blushed deep red and jumped down all four porch stairs, landing on the ground in a perfect jungle crouch. Someday her sister would be begging for a drop of water for her tongue.

"What a Friend We Have in Jesus!" Colleen bashed the keys.

"Miss Colleen Fish!"

Roxanne accelerated, running past the basement windows of Sunday School Room Three, where the stuffed horse had been, over the church lawn and across Carroll Street, aiming toward the Beardshear School swings at ninety miles per hour, pretending to be a cheetah. As per usual she communed with all animals and one or two plants. She leaped over the seesaw and veered left, following the fence and running around the whole school, back across the baseball field to Carroll Street, where her Woolworth lookout point lay. In the animal kingdom there was no sin. A bumblebee went by, and Roxanne waved. Coming down the last stretch of sidewalk, she got up to one hundred twenty miles per hour, the fastest speed ever achieved by a cheetah! At the last moment, only by jungle-lion effort, she put on the brakes and flung herself into the bush next to the fire hydrant, directly across from the Woolworth's tool shed.

She peeked.

The shed door was half shut, making it impossible to see if the red lawnmower was waiting to come out. She crawled farther to the right, enjoying the smell of dirt. Now she could almost see inside the shed. The bush enclosed her totally. A branch scratched her collarbone, but it didn't matter. You could see their air conditioner from here. The Woolworths were not exactly Satanists, but they worshiped their appliances, which was the same thing, putting idols before God. They did not attend church. Their kitchen had a dishwasher, something you did not need if heaven was your goal, and they had just taken down their clothesline and installed an electric dryer. It made no sense. Using her left foot to push, she heaved herself forward on her stomach.

"Roxanne Fish, is that you?"

Roxanne turned her head slowly, unbelieving. Her eyes widened. Miriam Woolworth's feet, in lavender flats, stood on the sidewalk in front of Beardshear School, not ten steps from Roxanne's legs sticking out from the bush.

"Oh, hello!"

"What are you doing? Spying on me?"

"Gardening," said Roxanne.

She leaped up. Pure humiliation propelled her across Carroll Street, past her true friend the hedge and down the church wall to the Fish front door, where she yanked the screen almost off its hinges. It bounced shut and open again.

"Mother!" she screamed. "Mother! Mother!" She hopped from foot to foot.

When Zelda limped in, one shoe on, holding the other and a nylon, Roxanne jumped on both feet. The floor shook.

"She saw me!"

"This is *exactly* what I knew would come to pass," said her father. There he stood, direct from prayer, his new tie a rich, dark red, fired up to preach. His eyes looked powerful and mad. He put his Bible down on the piano bench with a slap. "Now you've done it."

Chastised, Zelda smoothed her skirt. She put on her other shoe, starting with the nylon. "Oh my. What did you say?"

"I was gardening."

"That's a *lie*." Pastor Fish shook his head. "She'll have to go tell Miriam Woolworth the truth."

"Well, Winston, she *might* have been gardening." Zelda turned toward her daughter, hopeful. "Did you move any dirt around?"

"Sort of."

"Oh dear! Communion! The empty glasses! Hurry! Grape juice!" Zelda pointed toward the clock. "Church!"

Kneeling on the chair again, Roxanne aimed the Welch's bottle toward the tiny glasses, but the brilliance of her concentration was gone. Purple spread. She tried to grab a dish towel before God saw anything.

"Too late," said Fred.

Roxanne glared at the air where he was. If she ever did get saved, the demons could not talk to her. The little broken Saltine crackers were the body of Christ, but not while in the parsonage. She ate two.

"Oh! Your bobby pins!" said Zelda, pulling them out and fluffing Roxanne's straight red hair, momentarily curly. "There! You look adorable."

Roxanne peered at her reflection in the silver communion tray, the only elegant dish in their house. A cute girl looked back.

Quickly the family went out through Colleen's bedroom door onto the platform, Colleen in front, her ironed skirt swinging. Roxanne hopped on one foot. Pastor Fish stared straight ahead, avoiding the window that looked into the Woolworths' house, one hand balancing the communion tray, the other holding the crackers, Bible in his armpit. Pink corsage high on her shoulder, Zelda trailed across the platform fastening her garter, running back at the last minute to close the bedroom door. Her teeth held gloves. Winston set the communion items down on the table with its white cloth runner. The girls skipped across the platform and jumped off.

"What was she wearing?" whispered Colleen.

"Her halter top," Roxanne whispered back. "The one with speckles."

"Yikes."

Their father unlocked the front doors from inside and pushed them open. Sun flooded the church. Despite his righteous indignation, you could feel the peace of Sunday morning. How glad Roxanne was that the Lord had not yet come and they were still on earth. Strong sweet pea odor wafted in the open windows and filled the sanctuary.

The retarded Nedley car pulled up.

"This is the day which the *Lord* hath made!" cried Sister Fish. "Let us rejoice and be glad in it!"

• • • • •

When the girls returned to the platform to play their harmonica and cello duet, "Lord, I'm Coming Home," they looked left out the window, but the Woolworth yard was empty. Still, the Christians were on edge. They sang hymns and hid behind their songbooks, peeking through the side windows to see what Chick was doing. Nothing happened. They made it through Announcements from the Pulpit and the prizes for Attendance Drive.

"My text today," said Pastor Fish, "is taken from Matthew 3:1–3. Let us pray."

Winston was almost at the apex of his sermon when Chick Woolworth walked out his back door carrying a green lawn chair, the usual cigar in his mouth. The aroma drifted in over the sweet pea, making the Christians' noses wiggle. The lawnmower was not in sight. The silence seemed to tick, but Pastor Fish preached on.

"And John the Baptist cried, 'Make straight the way of the Lord!'"

Chick was shirtless, clad only in purple bermuda shorts. His huge stomach hung over the waistband. He arranged the chair and sat down facing them. Oily black hairs protruded out of pale white skin. He had stick arms and legs. He appeared for all the world to be listening to the sermon and enjoying his cigar, chair tipped back.

"As we are in Ames, John the Baptist was a voice crying in the wilderness."

At this moment Chick began to whistle. The ushers rushed to close the windows, but Pastor Fish sliced the air with his hand.

"We will not allow those people to dictate our lives," he said.

Roxanne squinted. By the set of his head, her father looked like a boxer in the Lord's army.

"Today," he continued, "is the third Sunday of the month. On the third Sunday of every month we take communion."

All the Christians darted their heads furtively between Chick and their pastor, except the retarded Nedleys, who stared out-right. "Tutti-Frutti," whistled Woolworth. Roxanne sat up straight. It was the Little Richard song from the *Farmer's Report*. She said the title silently behind her teeth.

"Only those who are born again should participate," said Pastor Fish.

Chick started in again on the same tune, embellishing it, slowing down and adding little curlicues of sound, driving the parishioners crazy. Christians twitched. Sometimes, during the week, Mrs. Woolworth offered Roxanne iced tea, and she always accepted, taking the opportunity to peek into the kitchen, which was how she had seen the clothes dryer.

"Would the servers come forward, please!"

The servers did, trying to act as if the horrid sound were not a presence in the sanctuary. Still, Chick had not fired up the lawn-mower.

"Search your hearts, if you will," counseled Pastor Fish.

Roxanne did not search hers. It was a sin to take communion if you were not saved, but she had to or the Christians would know. She checked her curls for curliness and took the little glass. When

God forgave her sins He would forgive this too. She took a cracker from the plate.

"Save me!" she whispered.

"Save me!" mimicked Fred.

"Quiet!" said Zelda.

Now all the Christians held forward their food, which had transformed itself, not the Saltine crackers Roxanne had broken and the juice she had poured. Despite the whistling each Christian looked upon the Saltine with a feeling of awe.

"'This is my body and blood which is broken for you,'" said Pastor Fish, his voice normal. Something in the sanctuary breathed. "'Take. Eat. This do in remembrance of me.'"

Woolworth continued to whistle, but the Christians hardly heard him. Even the retarded Nedleys faced forward.

"Now we will eat of the body and drink of the blood."

They ate and drank. Roxanne swallowed Welch's and looked to see which women had full skirts. The congregation prayed quietly. A fly settled on Sister Witter's hat. The mood was lighter now, for people knew their lives had meaning. They were lucky to be going to heaven. Euphoric at the blessed stillness all around them, strengthened until Wednesday, the Christians stood singing a hymn, their eyes closed. God had visited them in the crackers this day. While Assistant Pastor Weston gave the closing prayer, Pastor Fish tiptoed to the back door to shake hands.

"Hallelujah! God bless you!" cried Assistant Pastor Weston from the front. "Come tonight! Six o'clock!"

Sun flooded in. Pastor Fish faced out, but the wooden church door cut off his vision of the Woolworths' yard. Thus it was sturdy Sister Ransom who shook his hand, extendedly, turned, and froze.

"Sister Ransom?"

"Bop. Gumf," she said.

"Gumf?" said Pastor Fish.

"Joygup," Sister Ransom added, as if speaking English, and in a Christian handclasp she walked Pastor Fish beyond the door.

Naked Mrs. Woolworth stood behind a plywood stand with one hip out, showing off her rear end. It was barely covered by a tiny bit of fabric with green stripes, as were her exposed breasts. She had donned the first bikini in Ames. Chick stood in their open doorway drinking beer, smoking his cigar, his hairy stomach bulging.

Mrs. Woolworth waved. "Lemonade, anyone?" she called.

The sign did indeed say "Lemonade," hand-painted and nailed to the plywood, which came only to her mid-thigh. This setup exposed her naked body no matter where you stood, and when she bent to the pitcher her breasts hung. More beautiful than those on the Sinner Climbing Trees, though not as large, they were pink, and moved as Mrs. Woolworth moved, back and forth, for no reason anyone could see. Roxanne's eyes widened.

"Hoo," she said.

Eighty-seven Christians pressed together on the wide church sidewalk.

"Yikes. You can almost see the very *ends*," whispered Colleen.

All the Christians froze. Mrs. Woolworth had placed herself between them and their cars, right near the sidewalk where they must pass by. To walk all the way around the block to avoid her would be to admit defeat. Remorselessly she shifted her hip. The buttock closest to them stuck out. Dinners burning in the oven, the Christians stood as if turned to stone. For men became as wild beasts when naked women lured them. They could not help themselves. As if she were listening to music, Mrs. Woolworth was alternating knees rhythmically, which made alternate sides of her body push out. Roxanne's heart beat furiously. The situation looked hopeless.

Thelma Nichols saved the day.

"There is power! Power! Wonderworking power!
"In the blood! Of the Lamb!"

Up the street the Christians marched, past Mrs. Woolworth, following Sister Nichols, singing as they lifted their feet, all eyes glued to the crab apple tree, which leaned far over the sidewalk up ahead. Babysitter Schmitz lived there. Roxanne and Colleen waited breathlessly to see which men would go crazy.

"There is power! Power! Wonderworking power!
"In the precious blood of the Lamb!"

Eighty-seven people, almost half of them of the male species, were delivered that day, arriving safely at their cars, not only pure but with a new knowledge of God. They chose Zion. When the last Christians had driven off, the Fishes stood on the church lawn, not looking at Miriam Woolworth in her bikini. The home-made sign glared at them.

"I'd like some lemonade," said Colleen.

"Shhh."

Chick Woolworth laughed.

Pastor Fish locked the big wooden doors from the outside and led his family back along the church and up the porch steps, opening the screen door without saying a word.

●●●●●

"I'm going over to talk to them."

Usually a man with a good appetite, Pastor Fish sat slumped in his chair. Of his pot roast dinner he had touched nothing. Abruptly he stood up, holding his good Sunday napkin. It was perfectly clean.

Zelda rose too. "Winston? She'll just tempt you. She'll lounge there in that strip of cloth and bat those eyes at you." She imitated Mrs. Woolworth. "You girls get in the kitchen, and take the dishes with you. Careful with the communion things."

"It's not my turn," said Roxanne.

"This instant!"

Trying to listen from the sink, Colleen dropped a communion glass, which smashed loudly. Their mother didn't even notice. The girls edged back into the dining room, where Winston had picked up his Bible and put on his suit coat to face the enemy next door.

"Don't go," Zelda pleaded.

The door slammed. Zelda picked up *Das Kapital* and put it down.

"Dear Lord," she said, and knelt so suddenly it looked more like a collapse.

While Zelda Fish implored God to keep her husband safe, Roxanne moved closer, trying to get a grip on her mother's dolman sleeve in case the Rapture occurred. The skirt itself was straight. The two girls met each other's eyes, uneasy. Their parents never feared the devil or those in town in his employ, yet their father had been too nervous to eat. There his food sat. Colleen stood unraveling a ribbon on her dress, and when the door slammed again, she spun.

"He's back!"

Zelda rose, brushing off her skirt, and they all crowded together by the dinner table as he walked right past them into the living room.

Winston Fish's face in contrast to his new red tie was completely colorless. Slowly he lowered himself onto the ottoman. A bad hand gripped Roxanne's heart. What if heaven was not real? What if there were only empty planets? When she took a step back, her legs and arms felt like bones. She looked at her right bone hand. What if there was nothing, as the Communists said, except machines and empty planets in space? Her mother's face twitched.

"Winston?" Zelda held out both hands. "What happened?"

Winston stared out. "Why, they left the door open. They didn't care at all. I could see them."

"See them?"

"On the floor. *At* it."

"At what?" said Roxanne. She and Colleen exchanged blank looks.

"Girls? Out!"

"It wears you down," their father said, his voice flat.

Zelda turned on her heel and went into the kitchen. The girls followed her, but she shooed them off. They sidled through the living room past their father and ran into their parent's bedroom, hiding flat behind the bed with their ears to the floor vent. Their shoulders touched. They heard the telephone click in the kitchen as Zelda dialed it. Their heads bumped.

"Roland?" came Zelda's voice.

"Long distance!" mouthed Colleen.

Uncle Roland, Winston's healing brother, lived down in St. Louis, Missouri, where he prayed for trees, cows, sinners, saints, anything that breathed and had its being. Roxanne got lighter. When God told Roland to go buy gold coins, it always followed in a month or so that the price of gold went up, which was how he supported his family. For Roland Fish knew God.

"Roland, pray. Now. Drop everything. I'm worried about Winston," said Zelda Fish, long distance, by telephone.

Her voice softened, and the girls pressed their faces to the metal slats. When she hung up with a clatter, they jumped up and raced each other to the living room, slowing down to enter. Their mother strode out of the kitchen directly toward her husband, seams straight up the backs of her legs, white high heels like beacons. The girls hardly breathed. Sun moved across the Fish carpet. Their father's skull seemed to show beneath the skin.

"Winston?" Zelda put one hand on his shoulder, but he did not seem to notice.

"We are fighting powers and principalities on this street. Oh, I do believe in God. Yet He lets Woolworth do just as he pleases. No matter how many visitation calls I make. No matter how good my sermons are. Woolworth turns on his machine. *Vroom!* Mrs. Woolworth parades her nakedness. God looks down and lets them do it. Watching from wherever He is." Winston raised his head, his eyes despairing, not the eyes of their father who knew God personally. "The congregation is wondering where God is. I can see it in their faces. Zelda, I pray. But the Woolworths have been at it all summer. It feels like God has abandoned Ames." He sighed. "Attendance was down this morning."

Zelda smoothed a loose hair of her husband's back in place. He was staring down at the carpet again, his face white.

"I called Roland," said Zelda finally. "Just now."

Winston flinched, and then he sat up slowly. "I wish you had not done that."

"Stop it, Winston," said Zelda.

He slapped the end table, jostling a bowl of plums and a rare California pomegranate. His color had come back.

"Roland? I can pray as well as Roland any day. Who has saved more souls? Oh, Roland will tell you. He has! Mr. Hotshot. But I can tell you his conversions do not last. Once the fireworks are over his people backslide."

Colleen and Roxanne, standing side by side, entwined fingers without meaning to, their father's voice was so rough.

"Mr. Bring-Them-In! Souls by the hundreds! Nay, the thousands!"

"Stop it! God saves souls." Zelda stamped her foot, and the pomegranate rolled to the floor. Red seeds oozed from the crack where it split. "Not you."

Winston tipped his chair back, teetering dangerously.

"Girls," said their mother. "*Out.*"

• • • • •

By the time the Christians arrived for evening service at five-thirty, no signs of Mrs. Woolworth's astonishing display remained. This Sunday evening two new sinners from Des Moines were in church, and one familiar sinner, Roy McDuffy, Joy McDuffy's unsaved husband. That made three. The Des Moines sinners, women, sat together, hands folded in their laps, waiting for the Christians to do something loony, but tonight they were as quiet as Lutherans. The church orchestra sounded terrible, and at the end of their instrumental section Brother Weston dropped his trumpet. Roxanne glanced back at the Des Moines women, one of whom had beautiful long hair. In the July heat no breeze came in the open window. Chinese fans flapped. The Woolworths were being quiet, although you could just hear their radio. Occasionally Chick laughed. The sinner Roy McDuffy stared down at the carpet where Lyle Nichols had mended it with electrical tape. Roxanne cringed. Roy McDuffy, unsaved, unfailingly polite, never responded to the prayers of the righteous. He had perfect posture. When a car horn honked, the ushers rushed to close the windows, then stopped and looked at Pastor Fish, who was looking down at the pulpit. Despite the red tie he looked haggard and rumpled, as if his clothes had aged.

"I am preaching," said Pastor Fish, "from Luke 25:14–30. The parable of the talents." He cleared his throat, but something in the voice was not working. His shoulders had caved in.

There was a rustling of pages, and Zelda leaned forward. "Pastor Fish?" she called. "Not Luke. Matthew."

"Hallelujah!" cried deaf Brother Witter.

"Matthew 25:14–30," said Pastor Fish.

The Woolworths slammed their windows.

"Now, God gave one man five talents, and he went out and buried them." He cleared his throat again. "Now, we all deal with money. A talent at that time was a unit of money."

Pastor Fish stared at the air above his congregation's heads. It was not Blue Nose, they all saw by turning around. When they turned back, he was leaning on the pulpit, his head down. The two sinners from Des Moines glanced around nervously, while Roy McDuffy sat forward a little, finally engaged. Up the aisle a second bad spot covered by electrical tape caught the light. Like a dying man, Pastor Fish looked up.

"I don't want to preach. We sorely need a visit from the Holy Ghost."

There was a slight murmur in the church. Brother Ransom, although he seldom moved, tired from his work in the fields, shifted in his seat.

"Let's bow our heads and ask the Holy Ghost to come in."

Pastor Fish closed his eyes, shoulders slumped, hands folded against his chest, fingers interlaced. The congregation watched him. For he was their shepherd and they were the sheep.

"Holy Ghost? We need to feel your presence here tonight. Please come into our tabernacle and fill us. We will wait."

He stood there silently. The Christians waited and the electrical tape gleamed. Roy McDuffy was enjoying their discomfort, his eyes bright. Hands over their lipstick, the sinners from Des Moines whispered to one another as they looked back toward the exit.

Five minutes passed.

"I'm going to leave," said one of the sinners.

The Christians waited.

The smell alerted them first. Cigarettes were an abnormal phenomenon inside the tabernacle, and Christians had good noses. When they turned around, two police officers were standing in the doorway, an odd sight.

"Yes?" said Pastor Fish.

"How do." One large and one medium, in blue uniforms, they stood with their feet apart, arms across their chests. They were not from the Schmitz incident, Roxanne saw with relief.

The medium officer blushed and tossed his cigarette outside. "I'm sorry to interrupt, but your neighbors have complained about the noise. Disturbing the peace is a crime, to tell you the truth, but we just want to talk to you. The neighbors live here too, y'know." He looked confused because the church was so quiet.

"We're from Des Moines," the long-haired sinner said, fluttering her hand.

The big policeman ignored her, his expression blank as he scanned the room for suspicious characters, a big man doing his job.

"Just promise to be quiet so we can get going," said the medium policeman. "Do we have your word?"

Pastor Fish stood up straight, his face relaxed, imposing in his suit. Angels must have pressed it. He held the pulpit lightly with one hand and placed the other on his Bible, no bones showing anymore.

"Reverend?"

Pastor Fish looked them in the eye. "The Holy Ghost is a wind that blows where it will."

Sister Weston, the church pianist, stood up. "Shondorala loolah. Hipra shelala eebio. Seelah." Eyes shut, elbows out in front of her, fingers loosely up, she waited to see if there would be an interpretation. Sometimes it was just heavenly language, sometimes you got to hear it in English.

A presence ran through the sanctuary, strong enough for any human being to feel. The Christians sat there, feeling it. Pastor Fish laughed out loud.

Sister Weston squeezed her eyes tighter. Her lips moved. "O My people! Who are called by My name! Humble yourselves and pray, and I will do a mighty work in thy midst. For I am God! Siprah!"

"Hallelujah," said the congregation softly.

"Ahem." The big policeman took a step down the aisle. "We are just asking you to be reasonable."

"Excuse me," said Zelda Fish.

She stepped out of the pew, banging Roxanne's knee, unmindful. Her white shoes flashed. Every eye was on her, for she seemed to be moving not under her own power. She floated like a dancer toward the police, a mysterious purpose in her step. Hands near their holsters, the two officers stared at her. Their badges glittered.

"B.B.," she said.

The medium policeman blinked.

"You are B.B. Danner, pole vault champion of Jackson High. B.B. Danner, you and I are friends." Zelda laughed in the electric air.

The medium policeman's mouth dropped open. "Zelda Wellington. My God."

She tapped her fingernail on his badge, making little clicking sounds. The house of God was quiet as a pin.

"Thou shalt not take the name of the Lord thy God in vain."

He opened his mouth and closed it, like a trout. "Zelda! What in holy hell are you doing in Ames, Iowa?" A hand flew to his lips. "Oops."

"Serving God! Although I do miss the California mountains. What are *you* doing here?"

"I got married and my wife inherited a farm. She's from West Covina originally."

Chick Woolworth appeared against the light in his window. Images of California seemed to play against the tabernacle walls, green palm trees. At the piano Sister Weston's hands were at the ready, a gospel chord hovering exactly beneath her fingers three inches off the keys.

"B.B!" Zelda's voice was eerie. "I remember when you were on fire for God, although you were Nazarene. But the Nazarenes can make heaven, even without speaking in tongues. B.B! What happened to you?"

"Come on, Danner," said the big policeman. "I think they'll be quiet. Let's go."

"We won't be anything," inserted Pastor Fish.

"Just please keep the noise down. Thanks."

Zelda made a cry like a bird. The men stopped.

"B.B! We used to go for ice cream and talk about the things of the Lord."

"Right," said B.B.

"Chocolate chip!"

B.B. the officer burst into tears. The big policeman took his arm, but it was all over. B.B. listened as eternity ticked.

"Danner, we're on duty here. Vamanos."

B.B. started forward, his eyes two large holes, just as a third man appeared in the doorway. Colleen and Roxanne joined hands. The third man's hair looked like someone had cut it with a bowl on his head. His nose was flat, and he had buggy eyes. He stood perfectly still, staring out from behind round glasses.

"Hello, Engstrom," said Pastor Fish.

"Duck!" screamed B.B.

The knife sailed through the tabernacle, end over end, toward no one. It landed in the wall left of the piano, its point toward the Fish living room. Sister Beverly Cedars gasped. The two policemen tackled Engstrom. Roxanne caught his eye as they were handcuffing him.

Engstrom blinked.

Pastor Fish had stepped back on the platform and was looking at the knife, which still wobbled. Engstrom's bug eyes were now aimed at the church carpet, vacant, as though he could not recall what he was doing here.

"What's going on?" It was Woolworth, the fourth person to appear in the church doorway.

In shock for the second time that day, the Christians stared at him. Throwing knives was typical of sinners, yet they had not seen it coming. They regarded Chick suspiciously.

"'Let us run with courage the race that is set before us,'" said Pastor Fish, watching as the big policeman led Engstrom away. "'Looking to Jesus, the author and finisher of our faith.' All rise."

• • • • •

Roxanne got up from the altar, unsaved for the one bizillionth time. Stepping over Christians, she went down the aisle past B.B.

Danner, who was sobbing. His face shone. Outside, lost, she continued up Carroll Street. Behind her she could hear their voices praising God. Three houses north, she turned around and looked at the church. Light spilled from the open doors onto the lawn, but no one was outside yet. The thought that God would never save her drummed against her ears. She walked faster, past Babysitter Schmitz's car. A multitude of stars looked down coldly. She turned left at the crab apple tree and ran between the next two houses, which had facing garage walls with no windows. Moving fast, she took off her blue skirt, orange blouse, yellow slip. The Christians were still praying because of tonight's wild events. In the narrow space, nakeder than Mrs. Woolworth, Roxanne touched the middle of her panties with two fingers.

A car went by, its headlights dangerously close.

She moved her fingers faster.

Her skin cells tightened in the dark night air. Her cheeks burned. Her whole body trembled. Roxanne rubbed harder, the point beneath her panties on fire. If a car went by she could not stop now.

"Yikes!" said the pink part.

The Northern Lights exploded everywhere, against the garage walls, all through her arms and legs, out into her fingertips and toes. Her eyeballs tingled. Full of oxygen, she stood still, at peace.

"Hoo," she said.

In the dark she reached for her blue skirt, orange blouse, yellow slip. Now she could feel that God was going to save her. The Bible said so. Overhead the Milky Way gleamed. Back on Carroll Street, she walked lightly past the crab apple tree. The yellow car parked in front of Babysitter Schmitz's house was lit by fireflies. She gave a little skip without planning to. The Woolworths' was dark. When she got back the Fishes were just coming up the porch steps from church, heading straight for the kitchen, wide awake.

"Miss Bunny Rabbit, Miss Jump-over-Everything! Sit down!

We are celebrating B.B.'s name being written in the Lamb's Book of Life. Oh, I hope they do not abbreviate it."

Too excited to sleep, they chattered about the incredible events of the day. God was good. Engstrom's knife point stuck into the living room through the thin sheetrock wall, and they took turns examining it, marveling at how God had protected Winston Fish. If a Christian did die, he would go directly up. Roxanne looked sideways at her father as he sat at the kitchen table turning over the salt shaker. Now they were working on grounders, line drives, home runs. Roxanne marked the points off on separate fingers: keep the bat level, swing through, don't shrink from the ball.

"Well," said Zelda. "Well. I doubt you girls will become teenagers. The wars and rumors of wars are heating up, all signs of the Sooncoming of Christ. Hallelujah! We're going up!"

Roxanne checked out the window, but Archangel Gabriel was not in evidence. Tonight her mother wore a full skirt, gathered nicely at the waist.

"He has cheek," said Sister Fish. "Engstrom. I will say that one thing. Trying to kill one of God's servants."

"He had me confused," admitted Winston. "All I could think was he was late for church service. Of course, then he let go of the knife."

"Were you scared?" said Colleen.

"No."

"Praise the Lord." Zelda raised both hands to heaven, then continued putting pincurls in her hair on top. "Once we're saved, Satan cannot touch us. The real miracle is B.B. Danner showing up like that, all the way from Jackson High to hear about Christ."

Roxanne blinked. Sitting next to her, her father leaned forward, toward the dark outside the window. There in the backyard was the angel, touring past the brick barbecue with her nose aglow. Roxanne and her father shot up.

"Blue Nose!" Roxanne waved her spoon.

"I declare I saw her," said Pastor Fish.

"You saw her?"

"Her nose glows in the dark, apparently."

Colleen and Zelda ran to the back door, but Blue Nose had disappeared. Pastor Fish described her blond bun, but he hadn't been able to tell what color her dress was. Roxanne touched her father's suit sleeve. Zelda got out chocolate cake with brown sugar frosting, and creamy vanilla ice cream with chocolate chips.

"Two scoops for me," said Pastor Fish.

Her mother fished out a blob of chocolate chips for Roxanne. "My, it must gall Woolworth," she said, "that God *used* him to protect his worst enemy. It was Woolworth who called the police."

They tried not to smile. God was real no matter what Woolworth believed. They doubted he would dare to pull his stunts again. God was God.

Zelda turned to Roxanne. "Run and check if you can see their lawnmower."

"You stay right here," said Winston. "We need to pray. Lord, we pray for the Woolworths. Lord, we pray for Engstrom in his jail cell. Lord, thank you for your mighty hand, which protects us from the devil. 'If they drink any deadly thing, it shall not hurt them.' Hallelujah! Amen."

"Yuck!" Colleen stood up. "Those snake people." She rolled her eyes, which looked spellbinding. To Roxanne's knowledge Colleen was not saved, but perhaps God was going to let her in for being cute. Colleen pried open a huge bobby pin, placing it on her tongue.

"Just imagine!" Zelda laughed, a bell sound. "B.B. from Jackson High, saved! Colleen, take that bobby pin off your tongue immediately."

"I wouldn't be surprised if the whole Ames police department ends up making heaven before this thing is over." Winston chipped paint off the window. "Praise God!"

"Of course, up there we won't need police *as* police," Zelda mused. "Oh, and we need to visit B.B.'s wife."

"Yes."

"Tomorrow. My, this will be surprising for her." Zelda frowned. "But what about his cigarettes?"

Pastor Fish shrugged. "I told him he'd have to give them up. As of tonight. A Christian can't smoke, I said."

"What did he say?"

"Praise God!"

Everyone laughed, even Colleen, a rare moment.

"We must not rest until all have heard. We have to witness in the grocery store! At school! At the gas station, when the fellows are cleaning the windshield!" Zelda brightened. "Winston? If we're in heaven next Christmas? Maybe I ought to give you your gift."

"Now, Zelda. We don't know."

Above the Fish backyard, high up, the sky remained clear. It was doubtful Christ would come without some clouds to break through. The corn outside the window held three stalks, ready to eat. Roxanne smelled the sweet pea.

"Do you think the Westons will live near us?"

"Up there?" Zelda took a tiny slice of cake. "Take that bobby pin off your tongue!" She lightly slapped the air in front of Colleen's face. "The Westons? Why, yes, if they do not backslide."

Through the windowpane they all tried to see the streets of gold in the town where they would live. Next door the Woolworths were quiet. Of course, the whole town would be heaven. It would look much like Ames in summer except for the sparkling of gold and crystal. Even the trees might be diamonds, although Roxanne hoped for regular leaves. She passionately loved grass. Surreptitiously she wiped the fingers of her right hand on her skirt, getting rid of the underpants smell.

"Even the driveway will be gold," said Sister Fish. "Can you imagine?"

"Well, the Bible does not exactly say," said Pastor Fish.

"Well, it wouldn't make sense to have the street gold and then the driveway concrete," said Sister Fish.

"Will we have the thame ode ugly couth?" said Colleen, the bobby pin flapping on her tongue.

"Oh my, no!" said Sister Fish. "Take that off this minute!"

"Girls, girls, girls," said Pastor Fish. Lazy, he didn't move. "It's going to be eleven o'clock."

Sister Fish stood up. "Everything will be all brand-new. We can have what we want! I'd like those little flower patterns on the davenport I saw in Younkers!" She paused, holding her hands out to embrace the whole kitchen. "With pillows. What a day that will be!"

Winston scraped his chair away from the table. "The women in my house! This is my point exactly! The Bible does not say! Heavenly furniture from Younkers Department Store? Ephesians? What chapter and verse?" He waved his fork. "I'm being forced to put *Das Kapital* back on the shelf and war with the females of my own family."

"Oh, Winston." Zelda Fish beamed. "God is going to give us the desires of our heart."

"It'th funny how you never thee the topth of the buildingth," said Colleen. She sounded drunk. The bobby pin waved, but for the moment she had forgotten she was Baptist and adopted. "Shining. Juth thticking up above the cloudth. I wodder how come?"

"It's higher! The Bible does not say where. Go to bed!"

"Colleen! Off! Now! My, what a day this has been. From the Woolworths to B.B."

"Woolworths," said Pastor Fish.

Everyone looked next door. All was quiet.

"That gang is up to no good." Zelda sighed. "They are pills. Trying to lure the saved onto their grass in broad daylight. On the day of the Lord!"

"Go to bed!" said Pastor Fish, but no one moved. For the Fishes knew what most people in Ames did not, and indeed most people in the world: time was not real.

"Roy McDuffy was crying," said Colleen.

"He *was*?" Zelda looked startled.

"Go to bed!" said Pastor Fish, and pulled the girls' chairs out, and tipped his daughters off.

Temptation Strong

WALKING HOME from Superba's, Roxanne skipped on every third step, alternating right and left, enjoying the huge squares of concrete. How she loved sidewalks! Anything seemed possible there. Jumping on Superba's mother's bed had not nearly exhausted her. The sky looked like tornado weather, which meant they would not go up tonight. Of course, Christ could trick you. To get quick faith, she made her muscles so tight they shook, and prayed for grilled cheese sandwiches for dinner. Manna sounded too dry to her taste buds, terrible in fact.

"Oops, sorry." Roxanne apologized to God and began to hop again, watching for the Woolworths, who miraculously had not pulled a single stunt since the night B.B. Danner came forward last summer. B.B. Danner's wife claimed to be saved, but it was not genuine. She still smoked downtown in the park, where three church members had seen her puffing. Roxanne prayed once more for grilled cheese and executed several jumping turns. She and Superba were perfecting this move, a jump while turning, to show to Elvis Presley.

"Roxanne!"

"Ouch!"

She lost her balance and got up rubbing her knee. Sinners' voices always made you lose your balance because they were not spiritual. Roxanne stood where she was and tried to guess what Miriam Woolworth was up to this time. Mrs. Woolworth was waving at her from the walk in her yard, wearing a dramatic black vinyl coat that reflected the gray sky. At least her arms and legs were covered.

"Roxanne! What luck!" She pulled on a pair of thin black gloves and stepped closer, holding her purse against her breast and dangling her keys, darting her head toward Carroll Street. There Chick sat in the car, his belly stuffed up to the steering wheel, the usual cigar in his beefy hand. He honked.

"Can you stay with Ralph? We just have to run downtown to sign some papers. Oh, *please*."

Miriam was purring like a cat, and Roxanne heard warning bells. You must not trust anything they said, for they did not care if they lied.

"Ralph just took some medicine. Pet him and call the vet if he vomits. The number's on the kitchen table. Be a doll."

"Miriam!" yelled fat Woolworth.

"Do me this one favor." A black lace hand cupped Roxanne's shoulder and led her toward the Woolworth front door. "Be a darling?"

Miriam touched the door lightly, and it swung open. Inside, Roxanne could see the white Woolworth furniture, which called to her to sit down. Even the carpet was white! For a moment grilled cheese seemed too orange. Now the Woolworth car was driving off, but you could still go home. Roxanne stepped in and closed the door. She extended one foot to check for unsuspected trapdoors, for the Woolworths were capable of heinous crime. No one knew she was here. The thought thrilled her.

"Ralph? I'm Roxanne from next door."

Toes tapping ahead of her, she went into the living room and sat in one of the white chairs, feeling how it might feel to be a sinner. She shook her red hair and sniffed. The chair had a new smell. A television set faced her, its screen off. If the Lord should come! She jumped up and continued to the kitchen, stepping over Ralph carefully. From the window you could see Reverend Kelsey the Episcopal minister's backyard and his Concord grapes. As soon as they ripened, she and Colleen planned to steal some.

She caught her breath at the Woolworths' gleaming appliances, an electric mixer with its beaters up, a toaster, an actual electric can opener. The can opener was plugged in. She went close but didn't touch anything. These were useless! For they would not be here long.

Ralph continued to go up and down, up and down, breathing. Black, he had no distinguishing characteristics.

"Good dog," she said, bending down to pat him.

The kitchen smelled like perfume, but not White Shoulders. Roxanne traced the smell to an open jar that said "Cloves." She was about to look in the refrigerator when she heard voices in the corner, coming out a crack in the door beyond the table, on the wall toward the church. Roxanne's eyes widened. The Woolworth basement! This was where they did awful things! Last month, late at night, Colleen and Roxanne had crawled through the tiny new grass around the Woolworth house on their hands and knees, hearts beating fast, spying. Out a low vent above the ground they definitely heard noise, and it was not children. The Woolworths had no children. Something was wrong with Woolworth's sperm, according to Colleen, who knew everything.

Roxanne tiptoed closer to the door. It might be victims they had kidnapped. Worse, it might be Communists trying to take over America. She took another step. Ralph's tail flopped once, but he did not growl. Now she could feel air coming out the crack, a cool draft. She flung the door back.

"Do you need help?"

"Eeeeek!" she screamed.

"Leeeee-royyyy!" someone yodeled.

It was not victims. It was the old *Great Gildersleeve* radio show, which Satan had switched to television where you must not watch it. Relief flooded her. She fumbled around for the light switch, but the bulb when it came on was dim.

She peered.

The Great Gildersleeve yelled at Leroy again, a yell that always made her father laugh. The sound came from behind the basement stairs. In the murky light she could see what looked like a swimming pool. Although she couldn't swim, she did not turn back. Holding tightly to the handrail, she descended with her knees bent, eyes so wide open they hurt. On the last step she tripped and went flying, waiting for the splash, and found her rear end resting on polished green linoleum.

She whistled. "A dance floor!" she said softly.

This explained the no windows. The Woolworths had guests, and they all got drunk and began dancing and God knew what. Sometimes sinners took off their clothes when they danced. Pastor Fish had read about it in the *Des Moines Sentinel*. The huge green linoleum expanse glistened like a lake, waxed to a high shine by Mrs. Woolworth. It was as big as the whole house. Roxanne took off her new blue patent leather shoes and with a running start slid out onto it as far as she could.

"Leeee-roy!" came the voice of Gildersleeve.

She fell down again.

"Ralph? Are you all right?" she called, remembering why she was there, and then she turned onto her stomach in the middle of the floor. She rolled over several times, arms flat at her sides to keep going. You could not hear anybody moaning in hell underneath this basement.

She got up.

A television showing white snow reposed behind the stairs next to a table with an ashtray. This was obviously where fat Woolworth sat. The Great Gildersleeve had signed off, and a hissing sound came out.

Roxanne froze. In plain view across the shining green dance floor, on the side of the room closest to Beardshear School, was the plywood lemonade stand, Mrs. Woolworth's bikini draped over the handmade sign. Slipping a little in her stocking feet, Roxanne went closer. How she wished Colleen were here! She picked up the top, no bigger than a Band-Aid, and held it against her chest. Impossible! She picked up the pants. No bigger than a postage stamp! She held the scraps of cloth to her nose, smelled the stripes, and put them back. She could hardly wait to tell Colleen.

"Ralph? Good dog," she called.

Cautiously she continued her inspection of the basement. There were rows of shelves and two racks of clothes on cloth hangers, including a woman's red suit and several men's winter jackets. The defunct television hissed. On one shelf sat thumbtacks and a typewriter. The shelves turned a corner, and a square box in front of her eyes said "Partagas Robusto." She sounded out the letters as her father had taught her. She tipped the lid, and there they lay, wrapped in plastic: cigars! She touched each cylinder of sin. On the shelf above, Beefeaters gin appeared, followed by more bottles. They contained booze! Once you got it in your mouth it changed your personality for good. It only took one drop. Roxanne went by the bottles sideways, lest they fall forward. Laundry soap was next, and then what looked like part of a car engine. She turned another corner.

Staring directly at her were the violent eyes of Little Richard.

"Oh!" she said, and stared back.

Little Richard was looking at Roxanne as if he were her brother or an old friend. Time stopped. She picked the album up off the shelf and studied his hair, skin, nose, teeth. She walked onto the dance floor, holding Little Richard out away from her. Something surged inside her chest. Off to the right she saw a record player with an arm that could be moved to On. Little Richard's eyes followed her. She slid the album out, placing it on the turntable with Side One up. Her Christian hands trembled. It was not a sin to use a record player per se, and in fact she was an expert with the recorded sermons of C.M. Ward and also the Dearborn Christian Trio. In the quiet basement she lifted the needle and placed it on the record's edge. Little Richard waited. On the album cover his eyes connected with hers again.

"Lucille!" came Little Richard's scream.

"Lucille!" she echoed, and her voice made a sound like nothing she had ever heard, perfect and soulful.

"Lucille!" screamed Little Richard again. From the album cover tilted in Roxanne's hand, he smiled to encourage her.

"Lucille!" she sang a second time, and her blood changed. She had never met this personality before.

Little Richard's insane voice filled the basement with Lucilles, and Roxy stayed with him, each note rising from her belly button to her throat. She had never sounded this way in church. She sang out again, loud and then soft, and then with a screech that made her hair rise in its follicles.

She took a step forward.

Little Richard's voice went on, and Roxy went wild matching him with amazing sounds that came from her own throat. The two voices in the basement were from Africa, not church. She wailed up into the air, she moaned, she belted out a note with knifelike clarity. Each second seemed like a happy eternity. Her voice was an animal that lived inside her, and it was howling in the Woolworth basement. Powerful, it did things. It followed Little Richard wherever he went. She could not believe her ears.

"Aaoooo!" sang Ralph, upstairs.

"Lucille!" Roxy and Little Richard implored.

"Bravo!" said Fred.

"Thank you." Roxy bowed. There was a scratchy pause.

"Send me some lovin'," Little Richard sang.

Roxy stood on tiptoe, arms at her sides, and opened her mouth to let the animal out. This time the voice inside her chest was thick, like cream. Little Richard wailed up to the ceiling, long flights of a single note that broke your heart, and Roxy's voice flew too, slowly, full of the pain of romantic heartbreak, which she knew by some mysterious means. She let her hips move to the music, propelled by rhythm. Each beat went up through her feet to explode out her mouth. She shook her head as Little Richard had shaken his on the *Farmer's Report*. Eyes squeezed closed, she screamed.

She opened them and saw her father's shoes at the top of the stairs. They were Florsheims, punched with holes around the seams, purchased at a store in Des Moines at a discount of seventy-five percent. Although he had owned them since before Roxanne was born, he kept them like new, polishing them each Saturday night so he could wear them Sunday morning to preach.

Her voice died.

"Turn that off," said Winston Fish.

He came down the stairs. Behind him the Woolworths appeared. Her father must have been looking for her. Chick was swaying, suddenly light as air. Miriam stood on the step above him, one hand on his shoulder, her whole face dreamy.

"Keep going!" Chick cried.

"I'll wait for you," Little Richard wailed.

"Off," Winston Fish said.

Her feet moved automatically. She avoided Little Richard's eyes, although she could see his teeth. The music ceased. In the silence the television hissed again. She wondered if she should mention *The Great Gildersleeve*.

"Holy guacamole!" said Chick. "That girl can sing."

Roxy and her father both looked up. "Holy guacamole" was not exactly swearing, as guacamole was not part of the Godhead, whatever guacamole was, but calling it holy was idol worship. Roxy wiped her sweaty face with her arm.

"Listen, I know someone I could call," said Miriam. She had changed into her lavender flats, the same ones she was wearing when she caught Roxy spying. "I used to be in show business in Des Moines. I starred in a play in a theater two blocks from Younkers."

"We are going home," said Winston Fish, lifting his hand to

indicate that Roxanne should follow. Suddenly he stiffened. He was looking squarely at the plywood stand and the bikini dangling there.

"Lemonade," he said.

"Oops," said Miriam.

"Hell, preach. Let bygones be bygones." Chick put an arm up to embrace Winston and thought better of it. He scratched his stomach through his shirt. Ralph made a whining noise upstairs. "Christians forgive, right? I may be an occasional son of a bitch, but I know that much. Love your neighbor, love everything. Heck, I love you guys!" He slapped Winston on the back twice. The television could be heard dimly, like a snake. Chick pointed to Roxanne. "You got a winner there, preach."

"Your shoes," said Winston Fish.

Roxy walked up the stairs behind the Florsheims of her father, Pastor Fish, shoes in hand, afraid to put them on. A truly horrible odor was coming from her underarms. Ralph lay on the kitchen floor, still breathing. As they walked past him, toast popped up, smelling of sugar and something. Pastor Fish opened the Woolworths' back door.

"Cinnamon toast, anyone?" Miriam Woolworth threw out her arms.

They went around the corner into the yard. Through the wire fence along the driveway the Assembly of God Church shingles looked gray and dirty. Everything needed replacement. A plane flew over, but her father for once in his life did not so much as look up.

"Looks like a darned tornado!" called Chick, as if nothing had happened.

Roxy turned around and saw the Woolworths standing together in their driveway, Miriam in her flat lavender shoes. On the Fishes went across the church lawn.

Inside the Fish kitchen Zelda was peeling carrots. Meatloaf smell issued from the oven.

"Where were you, Miss Jump-over-Everything?" she cried. Then she saw Winston's expression, and her face went blank.

Pastor Fish sent Roxanne to her room, where she dropped her shoes and closed the door. The white shade was pulled down over the window that faced the Woolworths', but Little Richard existed over there, Little Richard's face smiling, his white teeth flashing, his eyes that knew her. She stared at the shade, and something turned over deep inside her belly, where the fierce, surprising voice lived. Roxy touched the old scratched dresser, a piece of furniture from childhood. Deep in the bottom drawer Jennifer Smith slept under a washcloth, waiting to go to Rome for dinner with her boyfriend. But her arms and legs were plastic. Roxy squatted on the rag rug in her full skirt, the new one out of the Missionary Box, and wrapped her arms tight around her knees, rocking. The skirt had small flowers. She could remember each sweet note of Little Richard's two songs. The voice crouched too, waiting to come out again.

"May I come in?" said her father.

He knocked while opening the door, and Roxy jumped up. She turned to face him, swallowing twice, backing away as he entered in his Florsheims. Behind him, through her parents' bedroom, Roxy could just see a slice of the kitchen; she had time to follow the seam up her mother's stockinged leg right before the door clicked shut. In her mind's eye a carrot peel still whooshed through the air. Her father had no Bible, nothing but his hands, and at first she thought he planned to spank her. But he merely stood, staring at her. His hands, carpenter's hands, hands that could fix anything, hung down at his sides. Everything in Roxy held still. New whiskers had grown out of her father's chin since they walked into the house only minutes ago. His face had lines she had never seen before, and the skin sagged.

"I would like to talk to you."

Roxy's heart sank.

"Snort like a pig!" Colleen pounded on the door.

"Go away," said their father.

"I was singing," said Roxy. His face terrified her.

He stepped toward her. He tried to loosen his tie, but the knot stuck. His big hands dropped to his sides again.

"Sit down," he said.

She backed toward the bed and sat.

"Stand." Beads of perspiration appeared on his forehead.

Roxy stood, wishing her shoes were on.

"Some people believe demons enter when you make that guttural sound, but I don't know. When you yowl like that it stands to reason, but that is not my point."

"Rock and roll is of the devil!" Zelda Fish called from the kitchen. The whole house was eerily quiet, as if the furniture were listening. Zelda's voice carried like a bell. "We preach against it! We pray against it! Yet *whump*, *whump*, there you were!"

Pastor Fish looked around Roxanne's room as if he had never seen it before. Then he looked back at her in the same strange way.

"Hello," she said uneasily.

"Oh, you can get your worldly acclaim." He kept staring. "That voice in there" — he pointed — "is nothing to sneeze at, demons or not. But what is worldly acclaim?"

"I don't know," said Roxy. "What is it?"

"The Lord is coming soon."

Roxy's hair stood up. His voice reminded her of Little Richard. When he spoke again, it sounded like a trumpet.

"Our job is to warn them. Human souls are on the brink!"

"Please lift her up," prayed Zelda, talking to God outside the door.

"In the Assemblies of God we do not have jobs, not like normal people do. But we are *not* normal. We are sinners saved by grace. And we see Christ." His eyes bored into her. "Our *one job* is to warn sinners that the Lord is coming. Now! There is no time to sing songs and hear the applause of the crowd. Christ is coming!"

Breathing heavily, her father pulled up his suit sleeve. She knew what was coming, and her torso flinched.

"You cannot love the world and be saved too. It is one or the other."

Now he unclasped his cufflink. There was nowhere to go. With some difficulty he took off his watch, the watch he had owned since he was eighteen, the one his mother gave him for the navy, made of gold with silver inlay. He threw it through the air between them, and her hands came out to catch it, just like in baseball. The watch clanked.

"We are on Heaven Time." Pastor Fish's voice was steady.

Roxy did not open her hands.

"Keep it. It is yours. Yes, your throat can sing, but that is empty. Life is an illusion. Heaven Time is real. We are trying to save souls."

"Howdy Doody Time!" called Colleen from her room.

He went out and closed the door.

"Six o'clock," said Roxy.

A Christian could not. Would not. She balled her hands into fists and did not cry for the loss of Little Richard and her own voice flying around the basement. Little Richard was gone. Her stomach churned. The watch bit into her right hand, weighing her down with its heft. She made her fists tighter, staring at the door her father had just closed. It opened.

"That voice has the voodoo drumbeat," said Pastor Fish. "I never, never heard it before."

"I didn't know it was there," said Roxy.

He stared at his daughter, her hand holding the watch, her mouth that had screamed "Lucille."

"You are grounded," he said.

Now she knew why God would not save her. For she loved the world and all the things thereof. She loved the bushes and the birds that flew. She loved the Iowa dirt. The truth slowly dawned on her. The thought of Velveeta cheese made her mouth water. God knew she lusted for the Northern Lights. Even in the dark, He had seen her!

Something thumped against the house.

Roxy picked up her blue shoes and followed her father to the kitchen, where her mother was pulling the light chains off.

"Oh! If one of my children missed heaven! I would not want to be there!"

"You would want to be there," said her husband.

Roxy placed the watch on the kitchen table and sat down in a chair, hurrying to put her shoes on. At the window someone's bicycle wheel flew by, and Colleen screamed.

"Tornado," said Pastor Fish calmly.

"Close that window!" Zelda yelled.

The light in the sky was funny and getting funnier. Winston Fish was standing by the table over the watch set on Heaven Time.

"I want to go up," said Roxy, her voice squeaking unnaturally. With her index finger she pointed toward heaven, where their friends were waiting and their house stood empty. The manna was not that good, though.

Pastor Fish looked at her. "To the basement," he said, and guided Zelda and the girls by their elbows, his eyes blue again, his carpenter's fingers big, capable. "Let's get going before this tornado hits."

They raced down the basement stairs, suddenly aware of the air, which seemed to have been sucked out of the kitchen.

"What was *that*?" Colleen's face was wild.

"Hold on to the railing," said Pastor Fish.

All at once the basement lights went out.

"Hold on. We don't need any broken bones."

Down here there were blankets and canned goods and plenty of dry milk, and water for a week. Winston went into the little study he'd built himself behind the stairs and found the flashlight. Roxy crawled behind the water heater, warm, wrapped in the wool blanket with the colored stripes, arranging it around her so the stripes were horizontal, watching as Zelda lit the candles and the Fishes' Christian faces appeared one by one.

"Hallelujah! I'm walking with the King,
"Praise His holy name,
"Walking with the King!"

Zelda started them. They all sang, but Roxy turned her head and allowed her skull to rest against the wall, trying not to feel the beast who lived inside her. The water heater gurgled. Her father's voice was off tune, but in every other way he was a genius of the Lord.

"Thank the Lord for radios," said Winston when the hymn was done. "When I was a boy in Minnesota we didn't have them. We just stuck our heads up and hoped for the best."

Zelda, always lucid in a storm, tucked the girls into their blankets, humming, looking at her watch to see if she should prepare a disaster dinner. Colleen burped. According to the radio the tornado was moving northeast, toward Waterloo. The water heater caught, and the Fishes waited in the flickering light until it was safe to go upstairs.

Afrique

IN IOWA you could lose your bearings in a moment. Roxy stood listening. She was on her way downtown to meet Superba at the restaurant where her mother worked. She turned, looking for landmarks. She was lost again, but with everything flat it was no wonder. In California, where they visited Grandmother Wellington, the blue mountains always meant north. But California also had potato bugs that hid in your shoe. A shudder traveled the entire length of Roxy's bones. She looked down at her blue patent leather shoes and wiggled her toes to be sure. There was nothing. It had squashed horribly against her skin.

"Are you lost?" said a man's voice.

"No!"

Roxy blushed and tried to pretend that she wasn't standing in the middle of the street. She looked at the man without seeming to as she backed sedately toward the sidewalk, feeling for the concrete curb with each shiny shoe. You must not trip! Demons could dress up in suits to fool the public. All they had to do to get a suit was wish.

"I am visiting my friend."

"Where do you live?"

When her right heel hit the curb she stepped up with care, still facing him. This, she now realized, could be the Antichrist. He stood with one hand on a green parked car. She must not give him any information about the Assembly of God Church or her father, who was important.

"I have to go now. Goodbye."

She fled, but at the corner she still could not remember where downtown was. Dark rain clouds were forming, and the trees looked like green monsters. Mrs. Bell the doctor's wife's house had just been here. She bolted to the right.

"Roxanne! Over here!"

She spun around and there was Superba, leaning out the back window of her mother's car, flapping her arms. There the open car door was! Giddy with relief, Roxy tumbled in, flattening her hair, which had gone wild. The curious man in the suit had vanished.

"Your mother wants you home right now," said Mrs. Andrews, her foot lightly on the gas to keep the car from stalling. It was old. The sky looked menacing. A few drops fell, raising the fresh smell of dirt. "Hurry up and close the door. I'm on my break, so I'll just drive you."

In the back seat next to Superba, Roxy's heartbeat slowed. The upholstery had loose threads that tickled their cheeks. Something smelled like vinegar. She tried to watch where Superba's mother turned, but again the green trees confused her. Then out popped Carroll Street. This was not Kansas or Nebraska. It was Iowa.

"I wonder what my mother wants."

"Can Roxanne come downtown for dinner later?"

"If she wants to."

Down the street Roxy could see the Assembly of God Church, the white cross, the hedge. Superba would not be at school tomorrow due to a doctor's appointment, and Roxy groaned. Without her friend beside her she endured recess in agony, trying to look busy swinging. Sinners discussed the shows on television, and she laughed in a strained high voice. Plus someone might ask her why her mother wore no lipstick. She decided to be sick tomorrow also.

"Call us if you can come back for dinner," Mrs. Andrews said, smiling at Roxy in the rearview mirror. "The special is spaghetti."

At the church curb Roxy scrambled over Superba, not saying goodbye. As the car pulled away she waved shyly. Mrs. Andrews was a lost soul, but she was nice to you. When the two had disappeared, Roxy jumped with both feet over the broad church sidewalk, landing as befitted a cheetah. Her mother called her Miss Jump-over-Everything.

Roxy ran to the hedge. "How are you today?"

The hedge trembled. Roxy broke a leaf and inhaled its mintiness, which was the way you shook hands. This hedge was very long and very intelligent.

"I love you," said the hedge.

She bounded up the stairs and zoomed inside like an airplane.

"I got lost!" she yelled at the top of her lungs, flying wildly, landing with a bump, hair in both eyes so that everything shimmered. Her problem with getting lost made her mother laugh, because Roxanne could get A's on everything. But being smart did not get you into heaven. Jesus Christ did.

She stopped short and almost fell over. The man in the suit was sitting on the divan.

"Save me!" said Roxy.

"Too bad, so sad," said Fred.

"And this is Roxanne," said Sister Fish. "She felt the convicting power one night down in Sunday School Room Three. The Lord has a special work for her, a mighty work. Hallelujah!"

"Has God called you yet?" He stared at her. He was extremely tall.

"No," pronounced Roxy.

"The devil would surely like to get her," said Sister Fish. "He would like to get both our children."

The man nodded, probing the air for her spiritual condition. How stupid she had been to run away. Here he was, a Christian. Her mouth dropped as the truth hit her. This was their evangelist! There was nothing demonic about him. You could see that now, in the living room.

"And do you have the baptism in tongues yet?"

"Not yet."

"But she's tarrying. Every day she asks the Lord to fill her with His precious Holy Ghost. Speaking in tongues is the right of every man or woman who finds Jesus." Zelda raised both arms. "Fill her!"

"Smite her, Lord," said Fred.

"I am tarrying," said Roxy. But you could not get filled if you were not saved.

"Well. I am *extremely* pleased to meet you," said the man in the suit. He rose and held out his hand. "I'm Drexel Eiberhaus. I went to North Central Bible Institute with your father."

"Oh yes," said her mother. "This is Drexel Eiberhaus."

"Hello," said Roxy. She blinked. They continued to shake, ignoring the embarrassing encounter on the street. Her arm was beginning to ache. Drexel had a good handshake, but nothing like her father's. People stood in line to shake her father's hand because an all-is-well feeling traveled up their arm after the first pump.

At last Drexel Eiberhaus stopped. "You're a lucky girl to have your whole life ahead of you to work for Him. So God has not yet called you to anything."

"Not yet."

"Well, hallelujah." Drexel Eiberhaus placed his hand on Roxanne's red hair. "Bless your soul. He will. I believe God has laid a hand on you for something special. Full-time labor! Not every Christian is called, of course. We can pray during this evangelistic campaign."

"Yes," said Sister Fish, eyes closed, hands raised. "Yes."

"Yes," said Roxy.

"Good golly Miss Molly," said Fred.

• • • • •

At dinner no one paid much attention to her, and she put enormous pats of butter on her mashed potatoes. It was a beautiful color and tasted exactly the way it looked, pure yellow. Colleen kicked her once, and she looked up to see food falling out of Drexel Eiberhaus's mouth. The girls choked, convulsing behind their napkins. The adults, though, were profoundly engaged. Roxy ate and thought about getting lost this afternoon, the hedge, Superba Andrews. The watch was in the top drawer of her dresser, set on Heaven Time. Clean socks covered it. Tomorrow she and Superba were going to jump for prizes on Superba's mother's bed. She sincerely hoped they did not break it. The adults continued talking about what could happen if revival fire swept Ames.

"And this," said her mother, "is the cake Roxanne has baked."

Roxy blushed.

"Winston, can you get some water and a knife?"

"My, my," said Drexel Eiberhaus.

"And Colleen plays the cello. She plays in the church orchestra and at school. Both our girls have gifts."

Colleen burped. Prettily her mouth said O; prettily her curls pranced.

"Colleen!"

"I can't help it. I had Pabst Blue Ribbon beer."

Zelda slapped her arm, which only made the curls jiggle. "Where on earth did you *learn* such words?"

For these were the things God did not like (Roxy counted them on her fingers): alcohol, tobacco, sleeveless dresses, all nudity, lipstick, fingernail polish, earrings, rock and roll, Elvis Presley, dancing, movies, roller skating, swearing, murder, lies. He did not like Partagas Robusto cigars. The rest Roxy tried not to think about.

Thunder sounded and made all the Christians jump where they were, expecting the Rapture, but no trumpet blew. Moments later lightning illuminated the room.

"Winston?" Drexel Eiberhaus leaned forward. "Is that an airplane propeller over there? That flash lit it up. Possibly it was my imagination."

"It's an airplane propeller," said Roxy.

"I am interested in purchasing a plane, a small one."

"Winston, we have no money."

"I am praying to God to send some."

"So," said Drexel Eiberhaus, "you will use the thing to reach more souls? Shondalalala seeleo. Hallelujah."

"I just want to fly around." Winston smiled. "See the corn from up high, observe Iowa from the air. I hear they're doing this circular farming up around Fort Dodge."

Zelda got up and came back with a pot of coffee, looking sideways for *Das Kapital*, to hide it if need be. "I'm excited about this revival," she said, pouring. "Maybe our neighbors the Woolworths will get saved."

Roxy swallowed. Since the fiasco, she had avoided the Woolworths like the plague, going rigorously around the block so as not to pass their house at any cost. Once she had seen Chick in Raker's Hardware Store and had changed aisles immediately.

"They're a bad lot, I'm afraid," said Winston.

Colleen burped again. "Mrs. Woolworth gives out lemonade in her bikini."

With a tearing sound the sky emptied. Rain smashed against the windows as Zelda cut Roxanne's good cake. Yellow, with yellow frosting, it resembled a warm light bulb. Solid water came down in a sheet. As the adults continued to drink coffee, that mysterious beverage tasting worse than mud, Roxy touched her father's arm with her fingers in a way he could not feel because his suit was so thick. The propeller gleamed. She watched him eat cake. Her father listened no matter what your age was. As of yet she had not told him about the hedge, how it knew more than humans, how it liked rain. The watch on his right arm was missing, of course. Pastor Fish her father could do anything: plant trees, extinguish kitchen fires, change a flat tire while telling his joke about the spotted dog. How their mother laughed! Yet his singing was terrible. But that was all.

"Delicious cake."

"Tell me, Drexel." Zelda signaled with her eyes that the girls should clear the table, and leaned toward the evangelist. She tapped her finger on the space beneath the plate Colleen had just lifted. Roxy took the butter and the bread basket.

Zelda's color rose. "Tell me, Drexel, what do you think? Since Roxanne has a special work cut out for her, I encourage her, when she is with me, to help pray for sinners. On visitation! At the altar! In stores! Now, Winston says no, leave her alone. But I think if the Lord has a mighty work for her, why not start now? She'll speak before the thousands. Oh, the devil would like to get our girls. Why, we even found this Woolworth, next door, trying to sway her. Of course, it was the devil working through him. Oh, they are pills!"

"God is not afraid of Woolworth," said Winston Fish.

"No," said Zelda. "But the devil scares me. And that is why I want Roxanne right in the thick, laying on hands, praying the lost through."

"I agree wholeheartedly." Drexel Eiberhaus touched Roxanne on the forehead with a long finger. She was still holding the butter and the basket.

They all stared at her. Colleen shot her a look of sheer contempt and went into the kitchen. "Cootie," she mouthed from the doorway.

Winston shook his head. "Drexel, you observe the letter of the law but miss the spirit of the law. By miles, I might add. You end up old dry wood."

"Dry wood?" Drexel lifted an eyebrow.

"Dry bones, then. Ezekiel 37."

"What are you, Winston? A liberal?"

"Fundamentalist."

"Indeed?" Drexel Eiberhaus wiped his mouth, which was too red. "A fundamentalist would let his daughter pray. For there is no day after tomorrow! Christ is coming!"

"Let Him. Children should be left alone to go at their own pace. I don't want Roxanne to be baptized in the river yet, either. I don't care if she is saved. She's too young. Look at that seven-year-old preacher from Atlanta, Larry. Or Harry."

"Lonnie," said his wife.

"Horse sense!" Pastor Fish hit the table with his rough-skinned palm, and Drexel Eiberhaus jumped. "That is just plain *wrong*. Children cannot preach!"

"I don't know." Zelda tapped her fingers on the table. "That Lonnie has such enthusiasm."

"Let the children minister!" said Drexel. He placed his hands on the table too, but the fingers looked soft, ishy. His eyes met Roxy's, as they had out on the street, though both of them pretended otherwise. "Sister Fish is right, Winston. The Assemblies have no policy on this, and yet we know one thing: you cannot block the Holy Ghost. Shondala seeleo!"

"Well, you're both all wet," said Winston. He leaned back, at ease, but his eyes were fiery. "The Holy Ghost is not going to be blocked by me. I'm just a preacher out in Iowa." He paused. "I will not allow Roxanne to pray with any sinners, and that's that. She's only ten."

"Eleven," said Roxy.

"Eleven? She may be saved, but yet she's a child, and she needs to get out there and play baseball."

"Baseball?" said Drexel Eiberhaus. He lifted both eyebrows.

"Indeed she does." Pastor Fish looked at Roxanne. It was raining like crazy now, with a roar like a train coming. Roxy put down the butter as her father pushed his chair back. "She has some real baseball potential, in fact." He turned to her. "Roxanne, there's still some daylight. Do you know where your bat is?"

"Winston!"

Roxy put the bread basket down and ran to her bedroom, not pausing to check Heaven Time. She raced back out with the bat, jumping over the coffee table, barely missing it.

"Ball?"

"I've got it."

"Well, you better get your raincoat."

"I've got it."

"Winston!"

"You ought to put that grounder right back into the garden this time." His cheeks were burning red. "No sense not hitting a home run!"

Winston put on his raincoat and galoshes. When he opened the door, the rain got even louder. They stepped out onto the porch.

"Winston, *church*," said Zelda. Her voice was slightly hysterical.

"Oh, I imagine we'll get there."

"But five minutes!"

"It's all right."

"Winston," she hissed.

• • • • •

When they came in the rest were ready, and they had to hurry. Her mother stood holding her gloves, Drexel Eiberhaus stood tall. They all had their Bibles, and Roxy went to her room to get her own white one, looking with tolerance born of a home run at its zipper, which made it seem like a toy. She felt fabulous. They had lost the ball, but she would find it tomorrow, as it was raining too hard to see. Her father had to change his suit. While they waited, Drexel Eiberhaus raised his voice to God for the Woolworths.

By coincidence, tonight was not simply the first night of revival but also the night the congregation bade farewell, forever, to the old carpet. Workmen were coming bright and early to install a new one, and the people of the church were mildly nervous. Sister Beverly Cedars had gone off the deep end yesterday, convinced the old carpet was Holy Ghost headquarters, but it was completely worn through. The electrical tape had peeled, and in places the church floorboards actually showed.

"I am not going to throw that carpet in the trash," Zelda was saying.

Pastor Fish emerged from the bedroom, dry, but with drops of rain on his eyebrows. He smoothed his pockets and laughed. "They think the Spirit comes out of the wool and the wood. I declare I have never heard such nonsense."

"Oh, Winston, I understand what they mean!" Zelda gazed around the room, her eyes pausing briefly on the bruise where Engstrom's knife had come through the wall. "I'd like to keep a little piece for us over there." She pointed. "Framed above the lampshade. Or we could keep it in the top dresser drawer next to your chocolates. By the way, who has been stealing them? Colleen?"

"It's idolatry to worship carpets!" Roxy could see exactly what her father meant. Idol worship was for Catholics.

"She's right," said her father.

"Roxanne, you think like a man! Oh, how I wish Roxanne could get the baptism in the Holy Ghost. Then she would have power to fight off Satan. Oh, those Woolworths live twenty feet away!"

"Praise God," said Drexel Eiberhaus. "We will pray."

"Winston, I'm going to take the scissors and cut a piece out of that carpet. And maybe one for Sister Beverly Cedars to take home, something she can put under her glass coffee table to remind her of the times she met God at the altar!"

Roxy tingled. For you could feel the Holy Ghost when it arrived after the sermon, making your hair stand on end. It was more exciting than roller skating.

"I'll cut it big enough that she can see it when she first opens her eyes." Zelda held out both arms, to measure. She had an excellent eye for fabric. "Something she can sink her *teeth* into."

• • • • •

That night everyone came in wet. The vestibule was lined with galoshes and raincoats, and open umbrellas on the landing sparkled with fat drops of rain. It continued to pour cats and dogs, the kind of deluge that forces cars over to the curb to wait, so some people were late. But up here in the sanctuary it was dry and the furnace was on. There it was, that extraordinary burnt-wood smell. Roxy sniffed.

"Let us turn to page two hundred forty-three in our hymnbooks," said Pastor Fish.

Roxy stuffed Kleenex in her ears. All singing made her sad now, and she kept a supply in her pocket for just such occasions as this. The saints turned the hymnbook pages, looking down apprehensively at the old carpet, loath to lose it.

"'Love Lifted Me.' Amen."

Ears stopped, Roxy watched the Nedleys singing with gusto across the church aisle. Her father led the hymn, waving his arms erratically. He had no sense of time. With a final Kleenex push on each side, she worked some red hair over her ears. Her family understood, and did not question her. Because God monitored your thoughts in order to determine whose heart was good. On Heaven Time, Roxy sat with both hands in her lap while the lips of the congregation moved silently.

She did not think of Little Richard at all.

The saints were starting on verse two, judging from the long pause. Little Richard did not matter, with his white teeth and bright eyes, nor did it matter how his vocal cords broke at the end each time he said "Lucille." Roxy looked straight ahead, wiggling the Kleenex to stop the sound of Little Richard. If thine ear offend thee, cut it off, Scripture preached. Suddenly her mother nudged her.

"Now the Fish girls have a special number for us," said Pastor Fish.

Roxy stood, blushing furiously. Kleenex balls lay on the pew.

Colleen dragged her cello forward by the end pin so it scudded, making a ruckus. Roxy picked up her harmonica. Instruments were boring compared to the human voice, and did not bother her. Colleen bumped her sister's hip on purpose, and the two girls began after the piano introduction. Below them, Roxy saw, was Sister Nichols, just in case the Lord came before verse three and she had to jump and grab a skirt. Colleen poked her with the cello bow, and Roxy temporarily lost the melody. Their notes were spiritless, but no one was listening anyway. The Christians were all staring at the old carpet, reaching for it with their feet. What if nothing happened with the new one? The Holy Ghost might take to this new carpet, or it might not. The Holy Ghost was a wind that blew where it wanted to. The whole congregation was anxious to feel the Spirit tonight. To live without being struck! It was too dry to think about. There was no excitement on earth like it. Being drunk was nothing next to it, reclaimed alcoholics agreed. Retarded Dolores Nedley cried noisily, as did Sister Beverly Cedars.

On the platform the Fish girls finished with a long note and looked left, toward their exit, Colleen going first past Drexel Eiberhaus, down the stairs. Roxy turned to follow just as Drexel Eiberhaus stuck out his unusually long legs, completely blocking her. The Nedley family giggled. Eyes closed, hands raised, Drexel Eiberhaus praised God in a monotone, and Roxy was forced to walk across the whole platform and exit right, past the *Afrique* map, which put her on the wrong side of the tabernacle.

She sat down in the first pew.

"Praise God!" said Drexel Eiberhaus, still oblivious, his legs and feet out.

"Thank you for that instrumental version of 'Amazing Grace,' Colleen and Roxanne. Two talented girls!" said their father.

On the wrong side of the church, facing the giant map of Africa, Roxy could smell the retarded Nedley family behind her. Her face threw off blush heat. Her mother, on the other side, held up one finger to indicate that Roxanne should stay put because Drexel was about to preach.

"I am very happy to be with you," said Drexel Eiberhaus. He grasped the pulpit, flashing his dark eyes at them, trying to hypnotize his audience. Roxy got up anyway.

"Are we all set?" said Drexel Eiberhaus, looking at her.

She sat down, her face neon.

"Thank you for inviting me. God sent Paul to the Philippians."

Without her drawing pad, which was on the other side, there was absolutely nothing to do.

"Amen," said Drexel Eiberhaus. "The Israelites had to live by *faith*."

Drexel Eiberhaus was boring. Only her mother kept you hanging off the edge of your pew. Glaring at Drexel Eiberhaus, she put her mind instead on Miss Jennifer Smith, who was in the parsonage sleeping in the dresser. Jennifer was plastic and therefore could do anything, even drink Pabst Blue Ribbon beer. A career girl, Jennifer flew by plane all over the world, wearing pink lipstick, often meeting Paul, her boyfriend, for dinner. Drexel Eiberhaus's voice was insinuating, too oily, and Roxy bent forward, gently putting both index fingers in her ears and rocking, to concentrate. She was out of Kleenex. Jennifer, international drill team trainer for football games, wore short skirts and white boots with tassels. Roxy closed her eyes. Now Jennifer checked into the Spain Hotel and took off her diamond earrings. Jennifer was painting her fingernails red. Outside the hotel windows the Spanish Mountains rose.

The telephone rang.

"Hello?" said Jennifer Smith. Her fingernails were still wet.

"'Allo?" It was a voice from Paris, with a French accent. "Oo la la. Will you be our Paris fashion consultant?"

Jennifer looked out the window. Sun glowed on the Spanish Mountains. "Oh, por favor. Si vous plait."

"But the Israelites *doubted God*!" Drexel Eiberhaus shouted.

Roxy sighed and removed her fingers from her ear canals. Even Kleenex probably wouldn't help. How she hated Drexel Eiberhaus! She could not even play Northern Lights, as pew one showed everything.

On the wall ahead *Afrique* was huge, a gigantic map depicting the whole African continent, with many different colors for the nations that were changing. This map was obsolete. French Equatorial Africa was now Gabon and some other tiny countries. A missionary passing through France had bought *Afrique* in a French store and hung it on the front wall long before the Fish family arrived. The word *Afrique* was like a sign over a bar. No Christians spoke that language, for the French loved only wine. *Afrique!* But it was simply Africa, the same shape in all Christian brains, for that was where the heathen played their bongo drums.

"Please save the Africans," prayed Roxy, looking up.

"Save yourself," sneered Fred.

With a groan Roxy leaned forward and squinted at *Afrique*. There the Nile was! Instantly she put Jennifer to bed and became an explorer on it.

One blue squiggle on the map, the Nile was in actuality enormous, with bright parrots and blue water that moved swiftly. She could almost touch it with her finger. She squinted again. Roxanne, explorer on the Nile River, stood up straight, conscious of her kneecaps. How beautiful they were! Teetering in her boat, which was turquoise, Roxanne the Explorer balanced first on one leg and then on the other. Drexel Eiberhaus vanished. Roxanne had on a loincloth, which was what all explorers wore, the skin of animals, shaped like Miriam Woolworth's bikini. One foot planted on the bow, Roxanne the Explorer waved her spear. The turquoise boat slid through the water, starting around the dangerous Nile curve. The sun was huge. Her legs were deeply tan. She had picked the turquoise color at the Explorer's Boat Store herself. Natives watched her thigh muscles. Sometimes Roxanne made friends with the natives, and sometimes she got killed. To each side was the jungle, everything lunatic purple. There was some green. Roxanne the Explorer's blood boiled. She came around the curve, and there the natives were, wading out! What to do! A brightly colored bird flew from the jungle and landed on her bare shoulder.

The dangerous natives stopped. The bird screamed.

"ROXANNE!"

She looked up.

Drexel Eiberhaus droned on. But the natives were waving. Friends! Arms above her head, Roxy flexed her incredibly beautiful knees and dove into the water, slicing through the Nile to meet them.

"ROXANNE FISH!"

Suddenly Roxy's blood ran cold. Against her legs the ugly fabric of the church pews scratched her skin. She sat very still and pretended to be listening to the sermon. Because the map was staring at her.

"Roxanne!" *Afrique* had come to life and was pulsing. It shone as if outlined by theatrical lightbulbs. "Look at Me! I see you!"

She looked.

"Roxanne, I have a mighty work for you. I am calling you to be a missionary to Africa. Go ye!"

Not scratching her nose, which itched, she waited. If she sat still maybe God would go away. The map stared back at her, omnipotent.

"I am not yet saved," she whispered on the wrong side of the church, unwilling to believe her life as an explorer was over, every muscle in her body still upon the blue boat. In her mind's eye she could feel the throbbing sun. She did not so much as blink.

"This is the Great Commission. Roxanne!"

She blinked.

"ROXANNE!"

She jumped and tried to hide behind her hair.

"Go ye into all the world and preach the gospel. Work, for the night is coming. Roxanne Fish, go ye! You must give up everything. By the way, Little Richard's singing stinks. Phew." The voice paused. "Roxanne? I am an angry God. I am waiting."

Only Roxy's eyeballs moved, slightly to the right. Had Drexel Eiberhaus not been blocking her, she would be drawing Sinners

Climbing Trees on the other side of the church, smelling her mother's White Shoulders perfume. But now God was calling her! She wished she could murder Drexel Eiberhaus. Fortunately the congregation didn't notice anything. In front *Afrique* breathed evenly. The red hair across her face was getting wet from runny snot. As a missionary you could not wear a loincloth. You wore orthopedic shoes. You could never marry Elvis Presley or go to Paris or play miniature golf. However, all missionaries went to heaven. In Tanganyika you lived in a hut and read your Bible on your cot every night. In Tanganyika you could not wear high heels. You must dress as an example to the natives. Roxy cried harder, trying not to let the Nedleys see. Some missionaries got martyred, stabbed by Bantus in the Belgian Congo revolution, gallons of blood all over the floor. Of course, your eyes lit up and you stood before God immediately. Roxy remembered Brother Leeds, to whom they had sent money. His wife came and told the story, looking down and never up. They had dug a hole and tied his arms and legs, then lowered him with just his head sticking out, in order to test his belief in Jesus. Then they poured the honey on and the ants began marching. Brother Leeds closed his eyes. It had taken a long time to get to heaven in that case. Roxy sat in pew one pushing all ten fingernails into her arms. Possibly they would just stab her outside her shack.

"Roxanne!"

Breath caught in her throat.

"I hereby commission you. The fields are white to harvest. Go!"

"God will not always strive with men!" cried Drexel Eiberhaus.

"Hallelujah," said the congregation. "Praise God."

The map jumped.

Drexel Eiberhaus raised his voice. "So God *smote* the Philistines!"

The map fell off the wall and landed on the floor.

"Well," said Drexel Eiberhaus.

Afrique bounced once. It stared at her from where it lay, half off the platform steps. Her father bent to put it out of harm's way. It had been there since the Fish family came. On the wall was one bright square of paint. Roxy's breath was coming short and fast. The map even had eyelashes.

"Roxanne," it said.

• • • • •

"Well, that was some altar service tonight," said Drexel Eiberhaus.

They were sitting in the dining room eating more cake. Roxy closed her eyes and chewed. Chocolate made you salivate. She sucked some through her teeth.

"Praise God!" boomed Drexel. "People wanting to surge forward even while I gave the invitation for sinners! They could not wait!"

"It was the carpet, not you," said Colleen.

"Young lady!"

A hammer banged and Zelda jumped. At this late hour Lyle Nichols and Brother Ransom were pulling out the old carpet, expressly to save it for Sister Fish. A huge rip was heard.

"Oh my," said Zelda.

"We'll see tomorrow with this new one." Roxanne's father took a second piece of cake. That made three today. "I like this plum ocher color. It's good we didn't get the red."

"Maybe, but I think red would get people excited." Zelda licked a cake crumb off her finger.

"You can smell it," said Colleen. The new carpet was sitting on the platform right outside her bedroom door, ready for tomorrow. "It smells like a new car, not a church."

Zelda speared some spare frosting. "My, I *so* wanted Roxanne to receive the Holy Ghost tonight. She needs power to fight the devil, and I don't know if she can get it on this plum ocher one! Oh, I hate to cry."

"Now, Zelda," said Winston.

Drexel Eiberhaus stood in his suit, both arms up in the air. "Let us gather round her as they did in the Upper Room. All rise, shall we?"

His fingers pulled them upward, except for Colleen, who kept on eating her cake. The baseball bat lay useless on the floor under the table as loud Christian voices rose in supplication to God. Drexel Eiberhaus and Zelda took Roxy's wrists and lifted them. Her armpits stank. Drexel Eiberhaus put one hand on her head to brace and the other hand to push.

"*Fill* her!"

Now he was shaking her so fast that her whole face wobbled. Her fury at Drexel Eiberhaus grew. He raised her arms higher. Her lips and cheeks shook.

"Let go!" Drexel Eiberhaus cried.

Roxy let her body flop, eyes shut tight.

"Let go! Let go! Let go!"

"She's going to get it," Zelda said out of the dark.

Roxy stood there, flopping. It was impossible to get the baptism in the Holy Ghost, for you had to have Jesus in your heart, and she did not. But they did not know. Her mother's giant dolman sleeve was comforting against her forearm, there to grab if the trumpet sounded. Roxy touched the cloth just in case. Eventually they wound down.

"Hallelujah. Praise God. I think she came close."

"Did you come close, Roxanne?"

"I think so."

"Oh!" cried Sister Fish. "The things of the Lord are good!" Absentmindedly she picked up her brand-new navy gloves and put one on. Then she took it off. She placed them by the side of her cake plate. "When I was a teenager I was pathologically shy." She smoothed the gloves. "If I had a new dress I would not go to the high school. Oh, I was so afraid someone would look at me! I had to give a speech in Mrs. Carlson's class. Why, I had on that plaid jumper with that white ruffled blouse." Lovingly she touched the ruffled sleeves. "Well. So there I stood, up in front. Mrs. Carlson said, 'Zelda? Your turn.' 'My speech is on orangutans,' I said." Her face grew tragic. The Fishes and Drexel Eiberhaus leaned forward.

"Then I threw up! All over the floor!" Zelda threw back her head and laughed, and they all laughed too.

"But *then*. When I got the baptism in the Holy Ghost, all that went. Oh! From that day forward I could go anywhere and do anything. Anything!" She waved her fork. "I could go to bus stations! I stopped people in department stores! Oh, I could preach!" She took in more oxygen. "My. Which is my water?"

"I believe this one," said Drexel Eiberhaus.

Roxy got up and went into the kitchen and stood by the sink. Her life in the turquoise boat was over, the possibility of ever splashing out to see the natives, cold water on her naked skin. She could never dance around their campfire. She could never sneak down into the basement next door. Out the kitchen window she stared at the backyard, where rain pelted down. She leaned on the counter for support.

"Delicious cake," said her father. "Want a drink?"

"Oh!" said Roxy, who had not seen him come in. "Okay."

He turned the faucet and filled a glass out of the cupboard for her, then one for himself. She could see her red hair reflected in the glass when she held it up. There were no curls.

"A good game of baseball, if I do say so."

Roxy took a sip of her water. It tasted delicious.

"God called me to Africa tonight," she said, and began crying again. "It was because of that map, *Afrique*." She tried to take another drink but couldn't.

"Africa," said Fish.

"I said, 'Not my will but Thine.' So I'm going."

Her father looked out at the rain. He was handsome in his suit.

"Roxanne. God gave us our brains to slow us down. Oh, people think we are fanatics, I know, yet we do not go off the deep end." He drank some water. "There is plenty of work right here in Ames, Iowa."

They considered that, and Roxy felt a ray of hope. Perhaps she would not be eaten by ants.

Her father spoke again. "How many people here do you think are going up?"

"Thirty-five?" said Roxy.

"If that."

They counted the people who were not: Raker from Raker's Hardware Store, the Woolworths of course, Reverend Kelsey the Episcopal minister across the fence, and all the sinners snugly in their houses up and down the streets of Ames: Episcopals, Lutherans, Catholics, Presbyterians, most Baptists and Nazarenes. Ames did not have Communists.

"So I could just go door to door?"

"Knock knock," said Fred.

Roxy shivered, and her father took off his jacket and placed it on her shoulders.

"Want to hear the joke about the spotted dog?" He crossed his arms.

"Dad," she said, "did she wear high heels?"

"Who?"

"Babe Ruth?"

Her father considered for a long time. Then he nodded. "After work. It is a well-known fact that she loved high heels. I bet she had more than you do."

A worry pierced Roxy's brain. "But I don't want any Africans to go to hell."

"God has other missionaries besides you. Don't worry, He isn't helpless."

"I hear a heresy," said Drexel Eiberhaus from the door.

Both Fishes whirled. There he was, leaning on one shoulder.

"Winston, I believe you know that to be wrong. You are *apos-*

tate here. When God calls a girl to Africa, He calls a girl to Africa. That is it. He doesn't make mistakes."

"Eavesdropping again, Drexel?"

"And another thing. Babe Ruth was a man."

When the punch landed on Drexel's chin, you could tell being hit was a new experience. He went down all at once, landing in the doorway with his legs sprawled out. Over on the couch Colleen climbed onto her knees, her mouth open.

"God forgive you," Drexel managed, scooting backwards toward the front door.

"Now, Drexel, get going and don't come back."

Pastor Fish tried to help him up, but Drexel Eiberhaus used the table. Zelda handed him his hat.

"We will see about this!" he said, going out the door. "God help you, Zelda! God protect the children!"

"He's gone," said Colleen.

"Winston." Zelda Fish wrung her hands. "Whatever *possessed* you?"

"Possessed me? That man is an idiot. Roxanne, get your bat. It's a full moon."

They went out the back door.

"Babe Ruth was a boy?"

"Certainly not," said her father.

"Winston! Come in!" It was Zelda at the window.

It had stopped raining, Roxy saw now. In the moonlight over by the sweet pea, she spotted the lost baseball immediately. It felt terrific in her hand. It was a softball, actually.

"Now, you have to learn to throw like this. Bring your arm back."

Roxy did so. He ran and caught the ball, laughing. She picked up the bat.

"Good throw! How about that singing situation?" he asked, winding up. "Maybe you could go ahead and sing in church."

"No."

"Why not? It might be good. The Lord wants us to use our talents for Him."

Roxy drew the bat back. "I hate that music," she heard herself blurt.

In the moonlight they held their positions, their faces brightly lit.

"Heaven is real," said her father. "Make no mistake." From the barbecue he pitched to her at the back door. Bat met ball, a satisfying whack.

"Stay even on your swing." He wound up to pitch again.

"I stole your chocolates," called Roxy.

He seemed not to hear her.

"Out of your drawer," she yelled. "It was me, not Colleen."

"Well, I'll be," yelled her father.

Under the full moon the ball came at her, very white, Iowa so quiet you could hear the beans growing back by Reverend Kelsey's Concord grapes, so quiet you could hear the nightcrawlers traveling.

The Damned

HIGH ON THE SWINGS at Beardshear School, Roxy clutched the note in one hand and held tight to the chains. That sinner Woolworth! Not five minutes ago, as she was crossing Carroll Street, he had dashed from his car and thrust a slip of paper at her. Not a word had been exchanged, although their eyes met.

"Help me, Savior," she prayed through her teeth.

The note from Woolworth burned in her hand, crumpled against the swing chain. She had seen it once, the red ink written on the scrap of newspaper: "LIVE BAND TONITE!! U SING."

"Send me some lovin'," she sang, swinging, mouth open wide, throat pulsating.

Her soul thrilled.

She pumped higher, looking down at the Woolworths', going over all the words to Little Richard's song. The air was a whole different world, on top of this one, where the birds lived. Up here you could see the flat church roof and the weeping willow tree in the backyard. She came down and went up, down and up. The sinner kids claimed you could go too high and sail over the top bar. Still she pushed higher, humming through her nose, until it seemed she must surely fly around. At the top she almost lost her grip. On a cloud straight ahead she had surely seen one of heaven's buildings sticking up! Out of breath, she dropped down. Then she knew. Satan had tempted Jesus in the wilderness for forty days and forty nights, offering him the kingdoms of the world.

"Get thee behind me, Satan," she said out loud.

When she opened her eyes again, there was Uncle Roland's black Studebaker, coming down Carroll Street from St. Louis, Missouri. Aunt Dora was driving. Uncle Roland was here to heal the sick, his arm sticking out the window, thumping on the door to some inner drum.

"Keep me true," she prayed, dragging her feet as the swing slowed. "Eeek!"

She landed in the dirt without breaking any bones and lit out for Carroll Street across the Beardshear School grass, barely looking for cars, sailing up the curb, where at the last moment she remembered the note in her hand and veered left to stick it deep in the hedge's leaves.

"Thank you," said the hedge.

Roxanne Fish of Heaven vaulted across the fat church sidewalk, making it, and went to stand impatiently on the lawn, note gone, waiting for the Second Coming and for Roland to turn into the driveway, a maddeningly slow process.

"Colleen, they're here!" yelled Zelda, coming out of the house.

Uncle Roland and Aunt Dora got out of the car opening their own doors, unromantic people with fourteen children, although somehow Dora seemed to get younger each year, her skin like a teenager's. She raised the fourteen children and Roland traveled, going where God said. Once, coming home from a long evangelistic tour, he arrived to discover that his fourteen kids had found the money to purchase a used television set.

"TV is the one-eyed monster," he said to Dora, setting down his suitcase.

They had it on upstairs.

Without kissing his wife, Roland walked directly to the staircase and up, where the fourteen kids were waiting for him, gathered in their defiance as one.

"We're going to watch TV," said Gunther, somewhere in the middle age-wise.

"Daddy!" cried out Ellen.

He put his big anointed hands on the box and threw it out the upstairs window into the vegetable garden underneath. The picture went out fast. There had been a game show on channel two, and they had been about to see who won. Dora winced as it crashed. There was going to be glass in among the green beans for a long while. Yet if you watched TV you would not make heaven. Its evil influence lay vanquished in the St. Louis, Missouri, Fishes' side yard.

"Land!" Aunt Dora hugged Zelda and turned to hold her arms out to Roxanne, frowning. "I saw you jump out of that swing. Zelda, she's like to break everything!"

"Thank the Lord His angels protect her." Zelda waved a hand.

Roland stood stock-still. A huge man, he took things in like a wily polar bear. To say hello he merely stared at people, as he was staring at Winston now.

Colleen skipped around the corner of the parsonage, her curls bouncing. Her immediate family let out a relieved breath. In her hands, at this time, she did not hold a rosary.

"Look how tall you are!" cried Dora.

They all hugged Roland, and still he did not move. His arms hung down, but you could feel the warmth from him. Beneath his suit sleeves just the fingertips showed, twitching slightly. For as long as Roxy remembered, Roland had smelled like newborn babies. That either came from healing things or not telling lies. Or possibly it came from huge amounts of milk. Roxy stared at him, excited. A real fisherman, he knew how to wait and watch. Even the tips of his shoes seemed to be listening. It was true the lives of fish did not fall within the sunlight of his healing powers. He ate them.

"Look at those sweet curls!" Dora hugged Colleen, who rolled her eyes. Colleen hated all affection.

Relaxed as a cat, Dora exclaimed over everything while Roland rocked on his big feet. An electric field crackled out around him about one yard.

"Let's go inside," said Pastor Fish.

The girls had set the table, and they just had time for tomato soup before church. Roland ate thick slices of Velveeta cheese, keeping his elbows close in. When Roxy went to the bathroom she did not look out the window toward the Woolworths', and in fact pulled down the shade for extra insurance against Satan and his minions. For sin seemed exciting at first but ended in disaster.

Back in the kitchen, there all the Fishes were, babbling about something.

"The what?" said Roxy.

"The Dewey Dumpster Heiress." Zelda passed Roxy a Saltine. "She called and said she's coming to church tonight. Well, we shall see."

The Dewey Dumpster Heiress lived in New York City, but she had read about the healings in the *Des Moines Sentinel* while visiting friends, how Roland prayed and got results, how he was in Ames for a special service, one night only, how it was not Roland but God.

"Your big vine is going good," observed Dora, looking through the priscilla curtains at the backyard. All over Ames the leaves were peeking out of their buds. "Provided it don't freeze."

"The radio said we may get late snow. The temperature is dropping fast."

"Well, let's pray it doesn't get much colder." Dora put a cracker in her soup. "Flowers don't need to freeze."

Roxy's feet found Zelda's Welcome Wagon folders, which Colleen had stuffed under the table. Colleen was going down, not up. Since turning Catholic last week, she spoke to them as little as possible and wore a pained expression in church. Roxy looked around the Fish table, where all you could hear was the slurping of tomato soup. They would sit like this in heaven, for eternity, except Colleen. Little Richard's face flashed in Roxy's mind, but she blinked it out firmly. Heaven was real! They were only here below a short time, waiting to get in, perhaps this very night, a Wednesday.

Because of butter, crackers and Campbell's Cream of Tomato was Roxy's favorite meal. She took four more Saltines. They hurried with dessert, a white cake she had baked. To accompany it was chocolate chip ice cream. She watched, hoping there was enough for later on, after Roland's sermon, when they would be all worked up. No matter how little the Fishes had, they always spent money on cake mix for the visiting missionaries. In Africa, Betty Crocker was scarce.

"Good cake," said Winston.

Roland ate in silence, gathering energy like a machine, eyes moving around the table.

"Chew fast," exhorted Zelda, looking at the clock on the wall. "How rich is this Dewey Dumpster Heiress?" From the ice cream carton she dug out a spoonful of chocolate chips and put it on Roxanne's plate. Roxy popped it in her mouth and closed her eyes.

"Way up there, I'd say." Winston took a toothpick. "Dewey Dumpsters are everywhere, all over the United States. She called from that big hotel in Des Moines. I wouldn't be surprised if she has more than one house."

"Well, my." Dora munched cake. "All her money isn't going to help if she's not saved."

Except Colleen, all the Fishes nodded. Colleen ate her cake with her head down. She was in trouble. A rosary, from the Catholic Church, had been found in her room. Knowing that there might be demons in it, the Fishes had transported it to the town dump, and Zelda Fish was heartbroken. Satan in person was better than Catholicism. Catholics pretended to worship God but worshiped idols, hypocritically.

"Chew," Zelda urged again.

Nobody hurried. They were always late for everything, but as long as you were not late for the Rapture, it did not matter. They ran out of ice cream, but Roxy didn't volunteer to run to the store for more. She could feel her uncle Roland gearing up, and she watched on one elbow. Soon he would retire to pray for the healing service tonight. They were all very curious to see the Dewey Dumpster Heiress, who was going to hell. A person from New York had never been inside the Ames church before, but the Lake of Fire would be full of people from the Big Apple, Manhattan. They mocked God and drank martinis there, laughing with breath that would knock you over.

"What is this woman sick with?" said Roland suddenly. These were his first words.

"Won't say." Winston folded his napkin. "She wants to talk to you. Well, we'll see if she shows up."

"Deliver me," prayed Roxy.

"I see you got *Das Kapital*." Roland had come out of his trance. "How's that going?"

"Almost done. This fellow's pretty blatant in his denial of Christianity."

Zelda dabbed bright yellow frosting with her thumb.

"Communist fellow," said Roland.

"Right."

"They are trying to bomb us," Dora worried out loud. "Let us pray they don't succeed."

"You look healthy, Winston." Roland stared at him. "You been fishing?"

"I've been taking flying lessons out at Boone Airport. I'm going to get my license if we don't go broke."

"Oh, it worries me," said Zelda.

"I'd like to go up sometime," said Roland. "See Boone from there."

"I'll take you. You caught any trout?"

"Some speckled. Up to Minnesota I went out in a boat with Ma. They was biting the whole day. Of course, you can't keep up with Ma."

"My." Zelda looked superior as she licked her fork. "Winston catches oodles when he goes. We eat for *months*."

They all stared at her, thinking oodles was a type of fish. Then it dawned on them.

Zelda held aloft the cake plate. "Who wants more?"

"Not I," said Winston.

Dora scraped the last speck off her own plate, and Roxanne, the baker, marked this, looking at her family in the golden light.

"Colleen?" Zelda tapped the table with her free hand. "Do not make faces. Put that tongue back in your mouth *immediately*."

Colleen, damned, licked her lips. Quietly Roxy took her mother's skirt, getting a good handful in case the trumpet sounded and the Christians started to go up, up, up through the air. The Woolworths were going to be screaming along with Colleen. Without drivers, cars were going to crash on Highway 30.

"Save me!" said Roxy.

"Fat chance," said Fred.

"I got to go pray," said Roland. He stood up but didn't move.

"The whole church is empty," Winston said.

"If you got a closet I could go in. That works best."

· · · · ·

A distraction of the first degree, the Dewey Dumpster Heiress sat in pew four, left side, toward the center aisle. She gleamed exotically, a bright insect with all but wings. The Ames congregation inclined a little toward her, as if under a spell. All beige, her sweater was almost certainly cashmere. From where Roxy sat in her best blue dress she could see the Dewey Dumpster Heiress's legs ending in perfect high heels. Also beige, with tiny beige straplets, they were the most exquisite objects Roxy had ever laid eyes on on the face of the whole earth, including Des Moines, almost like a religion unto themselves.

"What's her name?" whispered Ramona Ransom.

"I don't know. Madame."

Zelda Fish and Dora Fish were sitting together up front in pew one, right side, watching their husbands, which was why Roxy for once was sitting on her own, the Ransom girls on either side of her. Colleen was in the Catholic section, mumbling heresies. Cars pulled up at the Woolworths' next door, but that was satanic and Roxanne Fish ignored it, keeping both hands around her Bible, which had the power of a two-edged sword even if it was white. She unzipped it in order to let more power out. Restored to the wall, *Afrique* was quiet, and the new carpet, tacked down professionally, stretched away in all its ocher glory. The Dewey Dumpster Heiress simply sat, closely watching Roland.

"Shall we sing? Page one hundred and seventy. Stand, please. 'Are You Washed in the Blood of the Lamb.' Amen."

Roxy stood but only mouthed the words. Singing made you want to bounce with Little Richard. More cars pulled up next door, but she did not look that way, except briefly. The women wore long dresses, and their earrings sparkled.

Eileen Ransom nudged her. "Woolworths are having sinners." She raised her eyebrows. "Hoo boy."

"Keep singing," said Roxy, starting on verse two.

"I can't hear your voice," Ramona whispered. "What's wrong with you?"

Bobbing her head of bleached hair, the Dewey Dumpster Heiress was clapping enthusiastically on "Are You Washed in the Blood" as if she were a charter member here. She tried to sing, coming in on the refrain, her voice carrying. She used no hymnbook. From time to time she yelled nonsensically, "Hallelujah!" You could tell she was not saved. She did not clap like a Christian, with the total relaxation of someone who possesses eternal life, but sharply, with a desperate smack, like someone trying not to die. The congregation watched her as if she were a being from another planet, except for the two Sister Fishes, who were too far forward. The Dewey Dumpster Heiress smelled good, but it was not Avon and not White Shoulders. Noses sniffed all over the tabernacle. Once the Dewey Dumpster Heiress raised both hands, cheerfully, as Zelda Fish just had. The Christians stared. She was definitely not afraid of them, as many citizens in Ames were. Next door, no more sinners walked up to the Woolworths', and Roxy breathed a sigh of relief. For the devil offered fun, but the price of fun was your immortal soul.

"Tonight we have with us my brother, Roland Fish, from St. Louis, Missouri," said Winston.

The Dewey Dumpster heiress sat up straight. The congregation did too.

"We grew up on a farm together, and I guess we have a lot of stories to tell. But God has given him the gift of healing. I think I'll just turn the service over to him."

Roland always took his time. All he did was stand up from the chair, a grizzly bear, and lumber to the edge of the platform, but you could not stop looking at him. The attention of the congregation had left the Dewey Dumpster Heiress entirely. Roland stood there, just the tips of fingers sticking from his suit, which failed to civilize him. Roxy breathed in, happy to be in God's world. Roland stared out, the skin on his face aglow.

"My God is a big God!"

Faith waves hit you like a shock. Now he had power to move mountains. It was praying in the closet that did it. Without meaning to, Roxy and the Ransom girls leaned forward. Roy McDuffy, Joy McDuffy's unsaved husband, was leaning forward too. In the nursery the Ransom baby cried out just once. Those who had their arms crossed dropped them to their sides, uncovering their chests. The Dewey Dumpster Heiress did not move, but as Roxy watched, some of the tension seemed to hiss out of her shoulders. Wrapped in cashmere, they emitted a different frequency. All her fingernails were orange.

"He holds the whole world in his hands!"

Except for Pastor Winston Fish, the congregation seemed to grow lighter. Sitting on the platform, Winston looked unaccountably angry, but of course the brothers had grown up together, and a prophet hath no honor in his own country. Winston said in private that Roland could not preach, but tonight the Spirit was coming anyway, despite Roland's inability to follow any train of thought, and also despite the new carpet. On the left side Sister Beverly Cedars was beginning to twitch. In the past when the Spirit took her she had danced her hair down, pins falling all over the old carpet. Now they all watched her head. You could feel the Holy Ghost crackling. The Woolworths seemed boring next to this. Pastor Fish crossed his arms and closed his eyes. Roxy looked at her father's wrist, which did not have his watch. Roland merely stared at them, waiting. They waited with him.

"I started out praying for dairy cattle," Roland said.

"Dairy cattle!" The Dewey Dumpster Heiress almost stood up.

Roland waited, arms hanging, not moving except to rock slightly, front to back. Some inner pulse had ticked on, and the whole congregation sat within his sway, eyes glued on him. He began to snap his fingers with a soft thud. His entire face shone. He was trying to tell them something he knew, and they listened hard, like people trying to learn French.

"Some dairy farmers was too embarrassed to have faith, and they flat out give me those sick cows. They didn't want no part. I walked to where they was and laid hands on them cows and prayed until they was well enough to walk home with me. Then I milked them."

The things of the earth were growing strangely dim. Being near Roland, you could feel the possibilities of life: new limbs, money coming down the heat vent. Even Colleen had stopped mumbling. The Dewey Dumpster Heiress was now invisible, while Roland had taken on a peculiar light. The stiller he stood the more he demanded their attention.

"I got Richard Nixon's aunt's goiter in a jar."

"Hallelujah!"

The Dewey Dumpster Heiress clapped, childlike in her enthusiasm.

"I seen babies healed from thumb sucking. Thumb sucking is about the hardest."

"Yes!" the women shouted.

Roxy discovered gum under the pew, but for once she ignored it. You could feel the power moving in and out among them, touching each believer on the forehead, closing Little Richard's mouth when he started in on "Lucille."

"Twenty-seven babies healed of thumb sucking!"

"Amen!"

Roland put one hand upon the pulpit next to him. He stood clear of it to feel the people in the congregation better, he had once explained to Roxanne.

"Another thing that got healed was the elm trees." Roland stopped snapping his fingers. "This just happened last year, so you might have read about it in the newspaper."

"I did!" cried out the Dewey Dumpster Heiress.

Roland rocked. "Around St. Louis all the elm trees was dying of this Dutch elm disease, some in Iowa too. It comes through and kills them. There ain't no insecticide that works."

He was getting excited now, and quieter the more excited he got. A little jiggle was all you could see. Something burned inside him.

"One day last December when I preached, God said, 'Go out and lay hands on those trees in the church picnic ground, and pray. Do it now. Get every one.' So I done that. The congregation went out with me, and I put a little oil on my handkerchief and anointed all forty-five elm trees on our property, one by one. Dinners burned in the oven that day, but God was mighty. One at a time them trees waited for the oil to be applied. Christians all stood there believing."

"Do you like plants?" said the Dewey Dumpster Heiress.

"That depends. Not all of them. I said, 'Lord? I rebuke the devourer.'" Roland's voice was sure and calm. "And I laid my hands on each one, forty-five times, just like God said. All the Christians there were hungry, but they kept believing."

"Yes! Amen!" The Dewey Dumpster Heiress's ten orange fingernails wiggled wildly, and her platinum hair shook, but the Christians looked past her. Her perfume wafted out.

"That was in December. Now all the other elm trees in northern and central Missouri are dead. One died on our land, but forty-four are healthy! Some reporters flew in in their airplanes. Now my brother Winston is a flier. He might fly down and see me." Roland paused. He was sweating hard. "Praise God. It's sad when trees die too."

All the congregation leaned forward, wanting to be elm trees touched by Roland. Roxy leaned with them.

"God tells me what to do. Me and Dora got fourteen kids. God brings in money." He stepped out farther on the platform, toes sticking over the edge, but no one worried about him.

"God told me to collect coins. I made lots of money. I was up in Cedar Rapids one time and God told me, 'Roland, go up on Hillman Street.'"

"Amen," said Brother Bowman, a traveling salesman who knew Hillman.

"'Sell them two coins I had you buy up in Detroit to the dealer there.' So I went up Hillman Street, and there a coin shop was. And I sold them. God give me big money."

Someone honked a horn and laughed outside on Carroll Street. Not a saint stirred.

"So He give me big money for them. God takes care of me and Dora, and we got a house to live in. I prayed for everything, traveling all around the country. Blindness, deafness, some broken legs. Some God don't heal. My God is a big God."

He stared and he could see right through them, they knew. They sat motionless, redeemed on the plum ocher carpet. The Holy Ghost swirled all around them, liable to do anything. New carpet could not hinder it. Roland rocked a little harder now, a big man going back and forth. His eyes were filled with something you could not deny, even if you were Roy McDuffy. He rocked some more.

"Hemorrhoids, heart condition, coughing, born without a toe."

"Preach it! Amen, brother!"

"Richard Nixon's aunt. Crooked elbow, warts, some broken legs. People don't know what it's like to walk with God."

"Glory to the Throne!"

"Some God don't heal. One man was a Christian, but he could not stop swearing. In 1953 God healed him, and he ain't sworn since."

"Shadada eeleo heemen!"

"Asthma, no memory." Roland stared at them, knowing things no one could know unless God told him. He studied each of them like bugs. "Get in line."

The Dewey Dumpster Heiress was first, wearing, it now appeared, a tight knee-length beige wool skirt to match her sweater. Lyle Nichols behind her had hiccups that he hoped God would heal. Now the line stretched nearly to the back of the church and left less than half the people sitting. Roxy wished she had a withered arm or smallpox.

"Hallelujah!" said Zelda, appearing behind the three girls and making Roxy jump. "Don't miss out."

Eileen got up for her pimples.

"Hallelujah!" cried the Dewey Dumpster Heiress, smiling from ear to ear. Her fingernails looked like shiny car paint.

Dramatically, the piano stopped. Roland lumbered off the platform, his finger beckoning.

"Step forward."

With his hankie on top he shook his oil bottle. The Dewey Dumpster Heiress stepped toward him, bouncing as she came. Her eyes, the congregation saw now, were violet, wide and startled. She didn't blink. Her chest was large and seemed to float, as if filled with balloons.

"What's wrong with you?" Roland moved the oil bottle up and down, staring with peculiar vision.

"It's my dog." The Dewey Dumpster Heiress's voice was clear.

"He hasn't slept in three months!" Now her voice wavered, like a flute, and the Christians smiled, including the retarded Nedleys. "Please! We watch him every minute, between me and Louisa! My maid." Suddenly she put a hand on each cheek, perhaps to keep from falling. "Last Friday he started to shake. As of yesterday he has not stopped. Shaking." She calmed herself by brute force. "He's getting tired!"

"Three months is a long time."

The Dewey Dumpster Heiress's chin quivered.

"Where is he?"

"In the car." She started sobbing. It was not musical. "I've taken him to everyone. I can't stand it. When I wake up at night? There he is." Her violet eyes were bright. "Staring at me!" Lightly she grabbed Roland's sleeve.

"Dogs can't come in," said Roland kindly. "Sit down and wait until we're done with this prayer line, and then we'll go out there. What's your dog's name?"

"Poopsie."

Wiggling her fingers, she backed into pew one, still sobbing, and Roxy studied her shoes again. Each had a closed heel with a small seam, as delicate as fairies' work. The line moved forward. Several Christians from Boone were there, one leaning heavily on a pew. Colleen still sat in back, lost in Catholicism. Roxy believed as hard as possible, watching Eileen, tightening her muscles until they shook in wild faith. Now Roland was praying for Brother Weston, who needed money for a new car. His face aglow, Roland looked uncannily young.

"Do you use a certain skin cream?" said the Dewey Dumpster Heiress, raising her hand.

"You be quiet now," said Roland, and she nodded.

Now there was an unknown man with a withered hand, and Sister Nichols for indigestion. Sister Ransom's headache lifted even before Roland shook her. Each stated their name and ailment. Brother Witter pointed to his ears, and Roland put a big hand over each one. They were not healed, though. Roxy marveled at her good luck in being born into a family that knew the truth. You could feel the Holy Ghost and the godly power of it, mad with possibilities. The line went on. Weak heart, gallstones, hiccups, tiredness, polio as a child. Those who had been prayed for sat down to have faith for others. Roland dipped his oil bottle on the handkerchief and held it in the area of Sister Beverly Cedars' forehead.

"Hives," she said.

"You need a godly helpmate," Roland corrected.

• • • • •

Parked across the driveway, blocking it, the Cadillac nearly blinded them. Beige, it floated on the surface of Carroll Street like a boat. Roland, tired, dark around the eyes, stared at it. It was almost eleven. There were lots of cars around the Woolworths', although the house had but one dim light on. Roxy realized with alarm that she had left her white Bible on the pew. She started back toward the lit church doors.

"Don't go in," said Fred.

For the night was beautiful, with many stars and no moon and the smell of Iowa dirt. Roxy moved to stand beside a Christian, Thelma Nichols in this case, while the whole Ames congregation and the two Boone Christians spilled onto the church sidewalk to gape at the Cadillac. Extremely new, extremely long, it had one thin strip of chrome running its whole length.

"Is that a driver?" said one of the Boone Christians.

"He don't move."

The driver, dressed in beige too, seemed not to have heard them. He didn't turn his head but kept looking south on Carroll Street, toward downtown.

"What kind is this?" Roland asked the Dewey Dumpster Heiress.

"Coupe Deville."

"I ain't never touched one."

"Go ahead."

Roland put out his right hand, a loose fist, and touched the paint. As he worked his fingers down the fender, his tiredness seemed to lift.

"Where's your dog?"

The Dewey Dumpster Heiress jumped and looked around fearfully at the congregation, as if they were the enemy. The church people waited. Then her face cleared, and there the other Dewey Dumpster Heiress was, her eyes open and believing. The face of Little Richard flashed into Roxy's mind and flashed out.

"In the name of Jesus," said Roxy. Like the driver, she turned south and put the Woolworths out of her sight and mind.

"Come here, Poopsie."

The Dewey Dumpster Heiress flung open the Cadillac door and lifted out a small dog that was trembling violently. It only stared, its black eyes frozen straight ahead. Three moles like teardrops hung off one eyelid. "He's a Yorkshire terrier," she explained.

Poopsie continued to stare out at nothing, trembling, as if he had seen a wolf. His posture was peculiarly rigid.

"Poor doggie," said Colleen.

"Now I'm going to anoint her forehead with oil. You hold her."

"Him." The Dewey Dumpster Heiress made a face and bit her bottom lip, displaying little white teeth. "Okeydoke. Go."

People crowded close around the car, inspecting every facet. They had seen dogs before. No one else tried to touch it, although Roxy sniffed. Everything smelled like leather.

"Nobody talk," said Roland.

He overturned the anointing bottle on his handkerchief, then placed the oil spot on the dog's forehead. The small body shook. Had the black eyes blinked? Colleen moved closer.

"Dear God." Roland kept his hankie on the cute eyebrows. "This dog can't sleep. You made it. It needs to get some rest now. Also, these long warts hanging off his eyelid bother him. I am asking you to heal —" He opened his eyes. "What did you say his name was?"

"Poopsie."

"Poopsie," said Roland. "Pray, congregation."

"Coupe Deville," whispered Thelma Nichols. "That's French for something."

"God, we know you are a big God. The whole world is your footstool." Roland held the handkerchief in place. "Shhh," he said.

They all heard it then. Poopsie was snoring, a large sound for an object so small, sleeping in the Dewey Dumpster Heiress's arms. When Roland took his hand away the dog's mouth was open, his body relaxed, legs splayed out, belly moving gently to his breath.

"You need to get saved," said Roland.

"Aboriginal," said the Dewey Dumpster Heiress. She was staring at him, nostrils flared, holding Poopsie.

"What?"

"Primordial. The Land of Other Things. Some primitive —" Her voice cracked. With one slim hand she wiped her forehead. "Oh my God."

"You need to get saved," Roland said. "God don't always strive with men."

"We have to go!" The Dewey Dumpster Heiress handed Poopsie to Colleen, digging in her beige purse. Her voice was shrill. "Whom shall I pay?"

"God don't charge."

"Here." She found her checkbook, wrote out a check, and folded it.

Colleen, cradling Poopsie, kept shoulder to shoulder with the Dewey Dumpster Heiress's beige sweater. She wanted to leave with her. The Dewey Dumpster Heiress placed both arms around Colleen, Poopsie and all, and squeezed. Colleen's head relaxed against the cashmere shoulder. She was the dog's god-mother, it was obvious to all. Roland stood with both hands at his sides, staring at the world. With a sudden thrust the Dewey Dumpster Heiress put the check in the pocket of his suit.

As the Dewey Dumpster Heiress retrieved Poopsie from Colleen, Roxy found herself backing north along the sidewalk toward the Woolworths', without asking her feet. She could almost smell the cardboard of the Little Richard album, see the glint of his white teeth. There was to be a band, the note had said. She knew how to be invisible from playing Northern Lights in church, and she employed that secret knowledge now, pretending she was not there. The black sky with its stars and no moon helped her.

The Dewey Dumpster Heiress gave Colleen a kiss and opened the Cadillac door. Her eyes were too bright, violet doll eyes, as she got in.

"Praise God! Drive!"

The beige Cadillac with beige seats sped off down Carroll Street, right through the four-way stop sign. All praised God. Thumping came from the Woolworth basement.

"See you Sunday morning."

"If the Lord tarries."

"Come by for croquet Saturday. We can make a foursome."

Roxy's feet continued their backward advance. For a split second the Assembly of God Church seemed strange, the Woolworth household normal. She watched the congregation, but no one noticed as her shoes found the Woolworth grass and stepped sideways along their fence. Sister Nichols cried out once in a heavenly language. The last thing Roxy saw was Colleen, a bright spot of orange lipstick on her cheek, still waving after the departed Dewey Dumpster Heiress, her true family. Then Roxy darted down the alley between the Woolworths' and the church, and the Christians disappeared.

Now she could see the tool shed where she had once spied on the power lawnmower. She ignored it, intent on reaching the back door. She listened, her ears straining for Little Richard's bleating voice until they hurt. Turning a corner, she saw that the door was slightly open. She shivered. One needle of light fell out into the world which Satan ruled. She looked over at the Assembly of God Church, and then she thought she heard the music.

She went in.

Five drinks stood on the kitchen counter, and her arm reached out for one, lifting it to her mouth and pouring it in. It tasted putrid and she choked. Ralph the dog looked up at her and immediately went back to sleep. She drained the glass and grabbed another one. After finishing the remains of all five, she waited for the powers of darkness to close in.

Nothing happened.

She moved toward the basement, ignoring the appliances, not touching the electric can opener, the mixer. They had a new iced tea machine. Roxy took a ball out of the jar that said "Cloves," whatever cloves were, and had a momentary vision of her Bible on the church pew.

"Heebie jeebies!" screamed Little Richard from downstairs, and her system calmed, like a river meandering.

Lights flashed when she opened the basement door, blue-yellow-green, and Little Richard's scream got louder. She started down the stairs, holding to the railing, glimpsing tops of people's heads. She felt at home, despite the smoke from Partagas Robusto cigars. On the third step the beams of color hit her foot and danced onto her calf. With radar vision she saw the band, dressed in red jackets, not playing their instruments but standing around smoking cigarettes and drinking drinks. A shock passed through her. The bodies of the guests appeared and disappeared in wild gyrations captured by the light, their arms jerking back, their mouths jerking, everything jerking. It looked hellish. The cloves in Roxy's hand smelled very pungent. Little Richard swung into a higher register, shaking the contents of the shelves with his frenzied vibrato.

Roxy clutched the railing.

The song crashed to its end and the dancers laughed, the men bending the women backwards so that their hair hung down almost to the green linoleum floor, unless it was stiff with too much hairspray. Roxy could smell everything. Miriam Woolworth appeared for a moment in a long black dress with spaghetti straps and then vanished in the crowd. Little Richard stopped, and no one touched the record player. The band stretched.

One of the band members went over to the drums and sat down. He spotted Roxy and threw her a kiss, and at that moment she dropped the ball of cloves, which bounced down two steps and off the edge, landing on the bare shoulder of a sinner in a red dress.

"Where did *that* come from?"

"It's a little girl!" said her companion, a sinner in a plaid sport coat.

All heads turned.

"Hi," said Roxy.

"And she's a little girl who can *sing*!" said the drummer, with a flourish on the snare.

"Amen!" said Fred.

It was Woolworth himself, waving both his drumsticks at her. She saw why she had not recognized him. He looked different. Because of slacks his legs did not stick out. His hair was combed flat back, and beneath his red jacket a good shirt stretched across his belly, making him seem less repulsive, almost sophisticated.

"Band? 'Send Me Some Lovin'.' Do you want to hear some sounds? And-a-one."

When the introduction started she was happy to be wearing her best blue dress. Her knees were beautiful, she knew, although her straight red hair did not curl. She cleared her throat.

"Send me some lovin'," she began.

It was inexpressible relief to open up her mouth and let the voice out. Air moved through her lungs for this. Her heart pumped for this. A burn rising in her stomach, she moved farther down the steps. Her voice got clearer on the second phrase. The room was charged now, and the faces were bright, although of course they were still smoking.

> "Send it I pray —
> "How can I love you,
> "When you're far away?"

Now the faces became people she thought she knew. Their heads lolled on their necks, and their hips swayed. For a moment she loved Little Richard more than Jesus, a feeling she could hardly register. She would kill to do this every day. She moved down another step, opening her whole throat. The faces looked up. These were sinners, yet their souls were clearly visible, shining out like Christians'.

> "I'm here and I'm lonely,
> "I'll wait for you."

The last note stretched, the breath lasting forever and ever. On her voice went, stopping at an indeterminate point.
"Brava! Brava!"
"Encore! Another one."
As they continued applauding, Roxy grabbed the rail, suddenly dizzy. She was drunk, she realized, a condition she had never known before.
"Brava!"
Woolworth looked around proudly. His friends clapped with their hands high, grinning.
"Sing another one!"
"Roxanne Fish!" said a voice.
She ran up the stairs, but her body had lost all coordination. In the kitchen, when she fell, she understood what sin was. Everything was spinning. She held on to the stove and took a step toward the back door, but it was spinning also. It was hard to

tell which direction was home. Ralph the dog growled, looking toward what appeared to be the living room.

"Satan," she breathed.

"Where's the little girl?" cried the leader of the band downstairs.

"She probably won't be back," came the voice of Woolworth. "Her parents are religious nut cases, seriously cracked. Too damn bad."

She leaned against the wall and inched toward the living room. She had always wanted to see him. She made it through the hallway, but instead of Satan what she saw was Drexel Eiberhaus, slobbering on top Miriam Woolworth, whose legs were up. All her freckles showed. Drexel's pants had come unzipped, and the male part stuck out, but Roxy did not look. It was very indecent. Now she realized that Drexel Eiberhaus might be a demon after all. Or Satan himself! As she backed away she fell again, and the two adults looked up, the evangelist dapper in a gray pinstriped double-breasted suit and white tie, his bottom bare. A ministerial smile creaked onto his face.

"Roxanne Fish!" said Drexel Eiberhaus, and leered. A new moustache glittered, wet.

"Are you Satan?" Roxy stood unsteadily.

They exploded laughing, collapsing on each other, and Roxy placed sweaty palms against the Woolworth wall. However, everything was spinning so hard she had to crawl. She was damned. God could not forgive her drinking.

"Help me, Jesus!" she said, and threw up on the kitchen floor.

Blindly she pulled herself up. She was starting toward the paper towels, holding on to the appliances, when she froze. Abba, Babba, and Mo were hovering around the toaster.

Ralph the dog whined.

"How are you, Roxanne?" said Abba, his bat feet slimy against the clean counter tile. Babba used his horsie leg to push the toaster down, and Ralph barked. Mo eyeballed her.

"You're drunk," said Drexel Eiberhaus, looming in the doorway.

"Get thee behind me!"

"I won't tell if you won't. Partners in crime!" He lifted a glass, which made her stomach convulse. "Sin, sin, sin!"

Somehow Roxy stumbled outside. Across the driveway, behind the side fence, the church beckoned. There was no time to run for Carroll Street and go around. She remembered how long Drexel's legs were. Fortunately the fence was weak and blessedly collapsed on the church driveway. Roxy got up and ran ten feet across the gravel to God's house, saying "Jesus" over and over in a wheezy rasp. When she reached the gray shingles around the bathroom window, she yanked off the screen and climbed in, barely aware of voices from the church, still talking. She was alive. She landed in the bathroom on her hands, just missing the toilet seat. Blood was coming from her knees, and she saw that they were skinned.

"Save me!" she prayed, running bath water.

Fred was silent.

Roxy ran the water at full force, woozy, managing to lock the bathroom door, getting in the tub with all her clothes on to wash the smell of Partagas Robusto off. She scrubbed her blue dress with the Dove soap and a fingernail brush, scrubbed her skin, scrubbed her toes. Then she scrubbed her mouth. Eventually she heard her family come in, laughing and yelling for cake. She paused in her scrubbing and sat up straight.

"Who's in there?" yelled Colleen.

"Roxanne!"

She took her clothes off and scrubbed harder, panic in her chest. If the Fishes knew! They would surely cast her out. When Colleen yelled again, she got out, pulled the plug, and wrapped her offensive clothes in the bath towel, shoving them under the tub to hang inside her closet and dry secretly, after everyone had gone to sleep.

"Marble cake!" cried Dora. "What pretty pink frosting."

"Indeed," said Zelda.

Roxy put on her mother's bathrobe, which was hanging behind the door. Her skin smelled sweet, not like cigars. Walking a straight line, she went into the kitchen, sat down at the table, and looked with relief at the pink Fish family skin, the same exact texture as hers. Her mother's robe was warm to the touch. It was chenille with lines that became flowers, white turning to purple, huge cuffs and a collar that came up against your chin and made you look like Queen Elizabeth. Luckily it reeked of White Shoulders. Out the cuffs now she wiggled her fingers.

"How's that watch, Roxanne?" Pastor Fish passed her a piece of cake. She did not meet his eye, but concentrated on the pink frosting. "Still ticking?"

"I wind it regularly," said Roxy, speaking normally, she hoped.

"Where have you been, Miss Jump-over-Everything? We couldn't find you."

Sister Fish enthusiastically kissed the silky hair on top of her daughter's red head. Everything in the kitchen looked yellow.

Roxy laughed. "Nowhere."

"Sleepwalking," said Colleen.

• • • • •

When at three a.m. the phone rang, no one was surprised. Fighting off sleep (except Roxy, who was awake), the Fishes trundled to the kitchen door to hear Winston on the telephone. He managed to sound alert. Roland and Dora were sleeping in the living room, where the couch, folded out, almost hit the piano. Blinking, they all listened.

"We'll be praying for you," said Winston.

He held the phone, cupping one hand firmly over the mouthpiece.

"Them warts fall off?" Roland rubbed his eyes.

"They did. She's in Des Moines. She wants to send us a present of some type. From London, England."

"Give me the telephone." Roland walked over in his huge pajamas and huge bathrobe. He took the black receiver and studied it. He put it to his ear. "You ought to get saved."

They could hear her tone, cheerful.

"Well, you can send it here. Nine thirteen Carroll."

In the overhead light the colors of the kitchen and their pajamas glowed. Roxy stood close to her sister.

The phone clicked.

"Let them who have ears hear," said Zelda, and they all went back to bed.

In the morning Winston made pancakes for breakfast while everyone talked about Poopsie and the Dewey Dumpster Heiress. It was too late to go to school. When it came to arithmetic versus eternity, the Fishes knew what counted. They took their time with Family Worship, debating whether angels spoke or sang when announcing the birth of Jesus, and Colleen won. Roxy prayed silently for the clothes from last night, which she had smuggled into her closet; they had hardly begun to dry. Her head pounded dreadfully. They all prayed for souls to be saved in St. Louis, Missouri.

"Amen." Winston got up first. "Let's pray for Colleen's Catholicism. Roland, will you lead?"

"It don't seem that bad," said Roland. "She's just having simple growing pains."

"Is that right? Well, you're as bad as she is. Money falling from the sky! Hillman Street!" Winston snorted. "You aren't the only Fish with spiritual powers."

The brothers glared at one another. Winston laid hands on Colleen, and the entire Winston Fish family followed suit, Roxy trying not to get cooties. Dora stood beside the piano, praying but not touching. Roland stood silent with his arms hanging down.

"Lord?" Winston gripped Colleen by the shoulders. "Deliver this girl from Catholicism."

The Fishes minus Roland said amen and backed away.

"Hail Mary, full of grace," intoned Colleen Fish.

Zelda smacked her daughter's arm. "Go to your room. Immediately."

Colleen went, head bowed in prayer, hands folded.

"We will not have nuns in this house, and especially so close to the platform." Zelda clapped her hands. "You are grounded!"

"I'm going to take a walk," said Roland. He looked at Roxy. "Want to come along?"

Outside, Roxy brushed the hedge leaves as they walked down the Fish side path, quickly telling it what happened last night.

"I will never leave you nor forsake you," said the hedge in a determined voice.

Passing the Woolworths', Roxy pushed into her uncle Roland's bulk in case Drexel Eiberhaus was hiding behind a tree. She still did not know if he was demonic or human. She smelled Roland and felt better right away. Out of school, the day was lovely beyond belief. In the sky, clouds shaped like animals floated. Roxy skipped from time to time, happy to be alive and not in Outer Darkness.

"That's where Superba lives." She pointed.

"Who's Superba?"

"My best friend. Boys follow her."

He understood immediately, not so much as nodding. He was tired from the night before, but you could see him imbibing the grass and the air, which would rejuvenate him. Superba was at school today, as were all children the world over. They walked companionably on in silence, out to where the houses stopped. The fields were planted, and they tried to guess which crops were which. At their feet was spring grass. A worm crawled by, and Roxy raised her hand to wave at him.

"Ain't God good," said Roland, his eyes shining.

A crow hopped at their feet. No traffic bothered them out here, although you could see cars in the distance on Highway 30.

"People don't know what it's like to walk with God," Roland said, rocking forward on his toes.

Roxy started crying.

"You took a fright," said Roland.

"God hates me," she whispered.

"God don't hate you." Roland touched his red-haired niece's forehead. "But you got to listen when God talks. Go here, touch that sick person there above the elbow, and so forth. You can tell when it's Him. Folks don't listen, though. God was talking to the Dewey Dumpster Heiress last night."

They turned back. Roxy dragged on Uncle Roland, but he was too huge to pull down. She took a skip. If God loved her! All the grass stood up straight.

"How do you know God is God?"

"I don't know who God is. He's mysterious. He don't like TV, though."

They passed Babysitter Schmitz's house. Up ahead the black Studebaker was slowly backing out of the Fish driveway.

"That dog is still sleeping, I bet," she speculated.

"Dreaming about hamburger meat."

They picked up their pace, Roxy swinging Uncle Roland's large hand. With her other hand she secretly gauged the electric field coming out of his suit. From last night it had diminished by about two feet.

"Well, we got to go home."

The Studebaker rolled down the driveway, all the Fishes following it. Dora honked. Roland hated being at the wheel, preferring to pay attention to the harvesting, how fat the cows were, what loony new irrigation scheme some farmer was up to. Sometimes he prayed. At the open car door Roland put one big foot in. Everyone else stood on the gravel, except Colleen, who was kneeling on the grass, her curly head bowed, crossing herself. Zelda stepped over to restrain her daughter's hands by force.

"Well, I'm glad to have these parsnips." Dora hit the steering wheel and honked the horn again, by mistake.

Roland inhaled fresh air. The hedge waved its leaves from across the lawn. Separated by the Studebaker door, the Fish brothers thumped each other on the back, big boys raised on farming.

"God bless you, brother."

"God bless you."

Roland reached into his white shirt pocket. "Here this check is." He held it out, but Winston failed to take it.

"Well. How much is it for?"

"I ain't looked."

"Open it!" said Zelda.

"One thousand four hundred," Roland said, his face like a child's. God often sent money to him.

Even Colleen relaxed.

"Are you sure?"

"Two zeros."

"We can split it," said Dora. "Get in, Roland." And she let out the clutch and took off.

"Tell your brood hello!" Zelda called. "Fourteen hundred dollars! Winston? We'll have new songbooks!"

Roxy walked toward the hedge, waving at the receding St. Louis Fishes, and leaned gently into its green leaves. She was transmitting information, which was how they talked. The hedge said it missed rain and was hoping for some.

"Look there," said Winston.

The black Studebaker was back on Carroll Street, coming toward the church, pulling into the driveway. Roland got out.

"We turned the news on. A jumbo jetliner went down this morning early, out over the Atlantic ocean."

Colleen gasped.

"No survivors. The Dewey Dumpster Heiress was on it."

Zelda put her arm around Colleen.

Roland coughed. "The radio said her dog had his own seat, paid for. I guess Poopsie was in her lap, though, out like a light."

Colleen wrenched free and ran down Carroll Street, her curls unable to help her, her hands over her mouth. Zelda moved as if to follow her, but Winston touched his wife's arm.

"Not saved," said Zelda. "Oh."

Roxy stood staring at her friend the hedge's leaves, the sweetest green of any color she had ever seen. The thud of the plane falling, the bodies as they hit the ground and broke apart, waking up with the other New Yorkers in hell. She leaned deeper into the hedge's embrace, trying to hear God, as mortal as the Dewey Dumpster Heiress unless Jesus saved her.

Cadillac Faith

FOR THE NEXT SIX MONTHS the flying dream came each night, and Roxy lived for it. Each night she laid her head upon the pillow, happily anticipating. The dream never varied in its details of takeoff, flight, landing, and gallons of oxygen in your lungs. In it Roxanne Fish soared over the town of Ames, the sixth of a formation of five blue birds, the wind lifting her red hair, the Ames lights twinkling underneath her. At all times the largest bird, who knew her, flew directly to her left.

In the dream, first she woke. The hands on her small clock said three a.m., the minute hand exactly on the twelve.

Creeping past her parents' bed on tiptoe, hands out to balance, was nerve-racking. Her mother snored softly while her father breathed on his side. Each night she almost tripped over the rug but caught herself. Her mother always stirred once. In the kitchen, with the door closed, she finally took a full breath. The linoleum each night was the same temperature. She went directly down into the basement stairwell, where she sneezed twice. After a pause she sneezed again.

Then she sneezed no more. Down in the basement she felt weirdly safe, not afraid like in real life. In the dark there might be monsters, but they stayed behind the washing machine. The Iowa sky waited for her, Roxanne Fish. She hurried past the tornado provisions, the piles of dirty clothes, her father's study. Being near the water heater helped him think.

"Whoops!" Past the second timber on the left she always almost tripped again.

Going through the door into the church basement frightened her a little. The Sunday School rooms were dark and might contain demons. Roxy hurried past the third-grade classroom where God had not saved her. She could just make out the Walls of Jericho flannelgraph standing on its easel. The tile floor here was cold, and Roxy, barefoot, was relieved to reach the wood stairs that went up.

She did not look behind her.

Protected by angels, she unlocked the front church doors. Moonlight from the outside flooded her and washed over the floor. The Ames sky looked back at her. She ascended into the sanctuary, where she turned to face the open doors, shaking out her fingers, arms, and legs.

"I believe," she said.

Like Roland's healings, becoming airborne took profound mental energy. She tightened all her muscles until they shook, to tell God she meant business.

"I believe," she said through clenched teeth.

Then she started running, across the foyer and out the door and down the concrete walk, arms flapping, mind thinking up, up, up, up, up, defying gravity, concentrating on the five birds hovering over Beardshear School.

"I believe," she gasped.

She believed so hard her knees locked. Quickly she rebent them. She flapped her arms faster. It always took three tries, the first two ending in despair out by the center line of Carroll Street, flying a ridiculous notion, her body at least two tons.

"Okay."

Sweat poured down her face as she went back into the church and up the platform stairs and turned around.

The third time Roxy tried the hardest of all, and halfway to the curb she lifted off the ground with ease.

The air was home.

At first she hovered over the church grass, where the feet and legs of saints were often rooted. She rose gradually, on a slight slant, circling back to talk to her friend the hedge, zooming by the double church doors. The air was thrilling. The five birds waited for her, in no hurry, high above Beardshear School. Holding her arms out, fingers straight, Roxy raised her head, gaining elevation quickly now, afraid of nothing as she flew past the real fourth-grade class windows, peeking in to see the real desks.

At the Beardshear School roof she felt a surge of joy.

Here she flattened horizontal to the ground, arms out, tilting them to turn left in a wide circle. People could fly! The five birds waited for her in their spot above the Water Lily Maiden lake, which was really grass. Birds did not look at you directly. The long blue leader signaled with the slightest movement of his head, and Roxy and the group took off, flying low, near but not touching one another's wings, over Mrs. Bell the doctor's wife's house toward downtown, where they passed Raker's Hardware Store just below.

The train tracks stretched east and west.

"This feels good," the birds declared, without speaking.

Porch lights twinkled all over Ames. The sinners and the Christians were fast asleep. The formation glided up and glided down. There was no talking, just the feeling of air across their skin and the freedom of sweeping through it. They flew over the houses and the tennis court and the creek, over the Witters and Sister Beverly Cedars, who always left her bathroom light burning, past but not over the water tower, to Dog Town and the college and all the way to Brookside Park out on the edge of Ames. They flew over picnic tables and trash cans. The blue bird was huge. At the famous Swinging Bridge they flew back and forth, back and forth, crossing and recrossing it, the creek water sparkling in the moon. Finally they ascended. The entire sky was their habitat. Swinging Bridge changed into a toy. After many hours, cool, they turned their beaks toward Beardshear School, flying back over the railroad tracks and Raker's Hardware Store, then lower toward the bandshell and the power plant where Lyle Nichols worked. Birds understood each other's thoughts perfectly. When they reached the lawn of Beardshear School, Roxy angled down across Carroll Street through warmer air. "Till tomorrow night," the five birds indicated by thinking. Birds were happy to be alive.

Roxy landed on her feet, went back through the church doors, locking them, and retraced her steps to bed, laying her head on the pillow in exactly the same place.

· · · · ·

Roxy hated science with a purple passion, and except for not being saved yet she wished the Lord would come tonight, which would prevent her from attending science class tomorrow. Out the window the sky did not look that dramatic, to be truthful. Roxy sighed and squinted at the Duncan Hines cake, trying to see a volcano.

"Get moving, young lady! Time to finish Mount Vesuvius. And stop pulling on my skirt. What's wrong with you?"

Roxy stopped squinting, in case that helped. "Ick," she said.

On the kitchen table Mount Vesuvius sat ugly for all to see, ruining the entire house. A chocolate cake with chocolate frosting, it didn't look like a volcano at all, even with the middle bashed in. It was cooling now so it could receive varnish, but it was obviously a disaster. Fortunately science was of the devil and did not matter.

"I think it looks nice," said her mother, standing back. "Let go of me! I can just imagine lava coming out. And you are *not* staying home tomorrow." Zelda opened the window to let the November air in.

"Science won't count up in heaven," Roxy tried.

"We're on earth." Zelda tapped the cake plate. "Right here."

She pried the lid off a can of varnish with a table knife tucked inside a rag. The smell was overwhelming. "Let's get busy. Here's a brush."

Roxy sighed again and took up the brush. She attacked Mount Vesuvius, painting wildly, but the shine only made the ugliness show up more. The varnish began to run, pooling in giant blobs. Science was evolution, which was of Satan. She imagined mad scientists in white smocks, going up in flames, the shock of recognition on each face. The Assembly of God Church of Ames, Iowa, had been correct!

"I put thick newspaper on the piano bench. It can dry there overnight."

"Guess what," said Colleen, waltzing in with both arms up. She looked like Aimee Semple McPherson, or as much as she could in a black lace dress out of the Missionary Box, far too big. "I'm a genius."

Roxy inspected her. She was a genius of being cute. "What type?"

Colleen kept both arms lifted. "A genius of philosophy. And art. Statues." She looked inch by inch around the Fish kitchen, as if at a foreign country, and extended her arms in supplication. "That is why school bores me."

"I'll genius *you*." Zelda Fish stood with her hands on her hips. "I want you both in bed. Go say your prayers, *now*. Colleen? You hold this newspaper while your sister takes Mount Vesuvius to the piano bench. I'll be in to rub your backs."

"A rose is a rose is a rose is a rose is a rose!" declaimed Colleen, walking backwards, her fingertips supporting the newspaper, her voice unnaturally deep.

Zelda clicked on the lamp. In the dining room the table and chairs glowed.

"Thank you, Jesus, Colleen is not Catholic," Zelda prayed, supervising them. "Walk carefully, Roxanne. Don't trip."

Roxy was carrying Mount Vesuvius, Zelda moving obstacles

and Colleen holding the newspaper underneath so nothing dripped, when Pastor Fish came in the front door from the church board meeting. Roxy blushed. It was too late to hide it.

"Who tripped?" Her father took off his hat. "I hope we aren't going to *eat* that."

"Winston! She worked hard on that. It's Mount Vesuvius."

"Oh."

He looked puzzled. The varnish unfortunately caught the lamplight.

"I don't quite see it. Where exactly is the crater?"

"I *hate* science," said Roxy.

She put the cake down and walked out fast, crying, desperate to reach the bathroom before they called her back. She locked the hook-and-eye.

"Come out here! What's wrong?"

She knelt in front of the toilet, putting the lid down first. Not only was her volcano a disaster, but she feared her heart was growing hard. That was what happened once you had committed the Unpardonable Sin. No one knew exactly what it was. So far her parents did not know about her singing downstairs at the Woolworths' party. Drexel Eiberhaus had not told. She looked up at the ceiling, crying.

"Save me!"

"I'm a genius," she heard Colleen say from the living room. "Yes. Philosophy. And art. Statues."

· · · · ·

On the way to school in the morning, walking with Superba, Roxy dumped Mount Vesuvius in the Turner trash can all in one swoop, hidden from the Fish window by the edge of the Woolworths' house and in addition by Superba holding out her skirt. Her father said there was no crater! Anyway, science was a nightmare full of microscopes and apes that eventually became human.

Chick Woolworth came out with his shovel, ignoring Roxy.

Since the incident with the band he seemed to have given up on her. Whenever she ran into him, he shook his head and muttered, but that was all.

Their eyes met briefly now.

"Religious nut cases," he mouthed.

"Last bell!" cried Superba.

The two girls hurried up Carroll Street, raced across to the Beardshear School side, and jumped the curb just as the bell stopped. Snow made it difficult to land, and Roxy helped her friend up.

"We're going to get in trouble," said Superba. "Come on."

They ran in the Beardshear doors and up the stairs. Through their mittens you could feel friendship warmth. Outside the classroom they fought to get their galoshes off, hanging their coats on hooks.

"Don't look scared," Superba said.

They opened the door and marched to their seats just as the Pledge of Allegiance was ending. Each girl stood with one hand over her heart, trying to look like she had been there all along. Mrs. Hartly's eyes noted them and smiled anyway.

"Sit down, class."

All sat.

"Today Roxanne Fish has her Mount Vesuvius project."

All heads turned.

"Is it in the hallway, Roxanne? Go and get it."

Roxy stood up and looked for Superba, who turned to face her. They had not thought of an excuse. Up front, Superba's eyes shone out at her. Because her name was Andrews, Superba always sat in the first row.

"She threw it in the trash," said Tommy Barker, his blond hair sticking straight up. She imagined the flames instantly, plus the parched tongue, all swollen up. It would not be long before this happened. But they were on earth now. Tommy Barker's voice rose, insistent. "I saw her do it!"

Laughter burst out from the sinner kids, and Roxy looked

down at her feet. She had on purple shoes out of the Missionary Box, which had looked cute this morning, but now they felt too big. She blushed furiously, and the laughter increased until Mrs. Hartly clapped her hands.

"Enough! I'm sure she had a good reason to throw it away. We are going to discuss Amerigo Vespucci. Now, who knows who he is?"

"He sailed the ocean blue," said Isabell, waving her hand. She was Episcopal and did not know the truth.

Mrs. Hartly walked up and down the aisles, discussing Amerigo Vespucci and his escapades. Today she had on a red dress and red high heels. Her hair was jet black, and she did not think Roxy was crazy. She was not saved, of course, but Roxy was sure she was in a special category, exactly like Superba. This was extremely rare. God was going to let her in for wearing all red. Maybe God would let Roxy in for running fast. She prayed, closing her eyes briefly. When she opened them, she saw Drexel Eiberhaus walking down Carroll Street with a long umbrella slung on one arm. A thin white plume of smoke from what appeared to be a cigarette trailed up in the cold air. She leaned forward. It could not be! She could only see his back, but she was sure of it. Drexel Eiberhaus turned and looked up at the school windows. Then he got into a car and drove away.

"Now, Vespucci was not the first to see the New World," said Mrs. Hartly. "Who was it?"

"Magellan!"

"Columbus!"

"Probably the Siberians from Russia," Mrs. Hartly said.

Just then the atom bomb bell went off shrilly, making the children jump. They didn't want to blow up. They crawled under their desks, facing away from the windows, hands clasped behind their necks, happy to delay the Age of Exploration. Roxy tried to tell if this was real or only a drill. Underneath her desk she turned her head both ways. With the A-bomb, grabbing your mother's dress was useless, for you had to pass through death.

"Do not explode, do not explode, do not explode," she prayed. For if she died she would be lost forever.

"Keep your heads down," said Mrs. Hartly's voice. Red high heels went up and down the rows, click click click.

"Save me!"

"Do you have your fingers interlaced across your neck?" Mrs. Hartly walked on her high heels. "I'm checking."

"Save me!" said Roxy again.

When the all-clear bell rang, Roxy thanked God that the Russians had not dropped the bomb. Alive, all the kids got up and sat down.

Roxy felt the carvings on her desk, planning to pinch her skin tonight while praying at bedtime. She was going to burn for singing in the Woolworths' basement, voodoo sounds from Africa, and for hating boring church music, and once in hell she would never see her parents again. It was hard to tell about Colleen. Mrs. Hartly stopped and placed a hand on Roxy's sweaty forehead, and Roxy wished she could tell her everything, all about the singing and Drexel Eiberhaus's pants. The red dress smelled new.

"Save me!" she prayed as soon as Mrs. Hartly had moved on in her red high heels.

"Closed," said Fred.

• • • • •

Practicing their cello and harmonica duet, Colleen and Roxy winced. The song they were playing sounded more like people drowning than being rescued from the waves. They finished the last verse, both giggling. Unlike school, the living room was safe.

"'He will lift you by His love, out of the angry waves,'" said Pastor Fish. "Amen."

He plunked out the last chord on the piano, reading the music with some difficulty. Along with smiling sweetly and the other traditions of the preacher's wife, their mother shunned the piano as if it were a virus. She much preferred her worldly work as Welcome Wagon hostess for Ames, and in fact was sorting her manila folders, practically skipping around the dining room table. She felt good.

"Sunday night we'll play three verses, with the chorus in between."

"They can't hear the words anyway," said Colleen.

"But they *know* them!" interjected Sister Fish. She had been humming little tunes off-key all day, very unlike her. "'Love Lifted Me.' My, that was inspiring. Winston, why don't you play your trombone along with?"

Colleen put her cello in its case, rolling her eyes at the suggestion of a family trio. Cellos were large and awkward to carry, plus you were responsible if you broke them. The cello just fit behind the piano. Colleen fluffed the same black dress she had been modeling around the house for three days. It was voile, with lace around the collar and puffy sleeves. She pulled up the skirt and looked down at her feet, black shoes with white socks.

"I have to have black socks. Geniuses wear black. Period!"

"Look in the Missionary Box," said Sister Fish.

"I MEAN REAL ONES!"

Her voice stopped everyone, bouncing off the furniture.

"I am a genius of the first degree. There are all grades, but I am of the first degree." Her cheeks were flushed, her hands curled in fists. "I'm not kidding."

Both Fishes sat down on the couch. Colleen was begging for a spanking. Roxy watched with interest.

"We'll get you some black socks tomorrow at J.C. Penney's."

Roxy and Colleen blinked. The Fishes never bought anything new. Instinctively the girls moved closer to one another.

"We are thinking of taking a trip to California," said Zelda Fish. "In fact, we are. Just the two of us, by airplane. Just a short one. We are trying to think what to do with you girls."

Roxy's hands went cold and her face froze. What if the Rapture happened while they were gone? To never see her parents again!

The signs in Africa all pointed to His Sooncoming. The Christians would not see New Year's.

"Take us," she heard her voice say.

"We can't take you. You can't be out of school."

"Set us free," Colleen pleaded, arms out. She looked exotic, gold curls against the black. Her lips were suspiciously red, so she must have been biting them. "Release us from this prison!" She stretched up, up, on tiptoe, barely balancing. "Freedom!"

"Don't leave," said Roxy.

"What's wrong with you? Grandmother's sick. Besides, we have some business to attend to. We're going to use part of that seven hundred God gave us. It's too bad that Sister Nichols can't stay with you girls, but she's down with that bad flu. Let go of my skirt!"

"I'm coming with you!" Roxy sat down on her mother's lap. Zelda smelled strongly of White Shoulders.

"Miss Worrywart! You can stay with Superba, and Colleen can stay with Rachel Overhart. Oh, I *hate* that there are cigarettes there. If they light up, run outside immediately."

"What about the Rapture?" Roxy pointed up.

"Then we'll meet up there instantly! Hallelujah! In our mansion! At the kitchen table!" Sister Fish had tears in her eyes. "What a day that will be."

"I am going to be gone when you come back." Colleen's voice was jaded. "I am going to Paris, France."

"Oh!" Zelda Fish gave Colleen the evil eye. "If I hear you're being Catholic while we're gone?" She picked up a white doily from the sofa arm and inspected it, snapping it smartly to get out the dust. "You will surely live to regret it."

Winston Fish, inspecting the other sofa arm, wiggled it. You could see him thinking how to fix it. "Chick Woolworth will not be laughing when the trumpet sounds. You may count on that!" He pushed the sofa arm back in, then pulled it out, to nail or glue. "We'll be gone just like that! He won't be firing up his lawnmower then, you may believe. Roxanne? How was your Mount Vesuvius project?"

"She gave me a B plus," Roxy lied.

"You should do better than that. She couldn't see the crater, I suppose. Would anybody like some pecans?"

They moved to the kitchen, where the pecans were, Colleen nagging her mother about what time they could go to J.C. Penney's to buy socks. Slipping into the closet sideways, Roxy pulled the door closed slowly so it did not creak. Inside, it was not quite pitch-black, and when her eyes adjusted she could see the outline of things. This closet was the largest in the Fish house, taking up what had been some useless platform space on the other side the wall. She pushed the winter coats aside and knelt with her nose against the shelf where she had found six tomatoes, not wrapped yet, before last Christmas. She had no idea how Roland had fit in here.

"Dear Lord," she said.

You could smell mothballs, but she tried to concentrate. God noticed your mind wandering.

"Has anybody seen Roxanne?" Zelda yelled.

"Dear God." She started over. "This is Roxanne Fish. I come to you today with longing in my heart. I am not saved."

A rushing mighty wind filled the closet, so that two coats hit her in the face. One was still wet.

Roxy grabbed her arms, but she did not feel particularly afraid. At least God was listening. A long wool scarf blew by her.

"Is this God?"

The wind increased, and she had to brace herself. It made a noise so amazing that it seemed impossible they could not hear it in the kitchen. She felt suddenly hopeful.

"I HAVE HAD IT WITH YOU!" said God. "You will never go to heaven with the Fish family. Voodoo drumbeats! Wiggling your little hips! You are one hairsbreadth from committing the Unpardonable Sin."

"It's wiggling?"

"It changes," said God. "Hmmm. Depart from Me, I never knew you."

"Oh no, God," said Roxy.

"Ha! You think you're so smart. Lucille this and send me that. Rock and roll! And that guttural voice! How much did you think you could get away with? Ha! My spirit will no longer strive with you. By the way, the Dewey Dumpster Heiress says hello."

"God, don't leave me! I am sorry for my sins!" Roxy bit her lips hard. "I will do anything!"

"Anything?"

"Anything! Live in a hut in Africa! Have the ants murder me!"

"Well."

"Please! I beg of You!"

"Jump off the roof," said God.

"I beg Your pardon?" Trying not to be rude, for this was God, Roxy did not think she had heard right.

"Jump off the roof. Fly! F-l-y. Who do you think has been giving you those flying dreams? I made the air."

Roxy cleared her throat. "You're God?"

"There. I'm humming. Like the Buddhists want me to do."

"You like the Buddhists?"

"Don't be crazy. I am in the carpet. I am everywhere. Fly!"

"Yes, Lord," said Roxy, enunciating. She kept her fingers interlaced in prayer. This was not the time for hesitation. "Fine."

"Little Richard," said God. "Heebie jeebies! What kind of language is that?"

"I want heaven!"

"This is your last chance. After this I give up."

"My last chance," said Roxy.

"But you have to do it immediately. Tonight. You can take Superba. I will hold you up by My strong right arm."

The wind stopped.

"God?"

The wind blew once.

"I have spoken."

"But the *roof*?" said Roxy.

"Well, it's up to you. I must go now. Someone wants to get saved in China."

"I'll do it," said Roxy.

She knew where He meant. The church roof was long and flat, exactly like a runway, and lay across the street from Beardshear School, where the five birds hovered.

"Roxanne?" Zelda called, and screeched when the closet door opened. "Oh! Is that you? What are you *doing* in there?"

"I was praying for the Africans," said Roxy, pretending to wipe her eyes. She sniffed piously.

"Oh! I'm sorry! Go ahead."

A coat fell down and Roxy hung it up. Then she emerged. She had to find Superba, fast. Her own coat was on the porch, and she went out and put it on, her mother watching curiously.

"I have to get my homework at Superba's house."

"Can't it wait?"

"I have to get it right now," said Roxy.

• • • • •

"Men!" shrieked Superba.

They dove and swam hard for the lake bottom. There was still a little light left. In their underwater palace they tried on their new dresses and fixed their hair and put on earrings, their hearts beating fast. As a Water Lily Maiden you could wear sleeveless clothing!

A hunter grabbed Roxy's bare arm.

"Eeek! Help!"

"Eeeek!"

"Eeeeek!"

"Eeeeeek!"

"I'm hungry." Superba stood up to go.

"Wait!"

Roxy scrambled up from where she had been writhing, snow in her collar despite her best efforts to be careful. It felt horrid melting. She took a deep breath.

"Listen," she said, grabbing Superba's mitten. "People can fly."

Superba, who had been gazing up Carroll Street, turned her head. "What?"

"People can fly," repeated Roxy, listening to the strange words.

"You are crazy!" Superba put her mittens on her hips and shook her head.

"They can." Roxy's voice rose. "You don't believe me? Come tonight and see. You have to hold your stomach muscles tight and show your faith by jumping off something. I've already done it."

Superba's liquid eyes widened. "Really?"

Roxy looked across Carroll Street at the Assembly of God Church. The side was gray shingles, but above the double doors, behind the tall white cross, the long, flat roof stretched out like an airfield.

"Really. I'll jump off the roof tonight and then fly back and get you."

"The *roof*?"

"Then we can fly around Ames together. I'm not kidding. Oral Roberts says you can get anything by praying. You can get a Cadillac. 'If your faith be as a grain of mustard seed ye shall say to this mountain, be ye removed into the sea, and it shall be.' Be outside my window at three tonight."

Superba wiped her nose on the wool arm of her car coat. Both girls looked around. The streets they were familiar with, but not the air above them. They had climbed up to the Beardshear School roof, of course.

Superba scratched her nose, mitten on, getting snow on her face.

"Okay. Who's Oral Roberts?"

"A rich evangelist. He's famous!"

Both girls looked up at the church roof. Then they went their separate ways for dinner, to wait until night came.

• • • • •

Beneath the covers Roxy went over the flying dream, memorizing the details of the third try. This was not a night for sleep. Superba was coming at three a.m. The ladder was ready, hidden under the window. In between somersaults Roxy repeated the faith verses and prayed, to stay awake and not let doubt creep in. She fell asleep despite herself, and woke up shivering on the floor in position for a somersault.

"Psssst!"

With great effort Roxy got up, moving toward the window in her bare feet, trying not to think, tightening her stomach muscles until they ached. The air felt like thick mud. She wished she could call Roland.

"I believe people can fly," whispered Superba. Her breath made smoke. "It's after three!"

In a panic Roxy knocked the screen off and put one bare foot out the window, flinching at the cold. Then she put her other leg out and jumped down. Because of the snow the driveway gravel didn't crunch. Ames was silent.

"It's freezing out here," whispered Superba, who was wearing the same car coat over her pajamas. "Are you scared? Your face is white."

Roxy breathed. She had to take this chance. When God spoke you had to listen, or lose all hope. Hell crackled underneath their feet.

"People can fly. Right?" Superba looked up at the sky, with many stars.

"Of course they can."

Roxy shivered. Tonight she was wearing underpants, not like bed, where you had to air that part out. She snapped the elastic. Superba's nose was cold, but she had on earmuffs. The girls raised the ladder, which was bigger than they thought.

"Pull it toward the Woolworths'. Okay, now push it back. One, two, three, go!"

Through the window Roxy saw her own bed. How she wished she were in it! But God was going to turn His back on her if she didn't fly. She took a deep breath.

"This is fun," said Superba.

"If you want to we can fly out over Brookside Park. I'll come back and get you."

When she jumped, God was going to save her. About to get her name written in the Lamb's Book of Life, Roxy stepped on the first rung. The ladder creaked but stayed in place. Up she went. Her bedroom window disappeared. At the top she was surprised to see how ugly the roof was, with big clumps of tarpaper and trash peeking through the snow.

"Praise God," she whispered.

Tucking her long nightgown firmly in her panties, to free her knees, she climbed forward, onto the runway itself. Then she helped Superba, and the two girls moved toward the middle, which was not as frightening. It would show more faith to knock the ladder over, as they would not need it for landing, but that would make noise and wake her parents up.

"This is fun," said Roxy.

It was dizzying to be up here without a wall in front of their noses. Roxy and Superba held hands to steady themselves. Their hearts beat as one.

"If your faith be as a grain of mustard seed!" said Roxy.

"Jesus loves me, this I know."

Roxy could feel Superba's breath in her ear. From where they stood you could see the tops of the tallest trees, their branches bare.

"By faith Moses parted the Red Sea."

"Fourscore and seven years ago!"

"Faith is the victory. Cadillac!"

They moved forward. You would not have guessed a building of one story would put you this high up. Across Carroll Street the windows of the fourth-grade classroom glittered in the streetlights.

"We can fly over the school roof!"

"We can fly over the bandshell!"

Roxy laughed, then clutched Superba's hand tighter in an effort to be serious.

"By faith Moses led the children of Israel out of Egypt."

"I can hardly wait," said Superba. "Tomorrow let's not tell anyone."

"We can do it every night," said Roxy. It was now or never. She willed her mind to believe. "Or every other night, and sleep in between. Once I'm flying I'll zoom by the front of the roof and pick you up. Don't let your mittens slide off."

Holding hands, the girls felt how thick a thing friendship was. Overhead, the Milky Way stretched out, a brushstroke from the mighty hand of God. There was a crescent moon. At the Woolworths' Ralph stood staring at them, halfway out his dog door.

Roxy let go of Superba's hand and ran in place, her nightgown tucked in. She had to jump while her faith was at full blast.

"Daniel in the lion's den!"

"A car! Hide!" Superba screamed.

The girls ducked, giggling from sheer terror. The time was here. They stood up.

"Shadrach! Meshach! Abednego!"

"Rumpleskilpskin!" Superba cried.

Roxy's naked legs felt the freezing air. Her heart pounded violently, belief soaring.

"Okay. Here I go."

"I'll be on the edge," said Superba.

"By faith Moses!"

Roxy's heels flew up behind her, bits of snow and tarpaper spraying out. She was not cold. The roof flashed by. Birds waited for her in the sky, she remembered. She flapped her arms furiously. Here came the edge.

"Peter in prison! Lazarus! Shadrach, Meshach, Moses, Abednego!"

"By faith everybody! President Eisenhower!" yelled Superba.

At the last second Roxy's mouth opened wide. "Send me some lovin'!" she sang like one possessed.

She tried to stop her body, but it was too late. A light came on next door just as she sailed off the roof, screaming. Hell would be next.

Roxy clutched at air. A bright patch of ice caught the street-lights. She thought she saw Blue Nose just before a branch ripped at her face. She landed with a thud so hard her lungs disconnected completely.

"Help! Help! Help!" she hollered, but no sound came out.

In the haze of the streetlights Chick Woolworth wavered over her.

"What in the holy hell are you trying to do? Miriam, she's dead! Call the police!"

"I can't be dead," she explained. "Help!"

Then everything vanished.

● ● ● ● ●

If the white room was hell, it was awfully quiet. Roxy moaned and tried to flap her arms, but one of them wouldn't move. Now she saw it had a cast on it. A nurse peeked through the window on the swinging door. It opened and her mother walked in.

"Roxanne!" Zelda Fish hugged her daughter, tears streaming from her eyes. "I thought I wouldn't see my little girl till heaven. Oh! If my children missed eternity! I have *never* been so worried in my life!"

"Are you going to California?" Roxy asked miserably.

"Daddy's going by himself." Her mother's eyes shot out protection, love like a mighty river. "My little worrywart! Were you sleepwalking? Mr. Woolworth just kept saying, 'Holy guacamole!' What *is* guacamole? I swear I have never heard of it."

"I don't know," said Roxy, wiggling her fingers to make sure they were fingers, not cloven hooves.

"He kept looking at me in a funny way," Zelda said thoughtfully. "It might be conviction. I ought to take my Bible and go over and visit him today."

"No!" said Roxy.

Her mother looked at her.

"Stay here, I mean."

"You sweet thing. I will never forget the time you took the babysitter's car on that joyride." She sounded proud. "My children take the cake."

Roxy relaxed, reaching for her mother's sleeve with her good left arm. "I guess I was. Sleepwalking."

"Ma'am?" said the nurse.

"Sister Fish." Zelda held out her hand. "Come in. Hallelujah."

"The concussion tests are not conclusive. We'll have to do one more." The nurse had black hair in a ponytail. "But I'd say she's incredibly lucky. Only a broken arm!"

"She landed in a bush," said Zelda, "but it wasn't luck, believe me." Laughing now, she pointed up. "The angels protect this girl all the time, twenty-four hours a day."

Zelda smoothed her daughter's red hair back. Roxy closed her eyes, breathing in White Shoulders and hospital smells.

"That dog next door was licking her," came Colleen's voice.

Roxy kept her eyes closed. Her mother got up, and she heard her family talking in the hallway. Then the door swung again.

"How's Babe Ruth today?" said Winston Fish.

"Fine," said Roxy, but her father seemed far away. He belonged to heaven. She studied his face in order to remember every line. His chin was nice, and he had good ears.

"You like horsies, don't you?" He reached into the paper bag he was holding and handed her a stuffed horse, blue with pink ears and a green ribbon around its neck. "I found this on the dining room table. It must be left over from children's church."

Roxy recoiled so hard the hospital bed creaked. Two glass eyes drilled into her. Now her damnation was complete. She had summoned the demons. Their eyes did not have pupils. She looked around the room for the other two.

Her father frowned at her in concern. "Well, maybe you'll feel like playing with it later." He repacked the horse in the bag of goods to cheer her up, which included one baseball, the *Pentecostal Evangel*, and a puzzle of the Rocky Mountains, a cabin with a pink door in the lower left-hand corner. "Get that arm healed up in time for spring training, young lady."

"Okay," said Roxy, staring at the little bumps that were her knees.

The minute her father left, the phone rang. Roxy jumped and answered, stretching around painfully with her left arm.

"Guess who," said an oily voice.

It was a man's voice, and she had heard it once before. A sick feeling took her stomach.

"Here's a clue. I'm on a red telephone."

"Satan?" she breathed.

"I came myself. We're so happy you'll be joining us, O ye of little faith. You are ours now. Watch out for trucks!"

"What do you mean?" Roxy whispered.

"Do come for Christmas," said Satan, and the phone clicked.

Roxy held the receiver, terror in each separate body cell. A doctor, clad in white, peeked through the door.

"Wow!" said Superba, swinging in. "You sure can sing."

White as her sheets, Roxy put a finger to her lips, but it didn't really matter if her parents heard. She would only be here for a few more weeks.

"Oh!" Superba stopped dead. "Your cheek is cut. Oh, your arm!" She began to cry. "I miss Water Lily Maidens."

Roxy joined her hand with her friend's hand, and it felt warm. Superba cooed like a dove. Outside the swinging door, intent on saving lives, doctors bustled to and fro.

Storm Lake

EXCEPT FOR WINSTON, nobody in the Fish family could swim. That was not funny. Raised on a farm with pigs and cows, sinful (Lutheran), he had grown up swimming in creeks, and was convinced the other Fishes would all fall off a boat someday and drown. This always made Zelda laugh. She laughed now, thinking of it, as she stood in the shallows of Storm Lake splashing water on her legs.

"It's over a hundred degrees," said Sister Neehard. "I can't stand it."

Twenty-five Christian young women screamed, jumping up and down in the lake, naked in their bathing suits for the only time all year, astonished by the sun on their skin. Real Christians did not swim because the sight of naked female arms and legs could drive men to a bestial frenzy.

Roxanne Fish, young woman number twenty-six, stood still, letting Storm Lake swirl around her. She held one arm up, her left, the arm that had the watch with Heaven Time. (Her right arm had healed but was slightly crooked at the elbow.) She was worried. This year she did not relish the drops of water on her arms and legs, or catch her breath at the sun sparkling on the lake. She wished she were home in bed. Christians swarmed around her like insects. She was lost for all time. The eternal giggled, their names written in the Lamb's Book of Life. As she waded farther out, her foot hit a sharp rock. Angels were no longer protecting her, and she was still expecting demons to hit her with a truck, even though she had survived Christmas. In the long months since the flying incident, Roxy had noticed that her eyes were becoming as empty as the glass eyes on the stuffed horse. She avoided mirrors, looking down to brush her teeth.

Sister Dibbs blew her whistle. "Twenty minutes left!"

"God is getting people saved in Ames," Zelda was saying in a confidential voice to Sister Neehard. Too modest for a bathing suit, she stood in Storm Lake holding up her skirt. "My, it's hot."

"We need God to work in the Ottumwa area. Pray." Sister Neehard's voice scudded by her on the breeze.

Roxy waded deeper, making sure her left arm was straight. Sister Dibbs and Sister Neehard both stayed close to shore, lifelong Christians who could not swim an inch. The two women hunched self-consciously in their bathing suits, Sister Neehard occasionally dabbing water on her face. When a teenager from Des Moines splashed vigorously, Roxy moved toward the yellow rope beyond which you were forbidden to go. The watch was still dry. When she died, she would have it in hell to remind her of her family up in heaven for eternity, probably even Colleen. The Storm Lake water glittered, but now the expanse out beyond the yellow rope was just a place to drown. The voice still coiled inside her, she knew, but how she hated it. It had ruined eternity, for God had had it. She was damned.

"Splash war!" yelled Luanne Burbo, the preacher's daughter from Bettendorf.

Splashing, Luanne looked ridiculous. Roxy moved closer to the yellow rope, holding her arm higher. Luanne followed her.

"Splash war!" Luanne splashed. "Splash war! This is fun!"

"I am damned," said Roxy.

Luanne Burbo stared at her.

Eyes on the horizon, Roxy thought nothing. Beyond the rope something bubbled in the water, and she blinked. Demons were out there waiting for her. With her right hand she cupped water to her mouth, for there would be none down there. Her bathing suit out of the Missionary Box had a cute bust of gathered flowered cloth hiding wired cups that made it look like you had something. She poked one in. She supposed she would not be here to get six tomatoes this Christmas. Behind her all the Christians sounded like chipmunks.

"Brother Brenner from Davenport thinks Calvinists can go up." Sister Neehard's voice carried from the shore. "Once saved always saved indeed!"

"Why," said Sister Dibbs, "you could kill people! You could do every ungodly thing and still make heaven."

"Splash war, splash war!"

Girls fell down and girls jumped up, their hair streaming. All were saved, of course. Roxy had not told Superba or the hedge that she was in trouble. Either she would be hit by a truck, or her heart would stop, or a plane would fall on her in bed. In hell people screamed. For one second she felt oddly happy. All around her was the lake, and the sky with thick white clouds. Dreamily she let her right arm float.

"*Wheeeeeeet!*"

Roxy turned.

"*Wheeet! Wheeet! Wheeet!*"

Sister Dibbs stood knee-deep in water, whistling and waving both fat arms. Her face under her brown hair had gone white.

"Duck!" cried Sister Neehard.

Helplessly the women flapped their arms. A truckload of boys had turned up the dirt road fifteen minutes early, and now the girls were about to be raped. Sister Dibbs and Sister Neehard ran around.

"*Wheeeeet!* Oh, girls, girls! Stay down! In the lake! The truck! Keep out of sight! *Wheeet! Wheeet! Wheeet!*"

Unable to jump high enough, the girls showed off their arms and legs, madly aware of how beautiful they were, captured, conscious of the boys' eyes following them from behind truck slats. Roxy jumped too. Crouching in the deep water, which helped spring you, she jumped as high as she could, scissoring her legs. Girls leaped all around, their hair shining, water spilling off their skin.

"Stay down!" Sister Neehard's voice croaked like a warped record. "Stay down! Stay down!"

Slowly the truck backed up, slowly the boys' waving hands disappeared into a grove of pine trees. Slowly the girls ceased their jumping, happy to be young women, happy to be in Storm Lake, happy for the sun above. Out beyond the yellow rope, springs bubbled in the water.

"What *is* that?" said Luanne Burbo, preacher's daughter. "Yuck."

Roxy stiffened.

"Why, those are the springs," said Sister Neehard, struggling to regain her composure while Zelda helped the girls find their towels. "My brother used to be a swimmer back before he got saved, and he once investigated them. Springs keep this lake fresh." She stood up, baring herself, gesturing for the girls to follow her.

"I *told* them two-thirty." Sister Dibbs stomped her foot. "I *told* them."

The Storm Lake sun beat down.

• • • • •

Walking across the dirt with her mother, Roxy could still smell the lake on her skin beneath her ironed church dress. It stood out stiffly in the skirt but was already soaked under the arms from perspiration. Drexel Eiberhaus had not shown up so far, which seemed to argue that he was a demon, as demons were not allowed in Storm Lake campground. Dust came up around their feet, settling on her clean socks and Zelda's Missionary Box high heels, white patent leather with a gold strap. Walking past the central light pole, Christians from all over Iowa moved in unison toward the tabernacle. It was only day two of Camp Meeting, and saints were still calling out to other saints they had not seen since last year, ladies in their pastel dresses, men in suits despite the Iowa heat. All twenty-six Christian young ladies had survived their nakedness, and all over the campground young people smirked. Roxy and Sister Fish walked on, more dust getting into their purses and the zippers of their Bibles. The Christians were converging on the Storm Lake dining room, which did not serve manna but food. All the faces were relaxed, for within these gates no one said your mother looked as white as a ghost without lipstick, or called you nutty as a fruitcake. Christians told each other jokes and laughed and did not have to witness, for everyone was saved here.

Roxy shivered, cold suddenly.

"Sister Fish!"

"Oh my, Brother Burlap! I heard your wife made heaven. Hallelujah! She is getting your house ready. We will be there soon!"

"Sister Fish!" yelled another Christian.

A boy in a blue shirt smiled at Roxy. She blushed and almost walked into a telephone pole.

"Sister Fish! Where's your better half?"

People laughed everywhere. Her father and Uncle Roland had helped to build the dining room and tabernacle the year Roxanne was born. Both were cinderblock, connected to each other by a patio. Far across the dusty camp, Uncle Roland's great lumbering shape waved. All the Christians waited for the dinner bell, each holding a Bible, sometimes with a little ribbon sticking out. For this one week Christ's return was not expected. Here the Christians had fun.

"What is it tonight?" called Sister Harris from Le Mars, moving through the dust.

"Stuffed bell peppers, I think!"

"Why, Drexel Eiberhaus," said Zelda Fish. Her voice wavered slightly. "Bless the Lord."

Roxy turned and there he was, tall. Wearing the gray pinstriped double-breasted suit, but with a black tie, Drexel Eiberhaus stood in Storm Lake Camp with his hands on his hips. He smiled slowly. A vision of his bare bottom and Miriam Woolworth's freckled legs sat in the air between them, tangible. She felt dizzy and took her mother's arm. It didn't help.

"And how's the little girl? Miss Roxanne?"

"I'm fine," said Roxy.

"Well, how are things on the evangelistic circuit?" Zelda looked skyward for something.

"God is working, God is working."

They walked together through the campground dirt. People kept waving at them.

"Hot, isn't it?" said Drexel Eiberhaus. He looked at Roxy and licked his lips. "Not going to Africa?"

Roxy stared at him. Now it seemed his eyes had switched color, but perhaps they were greenish before. She racked her brain. The thin moustache was gone.

"I don't think she knows," said Zelda, shepherding her daughter into the dining room.

"Zelda Fish!" exclaimed a Christian in a lavender hat, and the two women embraced.

The evangelist stooped quickly down to ear level. His lips were bright red.

"Rock and roll," he said. "I won't tell a soul."

Zipper up, Drexel Eiberhaus departed.

"Smells like flapjacks," said Sister Harris.

"Flapjacks?" snorted Sister Dibbs. "Those aren't flapjacks! Those are stuffed bell peppers. You are losing your marbles!"

Aunt Dora passed outside the window with Colleen and five of the fourteen kids. She waved. Near Roxy's hip the Coke machine was humming, deep red, only for Christians. The Fishes never bought Coke, but she would not live past Christmas. Through the narrow glass, frosty bottles peeked out.

"Mom?" She tugged Zelda's arm. It was rude to interrupt, but otherwise there was no space. Zelda talked on and on. Inside, the bottles looked refreshing, otherworldly. "Can I have a Coke?"

"We don't have dimes to throw away. And this is my daughter Roxanne."

Zelda pushed her forward, and Roxy stood there blushing. It was impossible to make the blood go down.

"My, my! Is she the one who got saved in the church basement?"

"Hallelujah to the Lamb." Her mother pushed back her red hair.

"Oh my, let me look at her!" The lady in the lavender hat stared, intent on Roxy's eyelashes. "*Yes.*"

"God has a great work for her. We think she may be on TV. She will speak before the thousands. God has a mighty work in store for her, and I told Winston we should fix her teeth. Roxanne? We need to get busy and pray in that tooth money. Hallelujah."

"I'd like to have Roxanne come and preach to our Fort Dodge youth. Saved young people cannot start too soon!"

"No," said Winston. He had just walked up. "No. Is that understood? N-o. I will not have Roxanne preaching as a child. She is going to work on her home runs."

"Oh, Winston!" Zelda made a face and touched him on the cheek. "My hubby has a stubborn streak."

"God, keep your *mighty* hand on this girl's intellect!" prayed the lady in the hat, and placed her own hand on Roxy's head, making everything shake.

Winston turned away. "I would like to buy you a Coke, Roxanne. If I may."

"Winston! The money!"

At the Coke machine the coin went in and the bottle clinked out. This must be how rich people lived. With some difficulty she got the cap off, using the opener on the red machine.

"I believe I'll have one myself," said Winston.

"Dad," she said, "there are demons in the lake. They're scaring me."

"I see," said Winston Fish. He looked at her closely. "Well.

Demons can't hurt you, not if you're saved. Of course they can scare you."

"I think Drexel Eiberhaus could be one."

"Oh, I doubt it." He opened his Coke bottle, eyes on her. "Do you have any reason to think so?"

Roxy drank some Coke, considering. The liquid was delicious and cool. "No."

Sucking their icy bottles was wonderful, a rare treat. In between they held them to their cheeks. No cold Cokes in bottles came in the Missionary Box. A little ways away, her mother was saying that Roxanne would be like Aimee Semple McPherson.

Roxy upended her Coke.

"I'm going to buy you another one." Winston took the empty bottle from his daughter's hand.

"Oh! You'll spoil her," said Sister Fish.

"It's Camp Meeting," said the lady in the lavender hat.

Winston Fish held out another dime, and Roxy took it, wishing she could stand here and drink Cokes for the rest of her numbered days. The machine whirred when you pushed the button. Roxy jumped when the bottle rolled out.

"The *thousands*," reiterated Zelda. "We must tell God we need money for teeth."

More Coke trickled down Roxy's throat. She rubbed the bottle underneath her chin, eyes searching for Drexel Eiberhaus as the little group moved toward the trays and silverware, three Christians and Roxanne.

"You ought to put some vinegar on that sunburn, missy," said the lady in the lavender hat. "Your skin looks fried."

• • • • •

Roxy sat still in the tabernacle's back row of folding wooden chairs, trying not to wince as the Butter Lady used her fingers and her stick of butter to work the bubblegum out of Roxy's hair. The gum had been smashed there by Colleen, who was trying to impress Evan Randall. The church music was driving Roxy crazy with its boring melodies and stupid beat. She pressed her lips together and put one hand on her throat, trying to push the voice back down where it belonged.

The fingers pulled.

"Ouch!"

Roxy swung her legs. Other children sat beside her in the Butter Row, all with gum in their hair. The gum disappeared into the butter, but no one knew how. Down the row the other Butter Ladies worked, some fat, some thin, some normal. All were saved and going up, for none of them loved Little Richard and the things of the devil.

"Hallelujah!" yelled Brother Witter somewhere up front.

The Butter Lady's fingers partly felt good and partly hurt. Roxy liked being in the Butter Lady's arms, but the Butter Lady could not save you. She leaned into her anyway.

"You are a sweet girl," the Butter Lady said. "God bless you."

Roxy began crying. Out the tabernacle back door stars shone. Inside all the colors seemed abnormally bright. This was her last Camp Meeting, for Satan owned her now. She felt blinded by the sights and sounds. Earth had never seemed so beautiful, and there was a deep quiet under everything.

Now Ruth Bradshaw, of Quebec, was speaking on the platform. A petite woman full of fire and brimstone, she wore black patent leather high heels that threatened to fall off every time she jumped. After several shaky landings she bent down and took them off. Roxy looked up at her, remembering the Dewey Dumpster Heiress's high heels and crying harder. A dozen rows ahead Colleen was laughing madly as the Randall twins leaned toward her. This week Colleen was only speaking French.

"Zut alors! Frère Jacques!" Roxy heard her sister's clear voice.

"Am I hurting you?" The Butter Lady's black eyes snapped between Ruth Bradshaw and Roxy's red hair.

"No." Roxy wiped her tears away quickly. "It must be the onions."

"Onions?" said the Butter Lady. "Turn thisaway."

"Souls in Africa are dying!" On the platform Ruth Bradshaw bent forward in agony, then jumped back, her corsage bouncing. Around her electricity gathered.

Now the Speed-the-Light vehicle was on the way, racing through Kenya, down a jungle ravine, up a mountain, carrying news of salvation!

The Butter Lady was perspiring. Her fat hands glistened. Colleen and the Randall twins flirted back and forth, back and forth, back and forth. Debubblegummed, the boy next to Roxy was excused to go back to his parents.

"You got yourself a doozy," said the Butter Lady, "but she's winding down now, so we got to get it. Lean sideways."

Ruth Bradshaw was indeed coming to the altar call, you could tell by the sweet crescendo in her voice. Drenched in sweat, she wiped her face with a white lace hankie.

"There." The Butter Lady ran her fingers through the red strands. "We're all done. What a sweet girl you are."

"*Ching!*" went a chord on the piano.

"Get ready!" The fat hand patted her, aglow with butter. "Sister Bradshaw ain't going to spend a lot of time pleading for the sinners, 'cause there ain't no sinners here. She'll have us running down the aisle in no time." The Butter Lady began to rock. "Prepare your feet."

"Glory!" said the preacher. She undid the button at her throat. "Who wants to set the world on fire?" Ruth Bradshaw stepped forward on the platform, her small hands raised. She put her shoes back on and stamped her foot. "We are all Christians here. Stand up! The time is short! Who wants the gospel to burn out from Storm Lake Camp to the whole world? To break down the walls of Communism? To make the demons flee out of the afflicted?"

"Hallelujah!" cried all the Christians.

Like a mighty river, saints flowed forward, flooding the aisles, carrying Roxy along. Ruth Bradshaw stood, her arms up, yielded to the power. The Randall twins were fighting to walk next to Colleen.

"Shondala seeleo!" Ruth Bradshaw cried.

Wailing rose from all over.

Roxy knelt at a wooden chair halfway down the third row, people to all sides of her. Sawdust stuck to her knees. Children had to pray for fifteen minutes, and then they could go out and play with fireflies.

She peeked.

Facing backwards, she could see the other Christians kneeling, heads curled down. In the distance was the Butter Row and the back of the tabernacle.

She blinked.

Drexel Eiberhaus stood by the open door clicking his fingers. Behind him stars shone. Roxy put her head down, praying that he would leave, but each time she opened an eye he was still there. He seemed to be looking at her. The whole altar area was going crazy. With the Holy Ghost running things, Ruth Bradshaw stood aside to watch God work. A lady in a yellow summer dress collapsed, landing on her back. Her glasses went flying.

"Un, deux, trois," said Colleen, walking down the aisle to go outside. The Randall twins followed.

"Save me!" prayed Roxy.

Heaven was closed, as per usual. Roxy gripped the chair seat and placed her cheek against the smooth wood, tired to the bone. She did not know what to do.

"Got you!"

Roxy screamed.

It was not Satan but cute Evan Randall, she realized, wishing she could hit him with a croquet mallet.

"Your sister *said* you'd do that."

"What?"

"Scream." Evan Randall, immortal, hurried out to play.

A spider crawled by in the sawdust, gangly on its long, elegant legs.

"Be careful, be careful," said Roxy. For everyone had big shoes.

"Ask God now," said the skinny spider.

"Dear God, please save me. Also I pray for the heathen in Africa."

The lights almost knocked her over, they flashed so brightly. She stayed on her knees, both hands covering her face. Jesus was coming into her heart. Despite everything He was coming, just like He did in the Sunday School flannelgraph pictures, through the wooden door. Now He resided in her. Roxy knelt straight up. The bright flashes continued. Her sins were gone. All brand-new, she kept her eyes squeezed closed, her Savior in her heart.

She peeked at her forearms, which were immortal. Time was no more.

When she finally looked around, most of the Christians had risen, but a few still prayed. The tabernacle seemed familiar but unreal, oddly of this world, the chairs, the sawdust floor, the cinderblock walls.

Roxanne Fish, eternal being, rose to her feet. Her name was written in the Lamb's Book of Life. The Christian in the lavender hat was sitting farther down the row.

"Did you see a photographer?" Roxanne asked her.

"A photographer?" The lady shook her head. "No."

"Lights?"

"No," the lady said again.

"That's funny."

The lady in the lavender hat stood up. She placed her hands along the sides of Roxanne's head, over both ears, and shook. Roxanne clenched her teeth in order to protect her tongue.

"We are living on the hallelujah side!" the lady cried out.

Roxanne Fish, Christian, stepped into the aisle, kicking up sawdust. She giggled. The bodies that had been lying around prostrate were largely upright now and outside. The saints were chatting. She could not stop laughing; when she tried, her midriff still shook. Outside was the sky, where heaven waited for her with its gold driveways. The apostle Paul was there, and also Martin Luther, but without the Lutherans. Angels were rejoicing on Roxanne's behalf. She was going up! Now she could stay with Babysitter Schmitz or walk downtown. If the atom bomb went off it made no difference.

Overhead, the Milky Way stretched.

Roxanne began to run, down the green lawn along the lake, toward the outhouse in the distance.

"Hallelujah!" she said, trying out her new language. She had no one and nothing to fear. She jumped and seemed to float through the air, because salvation had put gravity behind her. She jumped again. At the outhouse she came down.

Despite the pressure on her bladder, she didn't enter the stall immediately. Instead she stood holding the Heaven Time arm out under the single bulb, studying the pores of her skin. She was going to spend eternity with John the Baptist and her family. And Superba, who must kneel down the second they got back to Ames.

"God save Little Richard," she prayed.

Entering the stall, she closed the door, pulled down her pants, and sat on the little hole cut in the wood. As urine fell into the filth below, it made a tinkling sound.

Relaxed, Roxanne did not hurry. Saved, she listened for the trumpet sound. Leisurely, she unrolled some toilet paper. She wiped herself and dropped it in. She rose, but before pulling up her pants she lifted her arms to heaven. Time stood still. There was no death at all.

"Come quickly, Lord Jesus," she said.

· · · · ·

The next night, when Roxanne got the baptism in the Holy Ghost, she spoke in tongues for more than three hours. A Christian among Christians, she lay on her back smelling sawdust, her mouth moved by a mysterious power, the peculiar language coming out, warm, on its own, at last. There were people gathered around her, she knew vaguely, encouraging her, discussing her great victory. She didn't blush. When her eyes finally focused, there her mother sat, clapping slowly, wearing her brown suit, and there was her father with both hands up. Uncle Roland and Aunt Dora stood quietly, Roland rocking on his heels. He was huge.

She sat up.

"Praise God," said Lyle Nichols. "You're filled."

When she left to be alone, each Christian understood. Outside there was a hum in the universe, one she had never heard, though it had always been there, she understood.

"*Hmmmmm*," she sang along. The hum did not make you feel the sinful voice at all, but neither was it stupid, like church music. It was in a category all its own.

"*Hmmmmm*," she sang once more.

She listened, crossing the Storm Lake grass, not running so she could hear it better. It came from everything, like a huge refrigerator. Tonight she even liked her red hair, and touched it to feel its silkiness. The peace that passeth understanding filled her soul. She had been saved for twenty-four hours, though she could not tell anyone, of course. Now that she was in eternity she took off the watch and put it in her pocket, gazing at the water where it showed between the trees. The stars were blinding. She did not fear Drexel Eiberhaus, whoever he was. She did not fear Satan and his red telephone. How surprised he must be! She was sure he knew already. Suddenly she turned three cartwheels. When she reached the chain link fence that marked the end of Storm Lake campground she considered climbing it. The hum was out there too. To her right, where a streak of light crossed the lake, a fish jumped.

"How's that Piper Cub?" said Roland.

"She's sweet. I'll have her paid off next month if the Lord tarries. There aren't many feelings like flying up through the air."

"You've got to give me a ride."

"I will."

Roxanne turned. Her father and her uncle were standing down beyond the trees on the grassy lakeshore. She could clearly see Roland's large head and her father's hat. She was about to speak when Roland's voice stopped her short.

"So God called you to California."

Her father's hat dipped slightly. "He did. We rented a big truck to pack our furniture."

"When?"

"Three weeks."

Roxanne pulled her ears. Her uncle Roland had said California, but that was impossible.

"Can't tell if there's fish here or not," said Roland.

"Blue gill and crappie." Winston turned as a large fish broke water. "Northern pike."

"You're in the will of God?" asked Roland.

"To a place called Glendale. They voted for me when I flew out there last winter. In addition to which they offered me another radio show, *Miracle Power*, on KXRW. You can come out there and talk."

"Ain't God good." Roland smiled in the dark. "Me in California on the radio. Roland Fish."

A voice pierced the night air with such profound sorrow they all three jumped. If Roxanne was correct, it was the voice of the substitute piano player from the Ottumwa church, a woman with pink cheeks. It cut like a knife, high and childlike, wailing in tongues.

"Shondala seeleo! Heeleo siprah!"

They all three listened to the message from God, waiting for the interpretation to come. In the silence Roland rocked.

"Go ye not to California! For the demons are powerful! The demons are mighty! Go ye not! Hoop! This is the Lord thy God!"

She stopped as suddenly as she had begun.

"That is a message in nonsense," said Winston. "The woman had too much to eat. Amen. The Lord our God is bigger than the devil. Even Christians falsely prophesy sometimes."

"What if it ain't false? Demons got clout. What about that wrestler fellow?" asked Roland.

"Don't make me laugh."

"Where is he?"

"In jail."

Waves lapped against the black Iowa dirt.

"Shondala!" the woman cried out. "Heeleo shibbala!"

Roxanne sat down where she was, dizzy. Nobody could make you leave Iowa. She decided instantly to live in Superba's yard and keep her toothbrush and toothpaste in the hollow up above the first branch of the sycamore tree, where even the police would never find them. She made a mental note to steal toothpaste the minute they pulled into the Ames driveway. Superba could obtain salami and Hershey's candy bars, and teach her everything she had learned in school. For they were not children. They were not Water Lily Maidens. She didn't know what they were exactly. They were souls. The plans they made were unyielding, not subject to anything. They were going to grow up together and marry Elvis Presley. Calmer, arms wrapped tightly around her knees, Roxanne smelled the dirt, the grass, the lake, the air of Iowa.

"Who told you about the move to California?" Her father's voice was strange, and made the night too quiet. "Zelda?"

Neither man spoke for a moment, but Winston's breath came in rasps.

"I got divination. God."

"Mr. Divination! Mr. God-Told-Me-to-Go-Buy-Gold-Coins. I am sick of your ugly mug. So there."

"I got that gift," said Roland, stubborn.

"You aren't the only one with divination. You're Colleen's daddy. Oh, it shows."

Colleen Roland's daughter!

In the twinkling of an eye, Roxanne saw this could be true. Her mouth dropped. That would explain Colleen's curls, her wide-set gleaming cheeks, her weird confidence. The two men faced each other like the elk and bear in the picture at Raker's Hardware Store. But why would God give her mother the wrong baby? Roxanne closed her eyes, trying to smell Iowa again. This was Storm Lake, but everything was changing.

"Ha," said Winston bitterly. "Ha ha ha ha."

There was an enormous splash as Winston threw Roland in the lake. Roxanne peered into the darkness for what seemed like forever, until finally a shape emerged: Roland walking from the water, in his suit, as though this were a baptism.

"So how about them flying plans?" said Roland. "Even your big brain cells don't know everything. Don't nobody."

"Sure," said Winston. "You're my brother anyway. I know that much."

Her father strode off, passing right by her, not quite close enough to touch. Roxanne stayed crouched like an animal.

The long grass moved. Roland stood there looking down at her, still dripping. He moved softly for such a big man.

"God saved you," Roland said.

"Yes," said Roxanne. She stared at him, seeing Colleen.

Roland stared back. "Don't nobody know everything." He rocked on his big feet. "My God is a big God. The whole earth is his footstool."

In the starlight you could hear the Storm Lake springs bubbling. Like a feather, his hand briefly touched her head.

Last Days

DAS KAPITAL COULD NOT be found amidst the boxes in the new house. They all suspected Zelda Fish, who at this moment was opening box one thousand in search of Winston's best tie. Boxes were everywhere, in stacks, although they had now been in Glendale for a month. When accused of hiding *Das Kapital*, Zelda pointed to the mountains up the street, the heavy bougainvillea outside, the weather without a hint of snow (ever!), the balmy air. Then she put both palms up and lifted, to demonstrate how the California atmosphere made them lighter.

On KXRW, Glendale 103, her husband's voice could be heard twice a week, the voice of reason in a sinful metropolis, latter-day Sodom and Gomorrah. Colleen called it Sodom and Gonorrhea, and Roxanne prayed for her, apparently to no avail. With her curls Colleen bounced along the California streets, collecting boyfriends.

Glendale, California, had a skyline at night, unlike anything you could see in Ames. The Fishes had a big house on Pecan Street, a real house, not a house behind the platform where a knife could shudder through the living room wall. This house had real bedroom doors with four panels and glass doorknobs, and closets you could walk into and turn on the light. Colleen and Roxanne wandered through it in amazement, touching the alcoves, the woodwork archways. It was nice but more like a castle, not the house of people who were leaving any minute, as they reminded themselves each morning at Family Worship.

Saved, Roxanne no longer wore the watch on Heaven Time, but she kept it polished on her dresser as a reminder never to backslide. Every night she prayed for Colleen, prayed for her teacher, prayed for the Africans and the kids at school. When rock and roll blared out of passing cars, she plugged her ears. She was finally on the hallelujah side. The other voice still called to her from the life she had left behind, but she kept her eyes on heaven. God tested the Christians. In church she made her voice thin and tuneless when she sang, and people looked at her sympathetically. As insurance she was memorizing Scriptures to quote, out loud if possible, whenever sinful thoughts of singing in the Woolworth basement reared their ugly heads. Also, she was studying Swahili, just in case.

"Look at those mountains," said Zelda.

It was Monday, and Monday meant school. Roxanne and her parents stood on their real front porch, waving goodbye to Colleen. Real mountains rose to the left, up the hill, within walking distance. Colleen disappeared behind a tree on her way to the high school, and the three remaining Fishes stood looking out over the devil's territory. In Family Worship this morning they had read from I Kings 14. Pilgrim School was closer, so Roxanne lingered on the porch another minute, holding the handrail, breathing the California air.

"Your daddy is getting a big following." Zelda tweaked her husband's ear. "Winston? How many fan letters did you get this week?"

"Three."

"KXRW, Glendale 103. *Miracle Power*. It still sounds like a detergent to me." Zelda held out her arms, to California, and inhaled deeply. "Oh, I love the mountains."

"Detergent?" Pastor Fish hugged his daughter goodbye. "Well, in a sense it is. I like that. *Miracle Power*."

Roxanne ran down the porch steps and turned south toward Pilgrim School. She had on a new dress from the Missionary Box, which had followed them to California. It was blue with a white collar, and not too big, she hoped. She tightened the belt.

Pilgrim School came slowly into view, far down the sidewalk. She felt lucky to be saved, for in California you could no longer race across the street and grab your mother's skirt if the trumpet sounded. Now she would rise from wherever she was. In her three-ring binder she had flyers announcing a Bible Club on Wednesday afternoon, 515 Pecan, but every time she approached a classmate her heart failed. So far she had not passed out a single one. She promised God she would pass out flyers on Tuesday. Because she didn't want to arrive early she took her time, stopping to investigate little weeds along the curb, but the plants in California were not the talking kind. She missed Superba with an actual physical ache. Pecan Street sported sinners' houses filled with lost souls who did not even bother to go to the wrong church. Some were atheists, she strongly suspected. In Glendale even the sky did not look Christian. The ragged clouds suggested not the Second Coming but Charles Darwin, Communism, dented Budweiser beer cans. Roxanne shifted her books.

"'Put on the whole armour of God, that ye may be able to stand against the wiles of the devil.' Ephesians 6:11," she said.

At ugly Pilgrim School kids were going in, and she picked up her pace. The first bell must have rung. The school was a low Spanish-style building with no second-story windows to hear leaves swish. Although the singing temptation was fading, she longed for the green of Iowa. She tried to think if running away was a sin. But run away how? When they visited Grandmother Wellington, whom God had healed of her weak lungs, they drove twenty miles by the speedometer and never saw a highway leading out of town. They passed Angelus Temple, but Aimee Semple McPherson was dead. Quickly asking God to save Little Richard, she turned into the school courtyard with her eyes closed, quoting Scriptures, peeking only when the Holy Ghost told her she was at the Spanish portico.

The last bell started ringing.

Running fast, she counted five doors down the hallway and

entered her classroom out of breath, keeping her eyes on her desk. Spanish style looked like a box of Ritz crackers. Roxanne checked her books while the Glendale children chatted. Finally the teacher clapped her hands.

Roxanne sighed.

"Good morning, children," Mrs. Inglehurst said, looking out at them from behind thick glasses.

"Good morning," said Roxanne. Out the open window sinners' houses lined the street. Ugly cars went by, filling the air with exhaust fumes. Here you could not smell grass. No matter how far you drove there were no pastures. She longed to see just one cow and make eye contact. She tried to breathe as Mrs. Inglehurst began the lesson.

"Children? In what year did Columbus sail the ocean blue?"

Roxanne stared at Mrs. Inglehurst, feigning interest. She had Hostess cupcakes in her desk for recess, in case the Lord came tonight. Heaven had no chocolate. She had borrowed money from her mother's purse, but would pay it back when her allowance came. Slyly raising the desk lid, she touched the shiny wrapper. Without Superba school was unbearable. She looked around at her classmates, who were whispering and passing notes, and for one moment she wished she were normal, with a normal family that went roller skating and to the movies. According to the clock it was going to be a long day. Glancing down, she pushed the Bible Club flyers deeper into her notebook, for fear someone would see the pink edges. She promised God again that she would pass them out tomorrow. All around her the lost fidgeted in their seats, souls that could not die, souls that would scream in torment for eternity, separated from God. The clock on the wall had not moved. Carefully Roxy slid the notebook off her desk and onto her lap, eyes bright with attention.

Up front Mrs. Inglehurst was sighting land, pacing up and down the decks of the *Niña*, the *Pinta*, the *Santa Maria*, which they had already studied in Ames.

"Dear Superba," Roxy began, "Glendale is ugly. Our teacher

got stuck under the desk during atom bomb practice." She was writing in small letters in the upper right corner so her arm would appear to be resting. With her left hand, for effect, she opened the textbook on her desk and ran her finger under "Columbus: Independent Thinker," page 232.

"Now, children, which explorer —"

"Bosco da Gama!" screamed Edward Miller.

"Rosco the Llama!" yelled Billy Tudball.

The class laughed. Roxy laughed with them. "Do not let them cut the hedge. *Promise*, okay?" she wrote.

"Billy Tudball, I will send you to the principal's office *yet*. I don't care who your father is. Roxanne, have you studied Vasco da Gama yet?"

Roxy drew a fold of her blue skirt over the notebook. "No, not yet," she lied.

"Then I cannot hold you responsible. But Californians, there is going to be a test. *And* I am calling on you. *And* whoever throws another spit wad is going to stand in the wastebasket for a week. One week."

"Bosco is for kids," whispered Joey Damato, a skinny boy with glasses.

Another spit wad flew. Mrs. Inglehurst looked sharply left.

"Please get saved," Roxy scribbled. "I miss you. I do not want you to go to hell either. Anyway I am praying." She drummed her fingers, watching Mrs. Inglehurst, and then looked out the window. "Here the church is not across the street from school, plus they do not have true clouds. Sometimes I think about the Communists, who believe there is no God." Roxy shivered. The Communists thought the universe was empty planets. "Many people here are atheists," she wrote furiously. "What if the Christians are wrong?"

"Roxanne?"

For a second she could not remember which state she was in. A fan whirred. Mrs. Inglehurst stood at the head of the row, apparently speaking to her. It was hard to think with all the Californians twisted around in their seats, gawking. Glendale was horrible.

"Roxanne Fish? If you don't pay attention I'm going to have to put you in front. Will you stand and pass these papers out?"

Roxy simply stared at her. The notebook was in her lap. The difficulty of her situation dawned on her.

"Me?" she said.

"Do you have another name? A secret Indian name? Something they use in Idaho? Pocahontas?"

All the children laughed.

"Iowa," said Roxy.

If she put the notebook on the desk she would be caught, possibly forced to stand in the wastebasket. Slowly she got up, shifting her left thigh, letting the notebook slide down her leg onto the floor, where it landed with a small thunk. She prayed for God to vaporize it.

"Hurry up!" said Mrs. Inglehurst, arm flesh jiggling as she thrust the white papers out.

Nervously Roxy walked to the front. The papers smelled of mimeograph as she counted out six sheets for the first row, one for each lost soul. In four minutes, when the bell rang, she could take her Hostess cupcakes to the bathroom, where she always spent recess. She hoped against hope for the loud bell, counting papers for the second row of kids. No one whispered. From the open window car fumes drifted in.

"She's writing notes," said Billy Tudball, nicely raising his hand. "Look. Under her desk."

Roxy continued to pass out papers, seven for row three. All the children sat up. Heat rushed through her body as blood rushed to her skin.

"Look how red she is," said Beth, a cute girl.

Holding her wood pointer, Mrs. Inglehurst walked toward Roxanne's desk. Dizzy, Roxy counted only five in row four.

"Billy Tudball? Pick that notebook up."

Mrs. Inglehurst gently hoisted the cover with the pointer tip. There the tiny writing was.

"Notes are for everyone to read. Hand it to me. Thank you, Billy."

"You're welcome, Mrs. Inglehurst."

The teacher tapped her stick and read silently. Then she spoke. "'Sometimes I think about the Communists, who believe there is no God. What if the Christians are wrong?'"

Roxy passed more papers out. The recess bell was ringing, but not a lost soul moved.

"Roxanne Fish." Mrs. Inglehurst tapped. "Aren't your parents ministers? On that radio show?"

Roxy swallowed hard. "Yes."

"I see." Mrs. Inglehurst approached and poked Roxy in the shoulder with her pointer. "I will not tell your parents this time. But one wrong move? One spit wad? One passed note not reported to me immediately? I'll have your parents on the phone before you can say Jack Sprat. Do you understand my English?"

"Yes," Roxy croaked.

Mrs. Inglehurst poked. "All right, Miss Judas Iscariot. You may go. Now that I know what your Indian name is."

• • • • •

All through visitation, going up and down the streets to knock on doors and invite sinners to church, Roxy worried. Billy Tudball would tell everyone! Or Mrs. Inglehurst would call! Carrying stacks of church programs, Bibles under their arms, she and Colleen walked down the strange streets, praying under their breath that no kids they knew were home. Certain people, as per usual, slammed the door on you.

"How long do we have to stay out here?" moaned Colleen.

"Till all have heard." Zelda stepped out from behind a car on the odd-numbered side of Gunther Street. The girls and Winston were taking the evens. "You two sound like the unsaved! Signal me before you go on to the next block."

When her mother's back was turned, Colleen rolled down her socks another fold, standing up slowly to look for boys while Roxy rang the doorbell. Their father was one house behind, talking to someone through a screen door and gesturing. Across the street they saw a curtain move.

"I don't think they're home," said Colleen, looking up at the green door.

"I hear footsteps."

"It's your turn to talk."

"It's not! I gave that woman the gospel tract!"

Through the open window of the house where their father stood, a man was clearly visible, sitting in an easy chair, drinking from a can. A radio issued the Dodgers score.

"But you didn't have to actually *talk* to her. That doesn't *count*." Colleen moved deftly sideways as the door opened.

A woman with a cigarette stood staring at them. She was wearing a dressing gown, and you could see a good part of her breasts. The girls backed up.

"What have we here?" she cried, throwing out her arms. Her red lipstick was smeared.

Roxy pushed her sister forward.

"My name is Colleen Fish, and this is Roxanne. We want to invite you to Sunday morning service and give you a tract about dancing."

Roxy nudged her.

"We're from the Assembly of God Church."

The woman blinked at them. "I'm Rayette from nowhere!" She threw back her head and laughed, a harsh sound. A peculiar smell came from her person.

"Booze," whispered Colleen.

Their father was advancing across the lawn, his hat at a tilt on his head.

Rayette stopped. "Who is *he*?"

"I'm Pastor Fish from the First Assembly of God Church down on Hill. We'd like to talk to you if you have a minute. May we come in?"

"Why not?"

Rayette picked up a glass of something golden and opened the screen door. The radio was playing Elvis Presley, and the hairs on Roxy's skin rose. She stepped forward, trying not to listen, but it came in anyway. Despite being saved, she smiled as Elvis told everyone to stay offa his blue suede shoes. Then she jammed her fingers in her ears, wiggling them, as they were not big enough to shut the sound out. All her Scriptures flew out of her head except their references, and she recited these now, keeping her head lowered.

"Hebrews 12:1–2. John 3:16. Deuteronomy 5:16."

The stench of cigarettes was overwhelming, profound. Somewhere a cat box had not been emptied, and the cat himself appeared, orange, huge, meowing in the doorway, his back arching. Elvis Presley wailed on.

"Luke 1:46. Revelation 12."

"Hey!" Rayette leaned down, holding her cigarette, halfway through applying more red lipstick. She stared at Roxy's fingers in her ears. "What's wrong with *you*?" Snapping off the radio, she reached for a chair to steady herself. The lipstick fell out of her hand. It rolled.

"This is no way to live," said Pastor Fish. He opened his Bible.

"So save me."

"The Scripture tells us that all have sinned and come short of the glory of God. Do you believe that means you?"

"That's a nice tie you're wearing, Reverend." Rayette lurched forward, trying to touch it, and almost tripped. "Oops."

"This is serious business. If the Lord should come today, do you know where you'd be?"

"Hell."

The girls looked at one another and out at the exotic living room. This was actual sin. Elvis Presley was silent. A garment made of feathers lay across a chair back. Colleen rolled her eyes.

"'For all have sinned and come short of the glory of God,'" whispered Roxy, trying to concentrate. Elvis Presley had made her want to wiggle and let the voice out. "'For the Son of man is come to seek and to save that which was lost.'"

Their father began reading from Colossians, and the girls kept looking around. Glasses crowded the table, black furry high heels leaned against the hall door. A pretty yellow bowl sat on the sink.

When Brother Townsend, board member of the Glendale First Assembly of God Church, came in from the hallway buckling his belt, no one could have been more surprised than the Fish family. Everyone froze. All you could see was the dust particles floating in the sun from the window. For some reason Brother Townsend picked the pepper shaker up off the little table that served as Rayette's dining room, and shook some out.

"Reverend," he said.

"Benny?" Rayette gestured vaguely to the kitchenette. "Get the reverend something to drink." She waved her cigarette in circles. "Soda pop."

"Ben Townsend?" Pastor Fish's face was ashen. "God has known what you are doing all along."

Sister Fish was calling for them in the street, and Winston gestured for the girls to hail her. Townsend winced visibly.

"I'll have to tell your wife," said Pastor Fish.

"Stay out of it," said Townsend.

"God can forgive anything, brother."

"Even me." Rayette clapped her hands, and her cigarette fell to the floor. "Oops. Better get that."

Townsend stooped for it and ran water from the sink over the burning end. His trousers were still half unzipped. Roxy tried not to look.

"Oh my," said Zelda from the door. "Oh my. Sister Townsend! May God help her! Brother Townsend has fallen."

"Sister Townsend? Who the hell is she?" Rayette took a drink, then held up her glass, toasting each Fish family member. "Here's to

Rayette, Slut of West Glendale. Where's my fucking lipstick?" Her hips switched, and liquid sloshed out her glass. "Oops! Pardon me."

"Jesus died for sinners," said Sister Fish.

Rayette hiccuped. "Amen. I mean ah, men! Boogaloo!"

Sister Fish approached. Rayette smiled, eyes glittering.

"Stay away from me if you know what's good for you. I'll call the police."

Sister Fish put an arm on Rayette's shoulder. "It's the devil who makes you mad. He doesn't want to see us here. He wants your soul for all eternity!"

Rayette could not stop laughing, and Sister Fish, who had embraced her although she was a sinner, jiggled with her. Rayette moved so suddenly no one saw her go, throwing up at the sink, her body heaving. She wiped her ragged nails across her mouth and stood up.

"Morning sickness," she cooed, and hiccuped again. Blood streaked her chin.

"I would like to read some Scripture," said Pastor Fish. He moved forward, frowning with urgency.

"Yes." Zelda cupped her gloved hands.

"If you do not get out immediately," said Benny Townsend, who had pulled up his zipper, "I am going to shoot you."

They all looked at him. It was obvious he did not have a gun, but obvious he meant business. Pastor Fish put a hand on each daughter's shoulder and steered them toward the door.

"God isn't afraid of guns," said Zelda Fish. "God *invented* them."

"We're going now," said Winston, reaching for his wife and encircling her with his arm.

• • • • •

"Oh, it's beautiful though," said visiting missionary Sister Zeng, running her hand along a window frame. "Remember the parsonage in Ames! And look at these lovely moldings."

"It's called woodwork," said Colleen.

"The girls miss Iowa," explained Zelda, stroking Roxy's forehead. The woodwork was a foot thick around the bottom, curved in a beautiful way.

"Not me!" Colleen's California ponytail swung. Several of her new admirers were outside at this moment, hiding behind several different bushes for a glimpse of her. But at least she was not Catholic.

"Well, this is a real house," said Brother Zeng.

It was true. This California house had more rooms than they knew what to do with, and contained an entire wall of tiny paned windows looking out on the mountains up the street. An actual fireplace made of actual tile showing a shepherd herding sheep existed in the living room. The Fishes walked around the house with the Zengs, shaking their heads, hardly able to believe they lived here.

"We must not lose our zeal for Christianity in a place this posh," admitted Zelda. "Hell is still waiting. I have heard the preacher's wife in Santa Monica believes in lipstick."

Sister Zeng narrowed her eyes. "'Watch therefore; for ye know neither the day nor the hour wherein the Son of man cometh.'"

"Heavens, it's Sunday morning. We'd better get a move on. Girls, go set the table. Immediately!"

Colleen tightened the scarf around her ponytail, strutting past the windows and out the front door. You could see her standing on the porch, hand on hip, surveying a world of boys. Roxy went into the kitchen and got out the plates.

"How are your girls doing?" asked Sister Zeng.

"I don't like Roxanne's face." Zelda's voice was thoughtful. "She's lost her color even though she got the baptism in tongues. Did you hear? The last night at Storm Lake Camp."

"She is on fire," added Winston. "She's memorized three hundred Scriptures since we got here. But she does look pinched. The Holy Ghost is supposed to relax you."

"Moving to a new state is hard on them," said Brother Zeng. "Or perhaps demonic powers are agitating her. But God is stronger than the tempter. Amen!"

When the girls came back in, all four adults laid hands on them. For Glendale was more dangerous than the Midwest had been.

"Roxanne? Say something in Swahili. Hurry or we'll be late for church. Roxanne is thinking of becoming a Wycliffe Bible translator."

"Say 'boys,'" said Colleen.

"No!" Roxy blushed. "Jambo," she said.

"Why, hello to you! Very good!" said Brother Zeng. "Jambo. Karibu watoto."

The Zengs, missionaries to Togoland, hurried off to change clothes for Sunday morning service. They were to preach, as they did each time they were in the United States on furlough, to raise money for the souls in Africa. Winston Fish was cooking his good pancakes and sausage. Grease smell filled the house.

Ten minutes later the Zengs approached the dining room table, stunning in their full African dress. Both wore robes with big sleeves and elaborate headgear, primarily red. They all sat down. Whitely the two Zengs looked out.

"Any luck locating *Das Kapital*?" Winston asked Zelda.

"Juice, anyone?" said Zelda, and kicked her husband under the table, which made everything jiggle.

"The Communist book?" Missionary Zeng filled his fork. He unloaded.

"Winston's correcting it," clarified Zelda.

"I'm annotating it, writing Scriptures in the margin to refute each point."

"What for?" said Sister Zeng.

"Fun," said Winston.

Sister Zeng reached across the breakfast table to touch Colleen's ear. "You're such a shining little girl. And those curls! I wish I had a little girl like you."

Glancing at her sister, Roxy could not help seeing Roland. Her eyes dropped to her plate.

"Both our girls are beautiful," said Zelda.

"I hope we get a good love offering for you today." Pastor Fish passed out more pancakes, fresh off the griddle, for the Zengs needed strength.

"A Speed-the-Light vehicle is sorely needed!" cried Sister Zeng, almost standing. Her headgear shook. "There are heathen living in the jungle worshiping demons. Demons!"

"Yes," said Brother Zeng. "Amen."

"Why, I've seen pigs fly." Sister Zeng took some butter. "Up in the treetops! It's voodoo. Why, the devil has a stronghold which is beyond anything." She stopped eating. "Every time Herman walks into that jungle I plead the blood of *Jesus*."

"Jesus' blood is powerful," Zelda agreed.

Winston pushed his chair back and disappeared for a moment, returning with an airplane propeller in his hand. The red Piper Cub had arrived last week, flown in by an aviator from Des Moines. Since then Winston had been flying a lot, looking at California, looking at the brush fires flaring around Glendale. He had his solo license and had even taken Uncle Roland up once before leaving Iowa. Now he sat down on a chair next to the sideboard and began polishing the propeller.

"Winston!" Zelda made a sour face. "Winston, *stop* it."

"And of course there's other things." Sister Zeng wiped her mouth.

"What things?" said Colleen.

"People changing into animals before your eyes, for one. Sounds in the night inside your house, but you turn on the light and there's nothing. Nothing."

"Don't scare the girls," said Zelda.

They were all uncomfortable with the specifics of voodoo, as if a demon within hearing might fly in through the paned windows.

"And then, of course, there's the Cannibal Threat," said Brother Zeng.

"Missionary soup," said Winston.

"Winston Fish!"

Unperturbed, Winston turned the airplane propeller on its edge. He and Herman Zeng could see their reflection in it.

"Here we sit, six ordinary people," said Winston, looking around the room. Colleen held up five fingers. "But if Christ returns soon, we are going to be the first people in history not to die." They all looked out at the blue sky, momentarily streaked by a jet plane. "Except for whom?"

"Enoch!" cried Roxanne and Colleen.

"Correct. 'And Enoch walked with God: and he was not.' Genesis 5:24."

"The quick and the dead," mused Herman Zeng.

"I'm the quick," said Colleen.

"Death is not pleasant." Zelda stared into space, a toothpick pressed to her lips. "At least in my imagination. No matter how much faith you have."

Winston turned the propeller around slowly. "Well, people who study Bible prophecy think the Rapture is near, and I think so too. The wars around the world are coming to a boiling point, and the parallels to Revelation are too strong to ignore."

They all hung on his words, even Colleen. It was a glorious accident that they were living in the Last Days.

"Look at Cuba," said Brother Zeng. "Look at the Congo. I can't believe we have much time. I want to see Him in the air!"

"Of course, no one knows save God," Winston finished.

"Amen!" Sister Zeng got up and went to her suitcase, taking out her big picture of a man who had been delivered of three evil spirits, to show in church. Roxy thought she recognized his green shirt from the Missionary Box, a Fish family reject.

"My, we're late!"

Zelda threw an old sheet over the dirty dishes to discourage bugs, and they all piled into the car. The pink Pontiac sped down the streets of Glendale, reeling around corners, protected by angels.

"Praise God. Sin is everywhere." Brother Zeng pointed.

Ahead of them loomed a billboard: a woman in a blue bikini smoking a Salem cigarette. Huge, she smiled down to tempt them, her teeth white.

"Don't look, children," said Sister Zeng, one hand over each girl's eyes. She did not have children herself.

"All these liquor stores!"

"Dear Jesus, dear Jesus. My my my."

The residential district north of church was no better. There Californians stayed at home, brazenly lounging in their front yards in shorts, mowing the lawn, washing their cars.

"Why, they can't possibly make church now," Zelda said, looking out of the pink Pontiac. "It's almost ten-thirty."

• • • • •

Today, unbelievably, Roxanne was flying. The Zengs were gone, and Winston Fish and his daughter were lifting, the earth getting smaller, Roxy bundled in a purple zip-up jacket from the Missionary Box and strapped directly in front of her father in the red Piper Cub. At this moment they were higher than the tops of buildings, looking down at little cars on little streets. The wings were over them. Roxy held on, carefully turning her head so that she could see her father behind her. She gasped. Sticking out of his shirt pocket was the new money Roland Fish had wired from the Dewey Dumpster Heiress, disbursed by lawyers from her will. The amount of five hundred dollars was being held together by a rubber band. The wind might take it! When she gestured madly with one hand to push it down, her father threw back his head and laughed. She said a prayer and faced front. Next to the open window her red hair blew every which way. The doctor's wife Mrs. Bell had called it wonderful, but that was nearly a lifetime ago. The wind going by the plane made it hard to catch your breath. Now they went higher, cleaving the air. In the hills of Glendale fires still burned, but you could not see them so far. A patch of upholstery on her seat was unraveling, and Roxy twisted around again, desperately trying not to shift her weight.

"The threads are coming out!"

"What?"

"The threads are coming out! Look! Is this plane old?"

"Don't worry so much!"

The engine shook, but the vista to each side was like a story illustration, all Glendale spread out in little flat squares. The fires reared into view and disappeared again. They could see the football field, and ahead of them the shopping district. Now the fires were off to their right. Heaven was above them, but a long way off still.

"The fields are ripe to harvest! Look down there!"

Roxy looked, taking care to hang on. Winston had to shout.

"These souls are as lost as the African with a bone in his nose. You want voodoo? Look at a car salesman! A dentist! A housewife! You needn't go to Africa for voodoo. They are lost right here as much as in Togoland. Look into the eyes of any store clerk!"

The plane tilted, but the seatbelts held them in. Roxy smiled hugely, to show she was not scared. If Christ came while they were up, they would beat Zelda and possibly Colleen to heaven by a few seconds. She held on anyway.

"Mrs. Inglehurst called!" her father yelled.

Roxy felt her shoulders stiffen. She wished a plane would crash on Mrs. Inglehurst. Pastor Fish's daughter looked straight ahead, in trouble now.

"Sometimes in our Christian life," he continued, yelling, "doubt creeps in. This is normal."

Roxy looked back at her father. Their eyes met.

"I myself feel doubt. It may last moments or hours. But this is when I get out the Piper Cub."

They flew.

"What holds us up? The engine?"

"No," peeped Roxy, not sure it would.

"God! God is responsible for everything!" Pastor Fish was getting hoarse. "Your teacher is a troublemaker, I'm afraid."

Roxy giggled in the Piper Cub's front seat.

"But is doubt a sin? No. This is all manual flying now," he added, unmindful of his vocal chords. "No instruments to rely on. Ready?"

They swooped up. His face, when she dared to peek, was happy.

"Dad? Where's the Pacific Ocean?"

"Farther out. We'll go some other day, after we get settled. I still need to find *Das Kapital*."

The plane banked and the fires got closer. You could smell burning. Below them a tiny truck labored up a toy fire road, reminding Roxy of Miss Jennifer Smith, who had not been found in the unpacking yet either.

"How's your singing problem? Are you getting any victory over those worldly desires?"

Roxy blushed. She had felt her heart speed up when Elvis Presley sang at Rayette the sinner's house. "I quote Scripture in my head," she yelled.

"Amen!"

Up they flew.

The very tops of Glendale's mountains were not on fire, but smoke trailed over their jagged outlines. This land was rugged and dramatic, the opposite of cornfields. The fires came back into their line of vision, and then they flew on over Glendale. There sat Pilgrim school, an air conditioner on its roof.

"I believe I'll give this to someone who needs it."

Roxy twisted in her small seat.

"God does not need Roland to support the Winston Fish family." With a casualness that was almost worldly, her father reached into his shirt pocket for the roll of money, snapped the rubber band off, and let a twenty-dollar bill go.

Roxy's neck hurt from turning so far. Twenty dollars was a fortune.

"Do you want some?" said her father.

"No. I mean yes."

He fanned the money out so the wind would take one bill at a time and carry it to the toughened sinners down below. It could land on anyone, a bum or Billy Tudball! As he let the money go he laughed, and Roxy tried hers, but her hand was awkward and the wind took it all. She screamed. In the dusk the twenty-dollar bills floated down through the California air. You could feel their happiness below as they looked up and wondered where the windfall came from. Winston Fish laughed again. Money fell, all over Glendale. Her father's face was peaceful.

The last bills flew out.

"So much for that," he said. "Let's land."

When the Piper Cub was safely settled in its hangar, they stopped off at KXRW, next door to the airport, to check the microphones for *Miracle Power*, Pastor Fish's broadcast heard Monday through Friday mornings throughout Glendale. Housed in an old hangar, KXRW looked industrial and thrilling. Roxy held her father's hand, although it was not dark enough to make that strictly necessary, and followed him up stairs and around sharp corners through two doors he unlocked with his keys. She skipped every third step, enjoying the heat of her thigh muscles. When at last they arrived at the broadcasting room, which had two walls of windows, top to bottom, the openness made her feel like running and sliding. She did.

"I just want to try these mikes," said Winston. "There's nothing worse than going on the air and having mechanical problems." He tapped one. "Hello! KXRW! Jesus Saves!"

"Miracle Power!" Roxanne said into the other mike. Her voice reverberated. "Washing sins!"

Her father nodded, and they gazed down at the parking lot four floors below. The setting sun streamed through the glass in gold shafts, over wires crisscrossed by light. It felt holy.

"Hello, Fish, you cocksucking toad. You ruined my career. You know I was a wrestler. I had the goods."

Pastor Fish and Roxanne froze. For a moment they saw nothing, and then Engstrom was staring at them from above a filing cabinet. His eyes were bleary, and they could smell his liquor breath, the odor of sin. Roxy shivered. A large knife rested in his hand, and now the metal blade began to clatter on the metal filing cabinet. Engstrom shook.

"I thought you were in jail," said her father.

"I escaped." He smiled, showing gums and missing teeth.

Pastor Fish stood exactly where he was, face taut, eyes shining, letting drop the pencil he was holding. Engstrom jumped. Perspiration stood on his forehead.

"Your day in the sun is done. I been waiting here all weekend for you." Engstrom took a step forward. His unsteady gait made the knife wobble in his hand. Larger than the one in Ames, it could hurt two people.

"Climb under the desk, Roxanne," said Pastor Fish calmly.

"I will kill the both of you." He reeked of booze.

Roxy's knees touched the floor softly. Engstrom brought back his knife hand.

Pastor Fish stepped forward in his Florsheim shoes. From beneath the desk Roxy could see just his feet. She prayed her father would not fall over.

"You can throw that knife." His voice was philosophical and strong, like on KXRW, Glendale 103. "Of course you can. Yet you can't kill me and you can't kill Roxanne. We'll both go straight to heaven and be at the right hand of God before you can turn around. We have a house waiting for us up there. So what are you accomplishing?"

Engstrom growled deep in his throat. He sounded like a killer.

Pastor Fish took another step. "You can go too, Engstrom. Why don't you put down that knife and kneel and ask Jesus Christ to come into your heart?"

"Jew preacher, harlot pimp retarded horseshoe asshole pimp!

I'm going to get you this time. You ruined my hand. My hand!" He groaned, and his voice dropped. "My hand was my ticket out. Now I'm going to ruin it for you."

From where she knelt Roxy could see the microphone cord snaking along the floor and up to her father. She heard Engstrom approach. It was like atom bomb practice, where you crouched beneath the desk waiting to be vaporized. It was true that you could be a Christian and still fear it.

Engstrom laughed. Now Roxy could see a pair of worn tennis shoes, the laces loose. They scared her.

"Throw your best show hold, you phony wrestler," Engstrom shrieked gleefully. The tennis shoes jumped. "This is it! I could take you from the day I was born." His voice cracked. "Go!"

There was a crash, and Roxy scrambled to her feet in time to see Engstrom lassoed with the microphone cord, which her father now pulled tight. One arm pinned to his side, Engstrom had fallen rather neatly into a swivel chair and rolled against the broadcasting counter. The other arm flapped.

"Get away from me," he snarled.

Winston stepped over the knife and toward Engstrom, who backed up, pushing with his feet against the KXRW floor.

"Pick up the telephone and dial 0."

Shaking, Roxy dialed.

"Ask for the police. Tell them KXRW at the airport, someone tried to kill us."

Roxy said these words to a female, and they heard sirens after what seemed like an eternity, although it was only one minute by the wall clock. The police station was beyond the airfield, visible to the naked eye.

"I'm going to tie him up good," said Winston, holding the looped microphone cord and walking toward the chair.

The scream from Engstrom stopped them both.

"Get them off me!"

It was Roxanne who realized what was happening. She recoiled at the look on Engstrom's face. He was furiously swatting at his cheeks, where Abba the bat must be. The Fishes could only see empty space.

"What in the world?" said her father.

Engstrom threw his head from side to side, his eyes bugging out, his free hand flailing. Now his fingernails drew blood. "Get away from me!" He punched the air.

Now he was rolling backwards toward the windows that went from floor to ceiling to let in plenty of light, four stories up. You could see what was going to happen. Pastor Fish tried to take up the slack in the microphone cord, but it was too late.

Engstrom crashed into the window, shattering it, shards raining all around him, the chair teetering, half inside, half out, suspended over the parking lot below. Miraculously unscathed, he stared at them. No one breathed.

"Help me!"

"Do not move," said Winston Fish. "God loves you."

Engstrom's eyes were wild as his head jerked around the broadcasting room. Pastor Fish held the microphone cord, trying not to break the doomed man's balance.

"All right," he said, advancing in slow motion, cord taut. But it could not save Engstrom. His fingers gripped the jagged window to his left.

"Get away from me, you eyeballs!" the crazed man screamed. "Stop speaking gibberish! Ouch! Don't bite!" He threw his one unpinned arm out wide. "God in heaven save me! *Helllp!*"

Sun came in the streaky windows as he fell, profuse, golden. There was the small, musical tinkle of glass, and then there was a bump, the bump of Engstrom's soul as it passed the fourth floor on the way to meet its Maker. You could hear the police coming up the stairs. When they reached the top they fanned out all over the room and looked out the window, which was open space.

"It's all over now," one of them said.

• • • • •

On the way home they got ice cream, peppermint with chocolate chips, two scoops each in old-fashioned cones. Pastor Fish paid with a twenty-dollar bill he had in his wallet.

"Keep the change," he said.

The scoop boy's eyes widened.

"And come out to the Assembly of God Church sometime. On Hill Street, by the Pontiac dealership. Sunday worship at eleven a.m. and five-thirty p.m., Monday and Wednesday at six."

On they drove through the Glendale streets, alert for anyone picking up money. For once they could not eat their ice cream. At a red light Roxanne took both cones and threw them in the trash, wiping her fingers on the paper napkin. She dashed back just as the light turned green. She longed to be in the Fish house with the Fish furniture and the Fishes themselves.

"Engstrom was saved once," said her father, hitting the steering wheel lightly with his palm.

"Engstrom was saved?"

"At one time he was living for the Lord, but he slipped."

"Dad? What if you got killed?"

"Well." He tapped the steering wheel again. "You'd have to remember several things. Let the ball come to *you*. Keep the bat level. Swing *through*."

"Dad!"

"There is no separation between those who love the Lord, Roxanne. If I got killed we would meet up soon, in heaven. Only sin can separate us, if we backslide. That is why we seek God daily. I guess you would have to help your mother."

That night, tucked in bed after the evening service, Roxy breathed and listened to her parents eating pecans and discussing Engstrom at the kitchen table. She and Colleen had the same room until the spare one could be cleared of boxes, and tonight she was glad to hear her sister chewing gum where she lay around the corner. The smell of the fires came in through the window, pungent. Colleen made loud smacking sounds. After school Colleen drank milkshakes, and secretly wore lipstick she kept hidden in a tree on Sycamore Street. Roxy prayed for her soul. In California Colleen had lost all interest in Catholicism, genius, being adopted, French. She had five admirers, but all in all the Fishes were relieved.

"Anyway, we'll never know if he got saved again. He had the chance, hanging there! We can only witness to the living!"

"Amen," said Zelda. "Oh, I wish we could call the Zengs. Togoland pales alongside Glendale. This is a mission field. Where are they, Winston?"

"Bakersfield or Sacramento." For they had dry-cleaned their costumes and were again raising money for the Lord's work in Africa.

"We saw a truck going right up by the fires. By the way, I threw the money out. That Roland sent. God will take care of us without Roland."

"You threw the money out?" Zelda's voice was disbelieving.

"Out. By the way, I've located another *Das Kapital* in Pasadena."

"Threw it out," said Zelda.

Winston cracked a pecan. He was still a little hoarse. "Yes. I'll buy it tomorrow night. They close at nine."

"You are an insane man," said Zelda.

There was the sound of muffled laughter. Someone whimpered and they laughed again.

"Look!" Now you could hear the freezer being opened up. "I bought some TV dinners on sale at the store. Only seven cents. I don't believe I've ever had one."

"TV?" said Winston.

"Well, you don't have to watch it while you're eating them."

"I don't know. We ought to avoid the very *appearance* of evil."

Zelda sighed and giggled once. A chair creaked.

"Who knows?" It was Zelda. "Maybe the Lord will come tonight."

Roxy tiptoed to the bedroom door. Her feet were cold, but

God was good. Quietly she leaned into the hallway, trying to see, but she could only glimpse their arms, which appeared and disappeared transporting pecans. Zelda laughed, and a pecan in its shell rolled into view.

"It will be nice to see the Westons, should that happen. I'm sure they have church news from Iowa. Well, the new pastor will be there himself."

More nuts cracked.

"Yes, and Winona Johnson. I didn't know her, but she knew Jesus. How long has she been up there?"

"Must be three or four years."

"Time is nothing to them."

"Let's let the girls stay home tomorrow if they're too tired to go to school."

"God is good," said Winston. "Have some more pecans."

Rock My Soul

IN THE MORNING both girls elected to attend school anyway.

"I saw him." Zelda used the pancake turner to dish up two eggs. "Not an hour ago when I went to pick up day-old cake on Colorado Street." She was talking about Brother Townsend, the board member who had been taken in adultery. "Right by the park."

"He lives down there," said Pastor Fish.

"Sister Thingamajig said she saw him going in the Presbyterian church in South Pasadena. She was driving by. She said his face was twitching. I say good."

"Well, Ben Townsend will someday meet his Maker." Winston wound his store-bought watch, a new one. "You can't hide from the consequences of sin."

"I'm late," said Roxanne, sleep in her eyes. She was tired from eavesdropping last night, but she had a test.

Colleen was pulling back her ponytail, an adult already, her socks rolled down.

"Girls! Wait!" Sister Fish laid hands on them. "Dear Lord, protect these girls. Put on the whole armour of God, that ye may be able to stand against the wiles of the devil. Amen."

Colleen pulled away and ran out, leaping down the porch steps, disappearing toward the tree that hid her lipsticks. Roxanne stood still on the porch, reluctant to leave. Mrs. Inglehurst did not like her.

"I thought you were late," said Zelda. "Get going. After school you can look in the new Missionary Box. I saw strappy high heels. Run!"

Roxy slid into the classroom through the back door seconds before the last bell, her books against her chest. Today she had on a white blouse and a plaid skirt rolled up at the waist. Already Mrs. Inglehurst was going on about photosynthesis, information you would never need in heaven. Roxy looked at the door, opening her notebook to begin a letter to Superba. Furtively she scooched out of the teacher's line of vision.

"Dear Superba, It is boring here." Her pencil drew a tree.

"Roxanne! Roxanne Fish!"

She jumped. Mrs. Inglehurst was standing up front with her hands on her hips. She snorted like a racehorse, walking in a small circle, her high heels clicking on the floor. Roxanne looked at her obediently, seething.

"Where are you? Off in the cornfields?"

The whole class laughed.

"It's a custom to pay attention in California, you see."

Billy Tudball snickered. Mrs. Inglehurst held up a note.

"This is from the principal, princi-p-a-l because he is your what?"

"Pal!" they yelled.

"Very good. He says there is a special singer here today. All choir members to the choir room. Choir members excused."

Two students gathered their books and left the classroom. As the door closed behind them, Roxanne stood.

"Miss Fish? Since when are you a choir member?"

"I have to go to the bathroom."

Mrs. Inglehurst looked at the clock slowly. It said 9:04.

"You may go. Hurry back so you may join our quest for knowledge."

Outside were more ugly palm trees. She was never going back to Mrs. Inglehurst, even though her books were there. It was blessed to be in the Spanish-style courtyard of Pilgrim School with sun on the sidewalks and no people. She passed the school nurse, trying to look purposeful, and detoured through the tennis courts. From here you could clearly see the purplish mountains. Roxanne shook her head. California was like a foreign country. She hated California entirely. She heard piano music coming from what must be the choir room, and almost giggled. She went down some steps and across a patio toward where the sound was emerging from a set of double doors.

The choir room was packed.

"Sit over there," said Mr. Biggs, indicating the chair nearest the piano. A pale man with limp hands sat playing it.

Roxanne stood silently.

"Sit *down*, please," said the choir leader. "Chop-chop. Don't just stand there."

Roxy sat.

"Children? Settle down."

Roxanne blinked. She had never seen an African before, not up close. The woman in green shoes was not ten feet away. Roxanne stared. The shoes were high heels, aqua like the sea, iridescent like seashells, something Water Lily Maidens might wear if they had feet. There were Africans living in South Glendale, but you only saw them from your car.

"This is Aretha Franklin, class. Her nephew, Benedict Harris, attends here. Say hello."

Roxanne breathed deeply. She thought the name was beautiful. The woman with dark arms and legs sat immobile by the blackboard, looking out at the children one by one. She was full of the Holy Ghost, like Roland. Sun came in the doorway next to her. A hum was in Glendale that was not coming from anything electrical. Roxanne cocked her head.

"Sing 'Twist,'" yelled a girl in back.

"Quiet, class," said Mr. Biggs. "Qui-et!" He clapped his hands too fast, face red, eyes threatening a few students still in conversation.

Aretha Franklin smiled. Sitting in her chair, she began to sing, each foot resting on the spike of its heel, forgetful feet, unlady-like. The voice went through Roxanne's bones and beyond. Now the woman in high heels was standing, although no one had seen her rise. Her green shoes glistened. She was walking back and forth across the room, back and forth, talking to you, singing "Rock my soul" over and over and over again. To her horror Roxanne's nose began running. She wiped it with her blouse and laughed out loud then. Aretha Franklin sang "Rock my soul" and laughed with her. When she finished, her voice lingered in the air, and they all leaned forward, listening to it, including the African.

"Well, that was absolutely fabulous," said Mr. Biggs.

Aretha Franklin kept listening, but not to him. Roxanne kept staring. She had of course seen pictures of the heathen in Africa with rings in their lips, and some in regular American clothes, which was how you could tell they were saved. When Aretha Franklin moved, her green high heels threw loose light.

"Miss Franklin is well on her way, well on her way, and some-day she may be a great-great. Today she is going to listen to our choir and give us some pointers. I'm sure we will never be the same!"

Aretha Franklin stared at them, not smiling.

"Now, are there any questions?"

"Do you know Elvis Presley?" said Roxanne.

Everyone laughed, but it was simply background noise. Sun came in the arched windows. A premonition told Roxanne she was going to be happy. Her shyness was nowhere. She watched the African.

"That's not the kind of question she means," said Mr. Biggs.

"Well, I do know him. He's a good singer. Do you think so?"

"Yes," said Roxanne.

"Sing 'ah.'"

Aretha Franklin was looking straight at Roxanne, so she must mean her, Roxanne Fish of Ames, Iowa. Her mouth went dry. She opened it, but nothing came out, and she sat there feeling stupid, like a real fish. The piano struck a chord.

"Ah," she said.

"Stand up. Now *sing* it."

This time it sounded like she was at the doctor with a popsicle stick in her mouth. Facing the black African, she opened up her body and let the sound issue forth. It came out stronger, like a train whistle approaching. Aretha Franklin held up one hand, closing her fingers slowly to pull the note out.

Roxanne gasped for breath.

"Do you sing?" Aretha Franklin said.

"Yes. No. Yes I do." Out the corner of her eyes she could see the green shoes, twinkly, Water Lily Maiden color.

"What songs do you know?"

"All of them. 'Heebie Jeebies.' 'Amazing Grace.' 'What a Friend We Have in Jesus.' 'Blue Suede Shoes.'"

"Let's go," said Aretha. "'Amazing Grace.'"

Together they sang, like sisters, and their voices flew around the Glendale room. It was more fun than jumping on Superba's mother's bed, better than flying. Roxy did not care if she went to hell. She did not pray for forgiveness. Even in the Woolworth basement she had not heard the voice now coming out of her, urgent and insisting, and she kept her eyes on the African's face for fear it would go away. On they sang, the purest Amazing Graces, Roxy resisting the urge to laugh wildly. They started again.

"You keep going on by yourself. I'll come in and out."

Roxy's voice squeaked.

"Just relax," said Mr. Biggs. Sweat blinded him.

Aretha Franklin stood still, exactly like Roland. She looked full of the power to shake things. "Don't hold your breath," she said.

Out came the voice again. Roxy opened her throat wider, singing the final verse, and her chest exploded with the Northern

Lights, going on and on until the choir room and she were one. Beyond the Rocky Mountains all the grass in Iowa listened, still and green.

"Well, well, well," said Aretha Franklin. "Sit down."

For the remainder of the hour the choir rehearsed while Roxy sat with goosebumps on her skin. Her chair next to the piano seemed out of time, eternal. She would sing or die. People were smiling at her around the room, she realized. Now she was a Christian, but she was something else too.

When the bell rang Mr. Biggs shook Aretha Franklin's hand profusely. Children who had been singing "The Battle Hymn of the Republic" danced out doing the Watusi, wiggling their hips, jumping over the threshold onto the patio. The patio itself had been transformed into an area of heartbreaking beauty, something Roxy had missed on her way in.

"Let's talk," said Aretha Franklin. "I have a proposition for you."

They were still talking when Mr. Biggs finished erasing the blackboard. For some reason he started again. They were comparing animal sounds, cows to owls. Aretha Franklin agreed with Roxy that the sound cows make is beautiful, moo. Chalk filled the air.

"Woo-woo-woo," Aretha sang.

"Doves."

Mr. Biggs erased at nothing.

"I have a tour upcoming that is called the Sanctified Sisters. You have a grown-up voice in there." Aretha Franklin tapped Roxy's breastbone.

"I do?"

"Coiled to spring. Sometimes that happens. Plus you got that porky sound, and one of my backup girls is getting married. She's out two nights, a fool for love. She comes back and we go north."

"The Sanctified Sisters," said Roxy.

At the blackboard Mr. Biggs kept erasing. Aretha Franklin turned and looked at him.

"Honey, *sit*." She swiveled back to Roxy. "Anyway, you ought to do it. Singing will sustain you. I need you in November for a couple days' rehearsal and two concerts. Just Los Angeles."

"What is backup?" said Roxy.

"The counterpoint, so to speak," said Mr. Biggs.

"Sit that fat ass down *now*." Aretha continued making soft sounds, cooing like a dove or like a mama to a baby. "Sha-na-na. Whoo-ee. Go down, go down."

The bad word floated off Roxy's back. She nodded.

"Want to?"

"Yes."

"Will your parents let you? Because you have to have their signed permission."

"Yes. They're very helpful."

Aretha Franklin scribbled on a slip of paper and handed it to Roxy. "Here's my manager's number in Los Angeles. You have your folks call him. I'll get Mr. Biggs the permission forms."

"Do you believe in heaven?" said Roxy.

Mr. Biggs stopped erasing.

"Only if there's plenty of singing." Aretha Franklin walked to the open double doors, feet twinkling in her green high heels. She looked up. "It's hard to believe in anything with these old raggedy clouds in Pasadena."

"Glendale," said Mr. Biggs.

Roxy loved California. She loved palm trees. She loved Superba, but she knew they would always be friends. Clutching the phone number, she reached out, unable to stop herself, and touched for one second the beautiful African skin. Aretha Franklin's arm said hello.

"Tell your mama. Call my manager."

"Okay," Roxy said.

Leaving the choir room, she walked back across the patio and off the grounds of Pilgrim School, although it was early in the day. Her books could stay with Mrs. Inglehurst forever. Truant, she continued up toward Sycamore Street, where the Lipstick

Tree was. She tried to hold it down, but the voice kept getting out of her despite her best efforts. She smiled at every passing automobile. The sky looked beautiful, and so did the mountains. When she reached the tree, she stood on tiptoe.

Within reach were Summer Peach, Siren Red, Tangerine Kiss, Baby Burgundy, Pink Passion. She unscrewed them one by one and smeared her hand. What she needed was a mirror. Filling the pockets of her plaid skirt, she ran back to Pilgrim School, trying not to clink. In the little bathroom off the main patio she tried on Pink Passion first.

"Heebie jeebies!" she sang, and shook.

She looked fabulous.

Tangerine Kiss was best, she decided, and then she realized that someone was in the stall she had thought was empty. She put Siren Red away. In the mirror she looked like a teenager of the world.

"Heebie jeebies!" she whispered.

• • • • •

She hoped Jesus did not come tonight. In fact, she hoped He did not come until she was an old woman. Nervously she pushed food around on her plate and wiped at her mouth. She prayed all the lipstick was off.

"Roxanne! Hold still. We're eating dinner."

"Is there any more of that spinach?" said Pastor Fish. "Colleen! Get back here so we can spend time as a family!"

Colleen rolled her eyes above the telephone receiver. "Homework," she mouthed, and spun around so that her ponytail swung. "The square root? Leonard is a square, if you know what I mean."

"Colleen!"

"Roxanne looks flushed," said Zelda. Her mother touched her forehead.

"What does it take to get everyone sitting down at once?" Pastor Fish banged the table.

Roxy made a well in her mashed potatoes. It would take a miracle for them to let her sing with the Sanctified Sisters. "Be ye not unequally yoked together with unbelievers," Scripture said. But miracles had happened. In agony Roxy clutched Aretha Franklin's phone number in her fist, CItrus-1402. She would die if they didn't let her. The thing to sound was casual. Tonight the Bergs, from Iowa, were starting a revival that they hoped would sweep Glendale, for the saints of California were lethargic. But the Bergs' car had broken down on the freeway, so Zelda was going to preach until they arrived. Roxy dished up extra spinach, for extra strength, and reached for the vinegar. The Fishes continued to eat pork roast, Colleen joining them. The tendrils of meat melted in your mouth.

"Finally," said Zelda. "Everybody here. How was the funeral, Winston? Eat fast."

"I think it went well." Winston nodded. "Girls, how was school?"

Roxy sat up straight. "Guess what."

Colleen looked at her sharply.

"Winston?" Zelda held up one finger. "Just a minute. While I think of it, we have *got* to do something about Prescott Hampton." Prescott Hampton was a retired Englishman who drank. He got saved Sunday night and backslid every Monday. A small, wiry man, he had been born again four times in the one month and one week the Fishes had been here. Christians were getting mad.

"I will talk to him," agreed Pastor Fish. He too loved spinach.

"He isn't taking his salvation seriously," reiterated Sister Fish. "In fact, he *enjoys* repenting every Sunday night."

"Roxanne, what were you about to say?"

"Aretha Franklin asked me to sing with her!" Roxy cried, standing up.

There was confused silence while they stared at her. She had yelled, she realized. Casually, she sat down.

"Let her do it," said Colleen.

"Can I, Mom? Can I, please?"

"Can you what?"

"Sing with the Sanctified Sisters on their tour." She forced herself to sit still. Aretha Franklin's telephone number actually felt branded into her palm. Across the table the Christian faces made her feel hopeless.

"Please. She wants me to sing with her in Los Angeles for two nights in November and stay in a hotel. *Please*."

"You mean she would want you to miss school?" Zelda dished some meat up. "Besides, you don't sing."

"La la la la la!" Roxy ran out of breath, looking down at her plate. She wondered if she could earn her own living. Her father looked at her strangely, as if she were not a Fish.

"I can witness to the people in the hotel!" she said.

Her mother leaned across the table, grabbed her shoulders, and kissed her loudly on the forehead. "Is this Aretha Franklin a Christian?"

"Yes! I asked her."

"Well, that doesn't necessarily mean anything."

"You're awfully young to go off in some vehicle overnight with a stranger." Winston twisted the top off the salt shaker and looked in.

Roxy gripped the table with enormous strength, being careful not to pull the tablecloth off.

Her father recapped the salt. "Maybe another time."

"Let her," said Colleen.

"Please!" said Roxy.

"Let's ask God," said Winston Fish, setting the salt down with a crack. Roxy and Colleen exchanged looks. "Right here. Right now in this time and place. We can put a fleece before the Lord. Let's do so before church."

"Praise God," said Zelda. "Let us run!"

They went into the living room, where there was a rug to ease their knees, and everybody knelt down and joined hands. Colleen found the barrette she had lost last week at this instant.

"Dear Lord, if You want our daughter to stand and sing with this Leetha character, make it known. We are asking for Your will in this matter. We are Christians. Now speak to our hearts. Amen."

"Los Angeles is a wicked city," remarked Zelda.

"So what?" Colleen ate a pork tendril. "So is Glendale."

"Hallelujah."

• • • • •

"I'm going to preach tonight, but first I want my daughter Roxanne Fish to sing a song," said Zelda. "Get ready! Roxanne?"

Winston almost stood to intervene, but Zelda had a certain look in her eyes. Roxy grabbed *Hymns of Glorious Praise* and began leafing through it, trying not to panic and rip the pages. All of them looked ugly. She started at the back and went forward, not reading the titles. She knew every song. This church was more a real church than the one in Ames, modern, with a sloping roof and colored windows along the side, yet the Holy Ghost did not seem to like it. The Glendale Christians were not on fire, and the tension showed in their shoulders and faces. They did not look friendly. Roxy closed the book and rubbed her face hard.

"Amen!" cried Zelda from the platform. "I am thinking of a missionary story."

Zelda's voice had changed, and Roxy looked up, her fingers laced into the songbook. Zelda was not beautiful, but light came out of her. She backed up from the pulpit with the energy of a young girl. Roxy and all the Glendale Christians leaned toward her.

"It was in Guinea, and the government had changed."

Her palm panned across the room, painting the Guinea landscape, which everyone could see: wild brushy trees and zebras, cobras coiled in branches, the sky enormous.

"One day officials from the government came through the village to the house of a young Christian convert."

All the Glendale congregation watched the officials knocking as Zelda's fist tapped three times. Her face radiated escape.

"This young convert's wife answered the door, but they pushed her aside. She had her three children, and a fourth coming. Up against the wall in back, for they had just one room, was the young Christian convert, staring at them. He had only been a Christian three months.

"'Renounce Jesus,' the officials said.

"'No,' said the young man.

"The officials brandished their guns. 'Renounce him!'

"'No,' he said again.

"So they dragged him by his arms out of the house, past his children. They dragged him through the dirt to the edge of town, where there was a ravine crossed by a plank bridge. The sky was very blue that day. They stood the young man on the bridge and backed onto solid ground themselves, holding up their guns. The ravine was quite deep.

"'Renounce Jesus,' they said, 'and you can go home to your family.'

"'No,' the young man said.

"Then the top official stepped forward. He was dressed in a uniform. 'Very well. Before we shoot you, you can say a few words.'

"The young man stepped out to the edge of the bridge and lifted his face to the blue sky. Then he sang, in his tribe's tongue of Soussou, while the men with raised guns waited. I can't sing, but I will say the words in English, for you know them.

> "There's a land that is fairer than day
> "And by faith we shall see it afar
> "The father waits over the way
> "To prepare us a dwelling place there."

"Oh, his voice was clear as it lifted out over the ravine, the words in Soussou.

> "In the sweet bye and bye
> "We shall meet on that beautiful shore

"In the sweet bye and bye

"We shall meet on that beautiful shore."

"When he finished they shot him, and his body fell into the ravine. I believe that we will meet him when we reach heaven."

Sister Fish sat down and the congregation sat there, hands raised. Roxy stepped forward. It was odd, but she knew just what to do. She put "Amazing Grace" down before Sister Sue, the pianist, and asked her to play high C.

"I thought you played the harmonica," said Sister Sue.

Roxy took her place behind the empty pulpit. When the pianist played the introduction Roxy missed the cue, it came so fast, like time was speeding up. She stood there and the piano played on, starting the introduction again.

"Amazing grace," sang Roxy.

It sounded creaky, but the congregation looked at her with some interest. She opened her throat.

"How sweet the sound

"That saved a wretch like me!"

Now the piano was following her, and not the other way around, a fact she noted with simple curiosity. She opened her throat more. For each note she had infinite time, Heaven Time. Her mother sat in pew one beside her father, dreamily hitting a slow tambourine against her left thigh, face still young. Pastor Fish looked at his daughter carefully, as if she were playing baseball. Roxy took verse two into a sanctuary full of faces come to life, shoulders relaxing, lips beginning to part.

"Sing something else," said Brother Bishop when she finished.

"Come home!" she sang. "Come home!"

As she held a long note, Sister Alma Jackson headed up the aisle in her red dress and stopped before the platform abruptly.

"I want to rededicate my life to the Lord," she said in an urgent whisper. She held out her arms but did not kneel down. "I have been spiritually cold!"

"Sing another verse," said Sister Thingamajig.

Roxy sang on, as no one came to take the pulpit.

> "See by the portals He's waiting and watching
> "Watching for you and for me."

Two more people were coming down the aisle now, from two directions.

"I have been prideful of my jewelry!" cried Sister Smith. Colleen had seen her in the drugstore buying lipstick. Now tears streamed down her face. "I am giving my rings to God." Three of them came off her fingers and landed on the platform floor, sparkling. One, red, looked real.

"I have took pride in my car and put my tithing money into engine parts!" The man with white hair threw down his keys and stomped back down the church aisle with his hands in the air.

Roxy had more energy than she had ever felt. She sang more songs, from memory, and the piano followed her on each one. Her parents sat emptied in the front row and let God work. Her voice soared, gliding down the aisle and into the pews, letting people stand up, letting people step out.

"I'm going home to get my new TV," cried a fat man. "I've been hiding it!"

Sister Ritter drove home, got her wedding dress, and brought it back in a bag with a zipper, dragging it behind her up the aisle. When she took it out, it exploded everywhere on the platform, a huge balloon of satin and lace.

"I have put my marriage before the Lord!"

The voice was everything. The power of Aretha continued to surge through Roxy. She sang from eight until eleven, which seemed like no time at all. Finally the Glendale Christians' faces were on fire. To Roxy's right, the platform was getting interesting.

"I have put my purses before God!"

"I been coveting my blender!"

"I have coveted my long hair. I am going to cut it off! Scissors!"

Sister Smith went to get some.

"I have been coveting the power tools in my garage, and they cut me off from God. This drill was in my trunk. I'll bring the rest tomorrow!"

Out the window the neon sign on the Pontiac dealership glowed.

Roxy sang all night, occasionally standing on tiptoe to stretch her feet. The items on the platform grew into a pile big enough to jump on. There were shoes and necklaces, the TV, the hank of hair, folded scraps of paper, a chandelier.

"I've been holding back a dislike for the new pastor," cried Sister Rosa Garcia Bishop. She sobbed. The relief in her voice made everyone breathe. "I thought he was a hick from the Midwest. Thank you, Jesus!" She took out a handkerchief and blew her nose.

They were laughing in the tabernacle now, laughing in the Spirit, that fine thing, something Roxy had experienced only twice in her life before, once at Boone and once at Storm Lake Camp Meeting. In Glendale they all sat in their pews and laughed where they were. They jiggled up and down, one body, the cheerfulest sound, tickled in the presence of God. Winston Fish and Zelda Fish laughed too, and Colleen Fish laughed where she sat in back. Boys laughed to her left and right, heedless of her now.

"I been coveting my Buick Electra, and here's the pink slip. Sell it for the building fund." Roy Jenson jumped, cowboy boots almost hitting his rear end. "I feel *good*."

"I have coveted my front lawn. I am going to put God first and let the weeds come!"

A lady in a blue dress brought a stunning string of pearls, all of them an identical size. Roxy met Colleen's eyes, and Colleen raised her eyebrows.

Revival fire was here in Glendale.

"I have coveted my jewelry. Lord, I give these pearls to Thee!"

When everyone was limp with exhaustion, Pastor Fish took the pulpit and said a final prayer. Roxy went outside and walked around the parking lot. Inside some Christians were still laughing. There were no fireflies, but how beautiful the white paint of the dividing lines was. She had never been so happy in her life. When the people began to come out, she stayed at the far edge, taking small steps, taking large steps, walking backwards. Even the lack of grass did not bother her. At last she saw her family and went to join them.

"That's quite a voice you have there," said her father, shaking her shoulder. "We want to think about this Sanctified Women project, Mother and I. Your voice is quite the something." He wiped his eyes.

Roxy looked at Colleen. She made prayer hands.

"Bringing in the sheaves!" cried Zelda. "Amen!"

"Shimmy, shimmy, ko-ko bop," said Colleen.

• • • • •

"My, this cake is delicious. Dee-licious," said Brother Berg.

They had just arrived, having had a broken water pump, and were sitting in the new Fish living room.

"Yes." Sister Berg tasted more. "Did you make it?"

"Well, I'm embarrassed to say. I got it at the day-old bakery down on Colorado Street. Things cost next to nothing, and you can't even tell. I mean, they aren't *used*."

They were having cake at nearly midnight and exclaiming over the mighty working of God in Glendale. There were so many items on the platform that Pastor Fish had simply locked the church. They intended to do something with them tomorrow. They sat in their new house (it was called Victorian), toasting by the first fire they had built there or anywhere. All their faces gleamed. Orange flickered around the room, over the sheet music on the piano, over the white doilies on the chair arms. Roxy prayed for God to make them let her go. Wood crackled.

"This suitcase is too old," she said.

She had dragged it from the basement and was checking out its straps. Zelda Fish shook her head. The concerts were in less than a month, and Roxy had written to Superba, a letter that consisted mainly of exclamation marks.

"So you're going to do some singing," said Sister Berg. She took another piece of cake, chocolate this time. "My."

"We shall see. Anyway, we ought to do something about her teeth. I have always said so."

"Mom? Can't we get a new one?"

"A new what?"

"Suitcase."

"Don't be ridiculous."

"God has placed His mighty hand on Glendale," said Brother Berg.

All nodded. Satan's days in Glendale were numbered.

"Where was Prescott Hampton?"

"Who is that?"

"A drinker. He gets saved too much."

The Fishes further described the people who had come forward, laying down their idols before God. The platform was heaped. For Christians must put nothing before heaven.

"This girl is awfully young to go off gallivanting," said Brother Berg. "With the who?"

"Sanctified Sisters tour." Zelda finished her vanilla ice cream. "Of course, she could have her Bible with her at all times and kneel down and pray if Satan shows up. If she's not too shy to pray in front of everyone."

"I'm not," said Roxy.

"I am waiting for an answer from the Lord," said Winston.

"The still small voice," Zelda added.

"This is delicious ice cream," said Sister Berg, and spooned some onto her cake. "Now, this Khrushchev thinks he can bang with his shoe. Temper! And the bomb right at his fingertips. Lord, come quickly!"

Around Roxy where she stood at the fireplace the air was jiggling, as if the atmosphere had gone insane. She racked her brain for how to make it through the zillion moments between now and three weeks from Tuesday, when she had her first rehearsal. She decided to put her socks in the suitcase tonight.

"I am worried about these elections," said Winston.

They all looked at him, alerted by a danger tone.

"I believe our Vice President is doing fine." Brother Berg scraped the last of his dessert up with his spoon. "Yet we need every last ounce of faith we can muster to get him elected."

"Of course, the Catholics have tried before." Winston put his fork down. Now Roxy saw that he had not touched his cake, and this worried her. The fork sat neatly on the side, the ice cream runny. "The Catholics would like to control the government. They have their own schools. I don't like the looks of this thing, not one little bit."

"They want us to worship the Pope." Sister Berg sneezed. "Excuse me."

"We will vote him down November eighth," cried Zelda.

"His wife wears cute hats," said Sister Berg, blushing instantly.

They all looked at the ceiling, where firelight played. Roxy looked at the clock. Ten minutes had passed, the slowest ten minutes she had ever lived.

"God can win against the Catholics," said Brother Berg.

The Christians resumed eating, but they had their work cut out for them. They would vote, but there were not enough real Christians to make a difference. Still, they could implore God to guide the voters' hands. They were weak but He was strong.

"I'm getting married," cried Colleen, bursting into the living room via the side door. Her cheeks were flushed, her eyes even brighter than usual.

The adults stared at her.

"Just kidding." She sat down.

"Roxanne?" Her father added a log to the fire, making it spit. "Lead us in a song of your choice, and then we'll get down on our knees."

"Yes," said Sister Berg. "I've got the joy joy joy joy down in my heart."

Roxy started out at a pitch all could accommodate, mindful of her voice, trying not to slide it like a trombone, but it refused to sound exactly Christian. Her father sang with his eyes closed.

"The wonderful love!" cried Sister Zeng, her hands up.

"These girls ought to get to sleep," said Winston. "It's way past their bedtime."

> "I've got the wonderful love of my blessed Redeemer
> "Down in the depths of my heart!"

They kept singing. Nobody wanted to stop. Roxy's voice sailed out in the open, bold, impossible to hold back. With her calf she touched the suitcase.

"Amen," said Zelda Fish just before they knelt down to pray. For a moment it looked like she was going to do the Charleston. "Oh! If even *one* of my children should fail to make heaven! I don't think I could take it!"

"Mom, you only *have* two," said Colleen.

Heebie Jeebies

FIGHTING TO WAKE UP, the girls sat eating toast and eggs at the kitchen table with the dark outside. It was five a.m.

They had missed Family Worship yesterday morning, an unheard-of event in the annals of Fish family history. Zelda was still agitated about it. She blamed herself for oversleeping after the Bergs' late departure Monday night. Despite the hour they had left for Sacramento to see the Zengs for a day and to pray for Togoland.

"This is the day which the Lord hath made," declared Zelda, spooning out sugar. "We will rejoice and be glad in it!"

No one answered. The sleepy Fish family continued chewing. To miss Family Worship was like inviting Satan into your living room. Satan tried to gain entry through any crack left open to him, which was why Christians had to be eternally vigilant: why their eyes avoided women in bikinis on billboards, why they attended church midweek and had revival every few months. For a while it had looked like God was not in Glendale, but now the Glendale Christians were on fire. On the platform in the church one mile away, their worldly objects made a small mountain, a love offering to God: all the things that stood between the saved and one hundred percent dedication to the gospel.

Clearing the breakfast dishes, Roxy thought about the pearls she had stolen off the platform when no one was looking. She had never done such a thing, ever, and it shocked her. Somewhere

Aretha Franklin was sleeping in her bed. Roxy walked quickly through the Fish dining room to the bedroom she shared with Colleen. Her chest was flat but starting to get sore, which meant something. Superba would know the answer, if she weren't however so many miles distant.

Zelda stuck her head through the bedroom door.

"Hurry, girls! I don't want to go another second." She clapped her hands, and the sound resonated through the entire house. "Hurry! We must stand against the wiles of the devil!"

Roxy stayed in the bedroom, waiting for her sister to leave. Not that they were exactly friends, but this once Colleen smiled at her, clear nail polish secretly on one finger, the finger dangling her Bible by its zipper chain. Roxy asked God to forgive her sister. Dangling was disrespectful.

"They better let you go," Colleen said.

Her sister exited, and Roxy turned back to the empty room. She slid the pearls out from under the mattress. Still white and round, they would look beautiful with her red hair. She slid them back.

"Family Worship!" Zelda called out in her best preaching voice.

Roxy grabbed her white Bible off her pillow. Time was short, but she dropped to her knees.

"Please make them let me go." She buried her face in her hands, the Bible against her chest. "Please, please, *please!*"

When the door opened she jumped, hitting her thigh on the bed frame.

"Oh!" said her mother. "I didn't mean to interrupt. Were you praying for the Africans?"

"Yes," said Roxy, getting up, brushing off both knees. Her knees were her favorite part of herself. "Hallelujah."

"Roxanne, you have a good soul."

Colleen sat in the living room, on the double ottoman, twisting her bracelets. She glared out at them to hurry so she could get back to counting her boyfriends. Even sleepy, she looked cute enough to be a movie star. Adorably she used both fists to rub her eyes.

"Let's *start*," she moaned.

"That will be enough from you, young lady. Eternity doesn't have a clock. Which way shall we go? First Chronicles 2:10, I believe. Find your places, everybody. Colleen? You can begin."

"And Ram begat Amminadab; and Amminadab begat Nahshon. I hate this. Prince of the children of Judah."

"And Nahshon begat Salma," read Roxy. She crossed her fingers, which was devil worship in a way. She uncrossed them. "And Salma begat Boaz."

"Interesting thing about Nahshon," said Pastor Fish, interrupting. "His relatives are mentioned in another part of the Hebron valley, which means he moved."

"My," said Zelda. "And Boaz begat Obed, and Obed begat Jesse."

It was Colleen's turn again. "Ha! But you would never go up to a sinner and say, 'Obed begat Jesse'!"

"You'd be surprised," said Winston Fish. He shook his head.

"The Word of God is powerful, and mightier than any two-edged sword," Zelda said dreamily. She raised her arms. "Lord, keep your mighty hand on Roxanne."

At the last verse of chapter two, Pastor Fish looked up. "And the families of the scribes which dwelt at Jabez; the Tirathites, the Shimeathites, and Suchathites. These are the Kenites that came of Hemath, the father of the house of Rechab." He closed his Bible. Roxy's heart clanged.

"I have prayed about this Sanctified Christians project," he said. "I went down in my study. It works to be alone with God. I might add that 'sanctified' is a Nazarene term."

Roxy held her breath. Her fingers felt stiff and cold. Colleen lightly touched one.

"A Nazarene can still make heaven," Zelda pointed out. "If they are saved."

"No," said Pastor Fish. "And that is final."

Roxy put her feet together.

"But she has a burden for the Africans." Zelda leaned far forward on the edge of their sofa. There would be new furniture in heaven. "I believe this woman is *from* there."

Roxy stared at the piano, paralyzed.

"Winston?" Zelda played her phantom tambourine against her palm. "Why, the whole tour bus might get saved if she took her pamphlets and her white Bible. Roxanne, use the passages that Jesus said. This is why they are in red."

"Zelda! A Christian cannot go *three days* out in the world. Three days is a dangerous length of time! It takes only a moment for Satan to creep in! What if the Rapture happens and her name has been erased from the Lamb's Book of Life? Seventy-two hours is a vast stretch. Nothing in the world is worth the Rapture. We do not miss midweek service! We do not miss Family Worship! We are living in eternity *at this moment*." Pastor Fish looked at each of them, his eyes bright. "*This moment*."

Roxy kept her eyes straight ahead. Zelda's tambourine had slowed.

"Is this worth your immortal soul?" Pastor Fish thundered.

"Hallelujah," said Zelda.

"Colleen, do you know this Aleetha Frankle woman? Do your unsaved classmates talk about her?"

"Nope." Colleen blew a huge bubble with forbidden bubblegum, an act her parents ignored.

"If she used the rhythms of her native Africa it would not surprise me *one bit*."

"Daddy," said Colleen.

Das Kapital lay open on the floor, Pastor Fish's handwritten notes running up and down the margins. Suddenly he stood up.

"Let us pray."

"I *hate* you!" screamed Roxy.

All four Fishes stopped where they were. Roxy was standing too, although she didn't know how she'd gotten there. She stared out and they stared back.

When the phone rang, Pastor Fish went to answer it. The remaining Fishes stayed in the living room, their Bibles open to Chronicles on the chairs. When he came back in, his face was white.

"Lipstick," he spat.

Colleen twitched.

"That was Mrs. Inglehurst. She says she saw you in the school restroom smearing it right on your face." His voice cracked. "Around your mouth."

Zelda's hands covered her eyes. "Oh my."

Pastor Fish stepped toward Roxy. He did not slap her. She took a step back.

"You have been lying all along." He reached out, but his hand did not quite touch her. "Is that what you were thinking about when you sang? About lipstick? Lust? I thought I saw something."

"Do you believe in God?" It was Zelda's voice that pierced the air. It rang out eerily between worlds, like the woman's voice out of the dark at Storm Lake.

"Are you the leader of a prostitution ring?" Her father took another step forward.

Roxy backed up.

"Are you the leader of a dope ring?"

His face held such contempt that Roxy stood trying to remember. She had been drunk at the Woolworths, of course.

"Glendale is an evil, evil city," said Zelda Fish. "I wish we had not come here. Where are the Zengs?"

"Sacramento," said Colleen. She sounded scared.

"We are going to baptize you." Pastor Fish spoke softly, so softly it felt violent. The Fish furniture seemed to settle. White music lay pristinely on the piano front. Pastor Fish's trombone shone.

"Next Sunday. We need to have a baptism anyway. Then you can dedicate this talent to the Lord. Aleetha Frankle can manage on her own."

Roxanne was still.

Now the look of eternity was on his face, manna falling through the heaven air, Jesus at the right hand of God. Light poured through the windows from His Throne. Aretha was no match for that.

"Sunday," he repeated, his voice vibrant. "Roxanne needs to be baptized. Real Christians must be buried to sin and come up new creatures in Christ Jesus."

"There's only one life," recited Zelda.

> "'Twill soon be past
> "And only what's done
> "For Christ will last."

"That lipstick is mine," Colleen said in a small, fierce voice.

"*Sunday*," her father declared.

• • • • •

East Fork River meandered gracefully, more a creek. In California they called anything a river. Still, it might have hidden whirlpools.

Roxanne waded in.

She had been sick all week. The old Fish suitcase was back down in the basement, empty except for crinkled newspaper. It was bad to miss so much homework, but the labor union in the 1930s did not matter in heaven.

Roxanne pushed down her Missionary Box skirt.

The five members to be baptized were holding hands, but it didn't help much: none of them could swim, being Christian. Roxanne still feared the water a little, even though she was saved. Gingerly she poked forward with her feet, in large shoes also from the Missionary Box, to check for holes. The water swirled around them. Onshore her mother clapped, swaying as if she had the tambourine, sometimes laughing. Underwater the men's pants clung to their legs while the ladies' dresses floated up, a baptism phenomenon, different from mixed bathing. The ladies used their fists to bat them down.

"Will those to be baptized come closer," said Pastor Fish, pulling with his fingers, just as Aretha Franklin had. He stood in the river in a white shirt, hands in the air, praising God. Butterflies flew around him. "Amen."

The five waded forward in the water, jumpy, holding hands, happy to be taking this step. For they were about to give up the old life. On the riverbank the congregation looked like flowers as they clapped their hands and sang. Methodists only got sprinkled, which did not count. Roxanne was in the middle, shortest of the five, behind Sister Cubbison. In front, first in line, was Dolores Ruiz. She had a sinful love of rock and roll on her transistor radio, but she had put the radio on the platform at the Glendale love offering. Pastor Fish had talked to her at length, for the devil was in the beat, which came from African drums. Brother Ritz, the fat man who had given up his TV, was behind Roxanne, followed by Brother Deerhart, whose lawn was filling with weeds.

"Amen!" yelled Sister Sue.

Onshore Zelda signaled frantically for her husband to take his tie off, but he ignored her. Voices floated out across the water.

> "Shall we gather at the river,
> "The beautiful, beautiful river!"

Roxanne could see her mother's white gloves hitting the tambourine, although she kept her hips almost still. Brother Townsend and his wife were absent, and probably Presbyterian by now. But the Presbyterians were cold and would take anybody. Water swirled.

"Dolores Ruiz!"

Dolores separated herself from the lifeline and waded out. On the road at the top of the ravine a car of unsaved stopped to watch, two women and two men. In their halter tops the women looked obscene. The Christians continued.

"Your name?" said Pastor Fish.

"Dolores Ruiz."

"Are you ready to be buried to sin and born in Christ Jesus? Are you ready to give up everything?"

"Amen!"

Pastor Fish braced Dolores Ruiz with his left arm and raised her left hand with his right. For a moment they looked like ice skaters. Ice skating was not sinful, although roller skating was the realm of Satan. No one knew why. Roxanne listened to the murmur of Christians' voices onshore. Her father brought Dolores's hand up over her nose, keeping it covered with his.

"I now baptize you in the name of the Father. And the Son. And the Holy Ghost."

Dolores Ruiz went down and came up.

Sister Cubbison was next. She waded out toward Pastor Fish. Now the people on the road were laughing.

"Your name?"

"Sarah Cubbison."

"Are you ready to be buried to sin and born in Christ Jesus?"

"Amen!"

Backward she went.

They all waited, including the sinners, while Sister Cubbison's old selfish desires were washed away. Underwater the mystery deepened. When she shot up, hair streaming, she screamed. Her arms flew heavenward. Now she could live for Jesus period.

"Glory to the Lamb!" She jumped, coming almost out of the river. "I'm new!"

The congregation sang Sister Cubbison to shore. She walked toward land with her eyes closed, arms up. On the rocks Dolores Ruiz waited in her wet dress, a towel around her shoulders, shivering, a new creature.

"Next!"

Roxanne swallowed. Fat Brother Ritz squeezed her hand and let go. She waded toward her father.

"Hallelujah," she said.

Above, the carload on the shoulder drove away. They would rue their laughter down in hell, where the Dewey Dumpster Heiress was screaming for a drop of water for her tongue. Roxanne reached her father's arm, now wet in its white shirt sleeve. They stood facing the congregation as the river rushed by. She was going to be baptized.

"And you are?"

"Roxanne Fish."

The congregation laughed. Somewhere nearby a bird sounded like Little Richard on the high notes.

"Are you saved?"

The bird tweeted again.

"Yes. I am saved and filled with the Holy Ghost. And I want to dedicate my life to Him."

"Talent," mouthed Zelda Fish from the shore.

"This girl is a singer, and she wants to dedicate her talent to Him." Winston Fish spoke out toward the congregation.

"Amen!" cried the Christians.

His right hand closed around her left, and he brought it to her nose, fingers over hers.

"Ready?"

"Yes."

"I now baptize you in the name of the Father! And of the Son! And of the Holy Ghost!"

She went down. She heard a splash. For a moment she opened her eyes underwater, and a minnow swam by. Now she was ready to come up, but her father was not bringing her. Her muscles strained toward the surface, but water was all around.

"Don't drown that girl!" called out Sister Cubbison.

With a wrench she broke water. Sun hit her face. She breathed huge gulps of air.

"Sing!" cried Sister Sue.

The congregation began on "Amazing Grace," waiting for Roxanne to raise her hands, waiting for Brother Ritz to go next. They swayed.

"Roxanne," said Pastor Fish.

She forced herself to look at him. Her father's eyes were blue, the same blue they had been in the Iowa backyard with the white softball flying past the clouds.

"I can lock the doors and call the police and do whatever I have to. They can't take you without our permission. I can handcuff you. You're under age. But I will not do this."

Water dripped from her ears. This was not an Iowa river.

"However, I would like to ask you not to go."

His eyes held her, the only eyes she knew. If she missed the Rapture, she would never see her family again.

"I want to sing with her," said Roxy.

Each Fish turned away from the other. Of course, Jesus might come before November seventeenth. Roxy sincerely hoped not. Pastor Fish clapped his large hands, which were rough from working around the house.

"Next!"

The Hallelujah Side

TWO WEEKS LATER, at six a.m., Roxy walked toward Mr. Biggs' car, staring at the pavement intently. The street did not look like Iowa because they used another kind of paint for the white line, plus the sun was not shining off it. It was cloudy. Colleen was still asleep, but Zelda and Winston Fish stood on the sidewalk behind, and she could feel her father's eyes on her. Because she was a Fish family member, she held her head up, and did not look back as they drove away. She answered Mr. Biggs' pleasantries with a cheerful yes or no. They were technically in Glendale, but to look out the car window they might as well have been in outer space.

A bus appeared. Painted blue, it sat at the curb. It had rained all night, and now the gutters were running so hard that the bus sported a plank from the sidewalk to the door, which was high up. Roxy slipped her Bible into the old Fish suitcase while Mr. Biggs held the car door open for her. Sequestered in the suitcase pockets were the pearls she had stolen and two lipsticks.

The bus driver honked. "We're late!"

Mr. Biggs took her suitcase and heaved it into the luggage carrier, from which fierce engine sounds came. "Good luck," he said with an encouraging wave.

Roxy boarded. As she walked down the aisle toward the back, the bus began to roll. When she looked around, Aretha Franklin was not there. Her eyes widened. She stood praying that she was not being kidnapped.

"Is this the Sanctified Sisters Tour?" she asked a woman with raven black hair, grabbing a seat back as the bus lurched.

"What are *you*?" said the woman, staring at her with sarcastic eyes. "A *dwarf*? Jesus!"

"Roxanne," said Roxy.

The woman gave a throaty laugh and dragged on a cigarette.

Roxy continued down the aisle, blushing.

There was nothing of heaven on the bus. Bare skin, whiskey, cigarettes, and strange activity filled the air. A man and woman were kissing right on their seat, their mouths locked together. Roxy tried to see if they could breathe. Balancing with difficulty, she moved toward a bare lightbulb in the back. Sinners stared out the windows, all with fire in their hair. She might be lost now. She found a vacant seat and plopped down, relieved that she hadn't fallen over.

"Shut the fuck up!" yelled the dark-haired woman's voice.

The vinyl seat was ripped. According to the sky, it looked like Christ might come today, unusual for California, but sunbeams were poking through the gray. She bit her lip. How she hoped He waited until after this event. The actual sun burst through a dark cloud just as they reached the 5 freeway, and Roxy twitched. But no Archangel Gabriel blew his trumpet. It was uncertain whether she was going down or up. Roxy looked at her arms and legs, fragile, like everyone's. She prayed a plane did not land on them.

"Abba? Babba? Mo?" she whispered.

"Whazzat? Swahili?" said the man behind her, whom she had not seen. Tall, perhaps Indian, he was wearing an undershirt that exposed much of his skin. There were no Christians on this bus.

"I'm sorry," said Roxy.

"Not to be. I am a Crenshaw from Jamaica and El Monte. Rita is a bitch. Hoo-hoo. Hold my hand."

"I'm a cheetah," said Roxy. "My name is Fish, but I am one."

"I see this is true."

He stuck his hand through the seat, enormous, and Roxy touched the skin with one finger.

"Crenshaw what?"

"Crenshaw."

She dozed with her cheek brushing the long bones of Crenshaw's hand, and dreamed the Fishes were in heaven eating manna from beautiful plates. Although there was an empty chair, no one spoke of her or seemed to notice. Angels flew by the window, and the streets sparkled gold, although there was no grass there.

When she woke up, Aretha Franklin was standing over her.

"So you made it." Her shoes were different this time, brown, like her legs, but her face had not changed. She smiled and went back up front to speak to the driver.

"If it ain't Los Angeles," boomed Crenshaw. "Bah ba-da-da. Here we are. Hello, Embassy Auditorium! Take four, you whore."

"How big?" yelled Rita.

"Twelve hundred seats."

"Candy from a baby!" Rita shimmied.

Bodies all around were moving, smelling of perspiration and cigarette smoke. Standing suddenly, Crenshaw punched the air.

"People! Go!"

Sun poured in. Now Roxy saw she had made a terrible mistake. Aretha Franklin had been wrong. Roxy was a Christian, and did not belong to the things of this world. The Catholics had won the election. She could not stop the tears that ran from her eyes. Crenshaw handed her his sunglasses, and she put them on. Into the aisle they tumbled, Crenshaw playing a small drum tucked in the crook of his left arm. She let herself be pushed forward, wishing she had a purse. If you had a purse you might look normal. But she did not, so she pretended to be carrying a monkey, and the monkey was hugging her. It was a spider monkey, brown, with bright eyes and fond spindly fingers. She gently tucked its head into her shoulder. The man in front of her, she saw in startled truth, was drinking Pabst Blue Ribbon beer.

"Do you know Woolworth?" she said.

"Woolworth? People," he called out, "who is Woolworth?"

"Woolworth ain't here!"

They did not know Woolworth. She walked down the aisle holding her monkey, who looked around curiously.

"You are crazy as a bedbug, and you can't sing," said Rita, standing by the bus driver and spraying her black hair. She glared at Roxy. "Die, midget."

The sun was blinding as they stepped off the bus and went right into a gigantic building surrounded by parking lots. Backwards out the doors you could see open space and a Los Angeles prairie sky. Roxy turned and hurried behind Crenshaw into an elevator, which groaned as it ascended. In a large room with wires, everybody began bouncing, as if God had breathed new energy into them. Crenshaw made rapid tongue clicks as he took his position on a stool behind the drums.

"Let's start," said Aretha Franklin, not bouncing. Her presence calmed the frantic feeling down. "Girls, line up at those microphones. Everybody? This is Roxanne. Help her out."

"Die," said Rita out the corner of her mouth.

First the band tuned up. All the passages that Jesus said were squashed into her suitcase, which was locked up in the band bus. She decided to wait until they got to their concrete hotel rooms.

"Teach her the part," said Aretha.

Rita snorted and sang a measure. Roxy opened her mouth, but only a squeak came out. She cleared her throat and tried again. The squeak got louder. It did not have that porkchop feeling. She bit her tongue violently and tried once more.

"She can't sing!" yelled Rita. "I knew the minute she got on."

"Ah!" Roxy squeaked. She rubbed her throat with all ten fingers.

Aretha stepped in front of her. "What's the problem?"

It was chilly in the room, but Roxy was sweating buckets.

"It won't come out."

It was not a nice slap, but neither was it mean. It stung. Out came the note, and Rita looked at Roxy sideways. Roxy opened her mouth wider, and the note became more fluid. Now the corners of Rita's mouth relaxed. Aretha Franklin wiggled Roxy's shoulders hard and walked off. The articles around Roxy were growing strangely bright, the music stands and electrical cords, as if they had light on them.

Aretha faced everyone in her high heels. "Rock my soul," she said.

The piano chords began. In the Lipstick Tree in Glendale, Roxy had left a note for Colleen anchored neatly under Summer Peach, Siren Red, and Baby Burgundy.

> Dear Colleen,
>   Well, I'll be in Los Angeles when you read this.
> Help! Don't drink too many milkshakes, ha ha.
> I think your hair looks great in a ponytail. I have
> Tangerine Kiss and Pink Passion.
>   Your sister, Roxanne

"Rock my soul," she sang, her voice twining around Rita's, and the two women moved a step closer.

· · · · ·

Roxy turned it in her hand. It was not a high heel but a boat to stand on, with a huge elevated bottom and a shocking four-inch heel, nothing like the Missionary Box had.

"Put me on," said the shoe.

Slowly Roxy stepped into it, and then the other one, both black velvet. The pearls from Glendale's love offering, property of Christ, were on under her dress, resting coolly in sin against her skin. She was in trouble heavenwise. The dress itself was blue velvet, short and swingy, and it exposed her shoulders, another sin. Rita looked the same, except that she was taller than Roxy.

Rita held her thumb up. "Nervous, little sister?"

Roxy nodded.

"Want a hit on the head?"

Roxy giggled.

The auditorium was huge. Roxy peeked through the heavy curtains, aghast. The stage itself was much bigger than a platform, the piano and the Hammond organ on opposite sides, Crenshaw's drums in the middle. The damned were tuning up. She had not turned to the passages in red in her Bible yet. The musicians and the singers had a wild energy that seemed to crackle just under their skin. All around her was bare flesh. She ought to speak, but they were talking to their instruments and did not care about heaven or hell.

"Do you know the way of salvation?" Roxy asked Crenshaw.

"Gimme B-flat."

"Thirty minutes," said someone.

The excitement was rising, and Roxy's stomach flipped. The bare thighs and arms were blinding. Behind the side curtains was a door open to the night outside, and Roxy walked carefully through it in her platform high heels, inhaling cold Los Angeles air.

"How do," said a bum. With his stubby beard and dirty clothes, he seemed all one color except for the bottle that said ninety proof. It held gold liquid. "Got a quarter?"

"I don't even have a purse."

At that moment she saw a sight that made her chest heave. Across the narrow space between buildings on the street passed Winston Fish, Zelda Fish, Colleen, and the Zengs, back from Sacramento, apparently. She ducked into the doorway.

"That's them," she whispered, covering her tangerine lips.

The bum squinted. "Damn fine-looking people," he said.

The Fishes disappeared. Suddenly Roxy missed Superba with a Water Lily Maiden's passion, but it was time to go in. She turned around carefully in her shoes.

"Merde," the bum called out.

She went to her place behind the microphone and waited in her blue velvet dress. Behind the black velvet curtain the musicians were still tuning their instruments, the naked V chests of the men glistening in the stage light. Rita stood behind the microphone to Roxy's left, toward the middle, being taller.

"Go, jailbait!" said Crenshaw under his breath.

When the curtains opened slowly, there all the sinners' heads were, hundreds of them, who knew how many, waiting.

In the quiet the floor varnish shone.

Now the subtle beat began, the beat of Africa coming through the floorboards themselves. Crenshaw hit the drums in agony, and she and Rita hit the first note.

"Oo-ahhh," they sang.

A smile took Roxy. Rita nodded, and her black hair shook. In their black velvet shoes Roxy and Rita stepped left to right, right to left. Roxy had her porkchop voice, and as it sailed out she saw her family, sitting in the middle partway back. Her mother's hands were up to heaven, and the Zengs were praying with their heads bowed low, invoking Jesus against demons, protecting themselves. Colleen bounced in her seat. Pastor Fish stared straight ahead, his eyes on the orchestra pit.

"Move," rasped Rita.

Left to right, right to left she stepped. The voice kept coming. The light caught Sister Zeng's hat.

"*Ching!*" crashed Crenshaw's cymbals.

The things of earth were growing strangely dim. The music swelled, and when the horns came in they made her arms rise of their own accord. Her body got lighter, and she thought she might levitate.

"Ooo-ooo," they sang.

When Roxy looked for her family again, she could no longer see them, but the love of Jesus seemed to be here. For a moment she could even smell Iowa, the cut grass, Superba's clean hair, the hedge on Carroll Street. A thunderous applause roared through the auditorium as Aretha Franklin walked onstage in gold shoes. Goosebumps broke out all over Roxy's arms, and for a split second she could see they were eternal, all the singers, all the sinners' heads, even the dear demons in hell.

Aretha started in.

"Rock my soul," Roxy sang, heart beating, throat opening, platform shoes stepping.

Acknowledgments

This book was written with a great deal of help. I am grateful to Peggy Reavey, Michelle Latiolais, and Bill Selby for their friendship and insight, and to Alison Gold, Joclyn Park, Joe Geare, Bill McDonald, Ruth Roisen, and Lynn Ordway for almost daily encouragement. Oakley Hall and Louis B. Jones gave invaluable criticism, as did Squaw Valley Community of Writers. Elaine Dundy's book *Ferriday, Louisiana* confirmed my feelings about the charisma of the Assembly of God Church. Tap Masters Leonard Reed and Cholly Atkins shared their broad knowledge of performing. I especially thank my agent, Leslie Daniels, for her true sense of story. My editor, Joy Johannessen, did for me what blues trombonist Peewee Whittaker did for Jerry Lee Lewis: "I just showed him how to stop and take his time and all like that."

DISCUSSION GUIDE

We hope the following questions will stimulate discussion for reading groups and for every reader provide a deeper understanding of *The Hallelujah Side*.

1. What things of this world does Roxanne love, including tree leaves, grass, and sidewalks? How does her love of these things conflict with the faith expected of her, and to what extent can it be reconciled with that faith? What are the consequences of her love for the things of this world?

2. Pastor Fish believes that "human beings had to get their blood boiling each day . . . to stay in top working order." How do Winston and Zelda Fish and others get their blood boiling? What might be the attendant dangers and benefits, if any?

3. How do Winston and Zelda Fish reconcile their faith's rejection of worldly things with the worldly activities that they enjoy (dancing, reading *Newsweek* and *Das Kapital*, and flying, for example)? To what extent are the expression and practice of anyone's religious faith determined by personal likes and dislikes?

4. We are told that Zelda Fish "was a perfect housekeeper, but when the Spirit entered she forgot housework." In what ways can the entrance of the Spirit interfere with the necessary, life-supporting activities of everyday life? What are the manifestations of the Spirit's presence in Zelda and others?

5. How unusual is Colleen's insistence that Winston and Zelda are not her true parents? What about her acting out of religious practices from other churches? How would you explain her behavior? Why doesn't Roxanne engage in similar behavior?

6. What do Pastor Fish and his congregation consider to be Holy Ghost power? How might that power be described in nonreligious terms? What instances are there in the novel of this power's operation, and what are its consequences?

7. What possible conflicts are there between Zelda's faith and her position as Pastor Fish's wife, on the one hand, and her job as Welcome Wagon Hostess, on the other? How do they reflect the greater conflicts between the actual world and the world of faith? How do details from Zelda's past help us to understand her resolution of these conflicts?

8. "Grownups were hard to fathom," Roxanne thinks as Zelda and Mrs. Bell giggle over dropping the logs. What does Roxanne find hard to fathom about the adults in her world? How does she go about *trying* to understand them?

9. How and why do Mrs. Bell's attitude, manner, and behavior change when Zelda mentions Winston's calling and invites the newcomer to their church? How do nonbelievers generally respond to the unsolicited advances of believers? Why?

10. How does Roxanne deal with the boredom of her father's sermons, the anxiety of waiting for the Second Coming, and the demands of her parents' faith? How do her discoveries about herself lead her away from the church and the fear of being left behind?

11. Why is it significant that the most frightening of Roxanne's three demons is "a stuffed toy horse, soft and fluffy"? To what extent, in the book and in life, does the malevolent take on the appearance of the familiar, amusing, or comforting? Does one have to be a fervent believer to accept the operation of evil in the world?

12. What role do Chick and Miriam Woolworth play in the novel and in Roxanne's development? To what extent is their be-

havior reasonable and understandable? Why do they behave the way they do?

13. Beginning with "putting idols before God" (that is, hoping for a ripe ear of corn before the Second Coming occurs), what "sins" are specified? To what extent are these "sins" part of everyone's day-to-day life? In what ways are they spiritually harmful or life-enhancing?

14. We are told that "in Iowa you could lose your bearings in a moment," as Roxanne — on her way downtown to meet Superba — does. In what ways, and with what consequences, do characters in this novel lose their bearings? In what ways might being reborn constitute as much a loss of one's bearings as getting lost along unfamiliar streets?

15. "Children should be left alone to go at their own pace," Winston Fish insists. In what ways does or doesn't Winston put these words into action? To what extent are Colleen and Roxanne allowed to find their way toward adulthood "at their own pace"? To what extent do they dictate their own pace despite their parents' actions?

16. What is Roland's effect on his brother's congregation from the moment he stands up? How would you account for that effect? What comparisons and contrasts can be drawn between a spellbinding preacher and a mesmerizing entertainer, and between the former's congregation and the latter's audience?

17. In what ways can we interpret Roland's advice to Roxanne — "But you got to listen when God talks"? How do different people experience this in different ways? In what ways does God talk to the people in *The Hallelujah Side*?

18. How would you interpret Roxanne's flying dream? What might that dream have to do with her hopes and desires, her rela-

tionships within her family, her parents' church, and Iowa? What is its importance in relation to the rest of the book?

19. How can we define the word *soul* in the novel? Which of the word's meanings and usages apply most importantly to Roxanne and her experiences?

20. How would you explain Roxanne's apparently otherworldly experiences — from hearing the voice of God and seeing Blue Nose, to talking to the hedge and seeing flashing lights at the Camp Meeting, to sensing a hum in the universe? Are they only the sensations and perceptions of a particularly imaginative and sensitive preteen?

21. Why does Winston insist that Roxanne will not sing with Aretha Franklin but will be formally baptized into the church and then leave the final decision to her? Why does he choose *not* to use any of the preventive means available to him?

22. What are some of the ways in which one may "rock one's soul"?

This Discussion Guide was written by
Hal Hager & Associates, Somerville, New Jersey